Sophie's Story

PENELOPE ABBOTT

Sophie's Story
Copyright © 2023 by Penelope Abbott

For more about this author, please visit https://penelopeabbott.com.

This is a work of fiction. Names, characters, businesses, places, events, locales, and incidents are either the products of the author's imagination or used in a fictitious manner. Any resemblance to actual persons, living or dead, or actual events is purely coincidental.

All rights reserved. No part of this publication may be reproduced, distributed, or transmitted in any form or by any means, including photocopying, recording, or other electronic or mechanical methods, without the prior written permission of the publisher, except in the case of brief quotations embodied in critical reviews and certain other noncommercial uses permitted by copyright law. Please do not participate in or encourage piracy of copyrighted materials in violation of the author's rights.

Editing by The Pro Book Editor
Interior and Cover Design by IAPS.rocks

1. Main category—FICTION / Historical
2. Other category—FICTION / Sagas

First Edition

TABLE OF CONTENTS

To Kate

CHAPTER ONE

TRAGIC NEWS

Sophie Anderson stood in front of her class, overseeing the young ladies working. She had written out English grammar exercises on the blackboard, and her pupils were copying them. The only sound in the room was the scratching of their pens on paper.

It was near the end of the summer term, and now that she was eighteen years old, she was looking forward to leaving her post as a temporary assistant at the girls' school and returning home. Sophie had done well in her training in accounts and was hoping to join her father in his wine importing business. Since her mother's death, her only wish had been to work with him to help reverse the recent losses he had experienced.

The morning sun slanted in through the tall windows of the schoolroom, shining on the old oak desks and lighting up floating specks of chalk dust in the air. On one of the walls, a portrait of the elderly Queen Victoria looked down on the young ladies.

Suddenly the classroom door opened, and Sophie looked up with a start. The school secretary, Miss Edwards, entered and informed her that the principal wanted to see her immediately and that she was to take her books and any other personal items with her. Sophie could not understand why she was being sent for in this way, before her lesson had ended, but hurried to gather up her belongings. Just before leaving, she told her students to continue with the exercises and asked Miss Edwards to remain with them until they were dismissed.

As she hurried down the corridor towards the principal's study, she wondered what this could be about. Her father was behind with her school fees, but the principal had given her teaching duties to help with that. She could think of no other reason the principal would summon her.

She arrived at Miss Turnbull's study door and gave a quiet knock, but as no answer seemed forthcoming, she knocked again more boldly, and on hearing a reply, she opened the door and went in.

The room she entered was light and spacious and furnished with a small sofa, two leather armchairs and Miss Turnbull's desk, which stood in front of a large rosewood bookcase. A vase of flowers had been placed on a side table, and Sophie caught their fragrance as she walked by. Two tall casement windows looking out onto a garden flooded the room with light.

She had been invited to this room several times to take afternoon tea with the principal and teachers after school, enjoyable occasions when she had conversed amicably with her colleagues.

An attractive woman, wearing an expensive-looking dress and with her hair coiled up in the latest fashion, sat behind the desk. Sophie had always admired Miss Turnbull and wished to be like her. Her principal's superior smile gave her an advantage over those she addressed, and it aways made Sophie feel deferential in her presence.

"You wished to see me?" Sophie asked quietly.

The principal smiled warmly and indicated for her to put her books down and take a seat. As Sophie did so, she noticed a letter on Miss Turnbull's desk, but her elegant, ringed hand was covering it. After Sophie had settled down and arranged the folds of her long skirt with her shaking hands, the headmistress began.

"I expect you are wondering why you are here?"

Sophie gave her a tentative smile. "Yes. Is there something wrong, Miss Turnbull?"

"I have just received a letter from your uncle, Mr. Christopher Anderson."

Sophie's face lit up in surprise on hearing this. "From my *uncle*?" Why had he written to her principal at the school?

As Miss Turnbull picked up the letter, Sophie gave her a slight frown. The principal said, “He requests that you leave here immediately and be taken to his house. He has sent a conveyance for you.”

“May I ask why he has asked me to go there? Why am I not to be sent to my home?” asked Sophie. She moved to the edge of her seat and leant slightly forward.

“I'm sorry, Sophie dear, I cannot tell you that. All I can say is that this has nothing to do with the school or your work here. Just stay calm and do what he requests, and I am sure he will have an explanation to give you.”

“I still don't understand why he has written to you. Something must have happened, and I wish I knew what it was.” Sophie looked down, distracted.

Rising from behind her desk, the principal came and put her arm round Sophie and gave her a gentle hug. “When you have gathered your things together, come directly to the entrance hall. I shall see you off myself.”

As she rose from her chair, Sophie tried to smile, but she felt full of foreboding. Something must have happened, and it distressed her not to know what it was. Why hadn't her father been the one to contact her? She concluded that he had probably been taken ill, but then remembered that she was not going home but returning to her uncle's house.

As she packed her trunk, her anxious thoughts began to weigh her down, and her movements became slower as she placed her clothes and belongings inside. A member of staff came to collect her trunk and bags, and she followed him downstairs to where Miss Turnbull was waiting for her.

Sophie stood in the vast entrance hall, clutching her leather satchel full of books and papers, and prepared to say farewell to her kind principal.

Miss Turnbull was holding a large envelope in her hand, which she handed to Sophie. “Sophie, as it is near the time when you were to finish your studies, regretfully, we might not see you again. Here are references and accreditations that may be of use to you. I am so sorry you must leave us so suddenly. You have done well here and proven to be a very good teacher. Be brave and face the future with fortitude and determination. I wish you well."

Sophie put down her bag and embraced her. She was now in tears, distressed at having to leave the school she loved. "Thank you for all you have done for me," she said, barely able to speak. "I shall miss you all. I have been so happy here."

Miss Turnbull accompanied her to where the groom and conveyance were waiting outside. Sophie wept as she climbed into the carriage. As they drove away, she turned around to take one last look at her school, and Miss Turnbull's receding figure waving her handkerchief.

The carriage rattled on, and Sophie leant back in her seat and tried to compose herself. Everything had happened so quickly, and she could hardly believe she was now on her way to her uncle's house. She prayed her dear father was all right, convinced now that this sudden request for her to leave her school must have something to do with him.

Over the last year, his business had begun to lose money. Her father had told her that he was "experiencing difficulties" and was unable to pay the fees for her final year at school. Sophie needed to take her final exams, so Miss Turnbull suggesting she stay on as a teacher had worked very successfully. Her father had always corresponded at least once a week, but she had not heard from him for a month and had put it down to his business concerns. She now realised that this might be significant but was unsure how.

Exhausted, she closed her eyes. She longed to reach her destination. After a short sleep, she awoke and looked out of the window. She knew the way home, having made it many times, but the route to her uncle's house was new to her. Her journey to school usually took four hours, but she had no idea how long she had been travelling since they left.

They passed several villages and farms. Sophie noticed the fields were nearly ready for the farmworkers to take in the harvest, as it was now July. Taking out her small watch, she saw that it was well past midday. Her father had given it to her when she had begun teaching, and she felt sad as she looked at it.

The journey continued with short breaks to change horses, and towards the end of the afternoon, she began to recognise the landscape. She had visited her uncle several times with her father and could tell they would soon be arriving. After a short while, the groom turned the horses slowly into the gate and drew up outside the house on the gravel drive. It was an imposing red brick mansion surrounded by laurel bushes and statuesque elms. Sophie looked out and saw the rooks circling round in the trees, and it gave her a feeling of foreboding.

The groom jumped down and opened the carriage door, and Sophie emerged, somewhat stiff from her long journey. She looked round and, as there was no one about, mounted the steps and pulled the iron bell handle. A young man, one of the servants, opened the door and asked her in. As she entered, a tall casement clock in the hallway chimed, and she saw that it was now four. She had been travelling for most of the day and was exhausted.

Once the groom had placed her trunk in the hall and left, the somewhat nervous young servant showed her into her uncle's drawing room. He left quickly after saying that her uncle would be informed of her arrival. Sophie sat down and waited, wondering what she was about to be told. She could hear doors opening and shutting and raised male voices, one of which she recognised as her uncle's. The sense of restlessness in the house made her feel uneasy.

The door opened and her uncle strode in.

"Ah, Sophie, you are here," he said, seeming agitated. "I have some very sad news to give you. I was—that is, we were all—very sorry to learn that your father passed away yesterday afternoon. It appears he took his own life. This is the reason you have been taken out of school and brought straight here today. We are all in a state of shock."

Sophie was completely taken aback by what he said. It was all very abrupt. Gasping, she put her hand to her mouth. She had never dreamed that the news would be this devastating. She felt overwhelmed, unable to say anything as she waited for him to continue.

"My dear girl, I am so very sorry. What can I say?"

She stared at him, feeling her eyes brimming with tears. "Uncle, why has this happened? I don't understand—he can't be dead. My father can't have done this!" She wanted words of comfort and reassurance, but they were not forthcoming.

"You are to stay with us until it is decided what can be done," he said. "I cannot say anymore at present. This is a dreadful business—a dreadful business!" He shook his head in disbelief. "My housekeeper will see to your needs, Sophie. You must understand there is a lot I must attend to. I will speak to you later."

He left, and soon Mrs. Adams, his housekeeper, arrived with some refreshments. She was a kindly woman who did what she could to comfort Sophie. She tried to encourage her to eat the sandwiches she had brought in on a tray, but all Sophie could manage was a cup of tea. Mrs. Adams suggested she go to her room to rest.

Sophie could not sleep. Her feelings were in turmoil, and she kept asking herself the same questions. Why had her father done this? Why had he left her alone? Why? Why? She hoped her uncle would be able to explain exactly what had happened.

She sat by the window and looked out at the late afternoon sky. The view was restful, and she turned her thoughts to the future. What would it bring?

Dinner that night was subdued. Sophie's cousin Robert was there, but not his younger brother, Frank. She did not know her cousins very well. They had met a few times during her childhood, but as she was a girl, they had not included her in their games and pursuits.

Robert greeted her and expressed his condolences. He had grown into a tall young man and had his father's slightly severe expression.

During the meal, Uncle Christopher explained that the funeral was to be a quiet affair. His brother was to be buried in ground nearby. He told Sophie that, as it was late, he would speak with her the following day.

After dinner, Sophie sat in her room and thought about her father's funeral. She knew that people who committed suicide were not allowed to be buried in church grounds. The last time she had seen her father was some months ago, when they had discussed plans as to what she could do in his wine importing business after she finished at school. He had told her about his financial difficulties, and she began to wonder if this could have anything to do with his death.

After breakfast the following morning, a maid knocked on Sophie's bedroom door and said that her uncle was ready to see her. She made her way to his study and found him standing by the window looking out, a silhouette against the light. The room was simply furnished, smelling of wood polish and stale tobacco and reminding her this was a very masculine household.

Sophie's aunt had been dead many years, and her cousins had been raised by a series of nannies and then sent off to school. She knew Robert now worked for his father in his manufacturing business. She could only just remember Aunt Margaret, a small, nervous woman whose main purpose in life had been to please her husband, who never seemed pleased at anything. Sophie found him stern at times.

When she entered the study, she wondered what her uncle was about to say. He turned towards her and began informing her of the arrangements he had made for the burial, asking if she wanted to attend. She nodded vehemently.

He continued, "You do understand, don't you, Sophie, that all this business leaves you in a very precarious position financially. Your father and I have always supported each other over the years, and we have always helped each other with loans when the need has arisen. Unfortunately, your father has died owing me rather a lot of money. He was declared bankrupt last week, and that is probably what precipitated his decision to end it all. I'm afraid nothing will come to you. All his creditors need to be dealt with, so there will probably be very little left, and then solicitors will have to be paid."

Sophie suddenly felt weak. It was all so overwhelming. Her future had been turned upside down, and she had no idea what lay ahead. All her plans of sharing her working life with her dear father were ruined. Whatever was she going to do? Where was she to live?

"What can I do if I have no money, Uncle?" she asked.

"Ah, good question! I'm afraid you are now in a position of having to support yourself. One way would be to become a governess. You are a well-educated young lady and should have no problem securing a position. I am happy to give you a good reference and can make some enquiries about finding you a suitable place if you wish. Of course, if you should marry, you will then be taken care of, but you must be realistic. You have nothing to bring to a marriage, and most young men look to marry someone with money. My own business is not doing well, and my health is not what it was. My will is in the form of a trust, and only my sons can inherit, so I cannot provide for you. You can stay here for the time being, and I suggest that after the funeral, you continue your studies as best you can, so you are well prepared if you do decide to become a governess or a teacher. You are welcome to use my library. I am sorry I cannot do more for you."

Sophie could not believe what she was hearing and felt resentment welling up inside her. She could not understand why her uncle was not prepared to care for her and welcome her into his family, seeing as she was still under the age of twenty-one and he was her only next of kin. Why could he not offer her a home? She could not imagine the future he had described for her.

She returned to her room and sat by the window. The sun was shining on the trees, and as she watched the clouds moving across the sky, she realised that her life was going to be very different from what she had expected. Although she had enjoyed teaching, the thought of becoming a governess was not appealing to her, but perhaps her uncle would find her a good position with a suitable family. She decided to go for a walk to think about all that her uncle had said. Her father's funeral was the following day, and she needed to settle her thoughts.

She set out along a path in the garden that led past some flower borders, down to a shrubbery and a small spinney. As she walked slowly along, she decided she would give herself a period of mourning and then put her shoulder to the wheel and try to make the best of things. In a single day, she had lost all control of her life. She remembered the good times she had shared with her father, the plans they had made to improve his business, and perhaps even increase sales, and feelings of regret overwhelmed her.

Later that day, her other cousin, Frank, arrived back from his university. He was slight of build, shorter than his brother, and with his boyish face, pale skin, and fair hair, took after his mother in looks. Sophie hadn't seen him for some time, and with surprise, she noted that he had grown into a handsome young man. At dinner that night, she asked if he was enjoying his time at university.

His reply was rather short, but she pursued the subject. "I should imagine that it is quite exciting meeting new people and learning new things."

Frank gave her a cold look, took a sip of his wine, and said, "What would you know about it?"

She started, taken aback and her face reddening, then glanced over at Robert and her uncle, who were engaged in conversation and had not heard this curt reply.

Next morning at the funeral, Sophie followed the small group of mourners to a corner of her uncle's grounds, behind the shrubbery. Her uncle and cousin Robert led the way in their dark, sombre clothes, followed by a few of her father's servants, who had arrived shortly before. Uncle Christopher held a large black Bible under his arm.

Bowing her head, Sophie wept as the coffin was lowered into the grave by four members of Christopher's household. The men then stood back, and her uncle read a verse of scripture, then Robert added a short prayer. They then joined hands and said the Lord's Prayer together. Sophie stepped forward, placed her flowers into the grave and, kneeling, said her silent farewells to her father. His servants came and spoke to her afterwards, offering their condolences and telling her how they would miss him. Sophie greeted them each by name and wished them well, saying she regretted they no longer had their positions and thanking them for all they had done for her father. They seemed to appreciate her words. Departing, they walked in a small group back up the lane. Sophie followed slowly, her head bowed.

The day after the funeral, when Sophie came down to breakfast, she found Frank already there. Her heart sank, but she greeted him with a "good morning."

After he had filled his plate from the sideboard, he turned to her and said, "My father is not at all well, you know, and his business is struggling. Your father has caused him a lot of problems, and now he must deal with you."

Sophie was very upset when she heard this but determined not to show it. "I am very sorry for it, Frank," she said. "I am grateful for the help your father has given me. I have lost everything in my life, and I know I am dependent now. I hope I shall be leaving as soon as I have a position as a governess."

"It's a pity your father didn't think of you."

Frank's words stung her, and she hurried out, making her way to the library. Distraught and silently crying, all she could think of was her dear father. What would he have said to her now? She imagined him putting his arm around her, telling her to keep going, that all would be well. But all had not been well with him. Why hadn't he kept going? Together, they would have found a way through his business troubles—she was sure of it.

Frank's accusations were cruel, and it was with a sense of relief that she learned that he had returned to university later that day. At least Robert was polite to her. He was the stoical one, whereas his brother seemed more outspoken with his emotions. Both Robert and her uncle would sometimes ask her how she was feeling, but neither offered any reassurance, their masculine reserve preventing any form of physical comfort.

Sophie spent most of her time in the library. She established a routine for herself. Each day she would begin by researching a subject and making notes and then wrote up what would be her curriculum. She could do the lesson plans later. She wondered if her pupils would require instruction in music and drawing. Sometimes visiting tutors were employed to teach these skills, and she hoped that would be the case. Her own piano lessons had ended when her mother died, and she was sent to school.

She bound the sheaves of paper together with cord and wrote the titles on the frontispieces, dating each one August 1890. She stored these carefully in her trunk, ready for her departure, whenever that would be.

Luncheon was a buffet set out in the morning room, and Sophie usually took hers to the library, as she wasn't overly fond of sitting down with her cousin and uncle if they happened to be there. Afterwards, she would take a short walk in the garden if the weather was fine. At five o'clock, she would close her books and go to her room to rest and dress for dinner.

She did not usually join in the conversation during the meal, as nobody seemed very interested in what she had been doing all day. She would rise from the table as soon as she could, leaving the two men to their drinks and business talk.

One evening, after dinner, Sophie asked her uncle if she could play the grand piano in the library. She explained that she might have to give some music lessons when she became a governess and she wanted to see how much she remembered. Her uncle readily agreed and told her where to find the key. His wife had been the last person to use the instrument, since neither of the boys was musical.

The following morning, Sophie unlocked the instrument and found some sheet music in the piano stool. She began to play, a little hesitant at first but then gaining some confidence played for about an hour. It helped her achieve some peace after the turmoil of the last few days.

She asked her uncle about her father's house, as she had been told nothing about her old home and wanted to know if she could obtain the rest of her clothes and belongings. He explained that, since her father had been declared bankrupt, the house and all his possessions had been seized by his creditors. She would be allowed to keep some personal things, so he suggested she make a list so he could ensure they were put aside for her. Sophie knew she would have nowhere to store any large items, but she needed the rest of her clothes, books, and other personal possessions as well as some mementos of her parents.

Sophie felt anxious to know what was to happen to her. It had now been several weeks since her father's death, and autumn was approaching. She was relieved when, finally, her uncle summoned her to his study.

He informed her that he had secured her a position with a family. Her pupils were to be two boys, one of seven and the other ten years old. Their home was in Devonshire, some distance from where she was now living. Sophie had never been to that part of the country, but she knew it to be a picturesque county with a lovely coastline. Her charges would be young enough for her to manage, and she was excited about the prospect. She was to leave at the end of the week, so there was little time to prepare.

The day before her departure, she packed her belongings in her trunk and bags and labelled them carefully. These were her only worldly possessions. Her uncle had managed to obtain the items she had requested, as well as a few extra things he thought she might like to have, including her piano music and watercolour paints.

Before she left, he asked to see her. "Well, my dear," he began, "to-morrow you will leave us to begin your new life as a governess. I hope you will settle in well with the family I have found you. Please let me know how you get on. Here is some money for the journey and a further five guineas to be getting along with."

Sophie thanked him for his generosity, then asked, "How am I to travel there?"

"My groom will take you to the railway station, and you are to purchase a second-class ticket to Plymouth. You will probably have to change trains on the way, but if you find a guard, he will be able to tell you how. Porters will move your luggage, and you should tip them one shilling. The name of your employer is Mr. Wilmott-Smith, and a member of his house staff will collect you. I believe he is a banker. I have written to tell them of your arrival. Here is the address in case there is some problem when you arrive and you need to hire a cab."

Sophie took the piece of paper and put the money into her small leather purse.

"Thank you, Uncle, for all you have done to help me. I will try my best to make a success of my new position, and I will write to you once I am settled."

"I wish I could have given you more, Sophie. I hope you have a safe journey tomorrow. I shall say my farewells now, as you will have to leave very early in the morning."

He gave her a brief embrace, and she could see he was visibly upset.

After dinner, Robert wished her farewell and handed her a small box. When she opened it, she saw it contained an expensive-looking fountain pen.

"Your father gave this to me on my twenty-first birthday," he said. "I want to give it to you as a going-away present."

"But it was meant for you," replied Sophie, looking up at him earnestly.

"I want you to have it," he answered.

Sophie felt moved by this gesture and accepted his gift.

"I am sure you will make good use of it," he added.

"Thank you. I shall certainly treasure it." She kissed his cheek, and he looked embarrassed. "Goodbye, Robert."

"Goodbye, Sophie."

The next morning, there was a loud knock at her bedroom door that woke her from a sound sleep.

"Time to rise, miss! It's six of the clock!" The maid entered with a jug of hot water.

How early these servants start their day! Sophie thought as she washed and dressed. She reminded herself that she must be grateful for her meals and the roof over her head from now on. After breakfast, her trunk and bags were strapped to her uncle's trap, and she was taken to the station to commence her journey to Devonshire.

Sophie left the house with few regrets—it had not been her home. Would she ever have a home of her own again, she wondered, or would she spend her life in other people's houses, teaching their children, until she was too old to do so? She was full of doubts, but she also felt excited as she travelled towards her very different life.

CHAPTER TWO

NEW BEGINNINGS

ONCE SETTLED IN HER SEAT in the train carriage, Sophie looked out the window. It was the beginning of September, and the tops of the trees were beginning to show signs of autumn. The smoke from the engine hid her view, but when it dissipated, she could see the ploughed fields, meadows, hedgerows, and woodlands passing quickly by.

Sophie's journey gave her time to reflect on all that had happened to her in the last few months. She was still young, and her father's untimely death had forced on her a way of life she had not anticipated. Her uncle, however kind he had tried to appear, obviously wanted her off his hands. Would she really have been happy if he had offered her a home in that very masculine household? Perhaps it was best that she was pursuing a life as a governess, at least for the moment.

She was curious about the place she was travelling to. Her uncle had not given her very much information other than that her employers were Mr. and Mrs. Wilmott-Smith and they lived at Clayden House in a village of the same name. She thought about the two boys who were to be her pupils and wondered if she would be expected to take on any extra duties. She recalled that her own governess had been a well-loved member of the family and had helped her mother by writing letters and reading to her when she was ill.

Lost in her thoughts, Sophie barely noticed the other passengers, but eventually she was left with two elderly ladies sitting opposite her in the compartment, with whom she engaged in polite conversation. The journey took several hours, and she was glad of their company, as well as the picnic basket Mrs. Adams had provided.

Eventually the train reached Plymouth, and Sophie alighted with a feeling of trepidation, unsure of what she had to do. The porter deposited her trunk and bags outside the station, and she remembered to tip him. People were crowding through the exit, and several carriage drivers outside were calling out passengers' names as they emerged.

She looked round for the stagecoach she had been told would take her to her destination, overwhelmed by the confusion going on around her. The two ladies she had met on the train must have seen her standing there looking bewildered, because they came over and helped her find her coach to Kingsbridge. Thanking them, Sophie paid for her fare and arranged for her luggage to be loaded. She climbed inside and waited for the other passengers to join her. Everyone was squashed together, and although it was uncomfortable, she was glad to have a seat by the window.

Many stops and two hours later, Sophie arrived at the small town of Kingsbridge, which was situated at the end of an estuary on the south coast of Devonshire. The coach stopped by the quayside, and she got out and waited for her luggage to be unloaded. She was exhausted but intrigued to see where she was.

Looking out over the inlet, she saw the evening sunlight reflected on the water. The fresh sea air revived her, and her spirits rose as she saw how picturesque her surroundings were. There were a few masted ships in the small harbour, and the whole scene appeared tranquil in the setting sun. She turned to look towards the narrow and busy High Street, which went up a steep hill, away from the quay. At the top, she could see a church with a pointed spire. It looked a very attractive place.

Sophie had been told that she would be collected outside the Harbour Inn, so she looked round to see where it was. There was a groom with a horse and trap waiting outside.

Waving, he began coming towards her. "Can I presume you are Miss Sophie Anderson?" he asked as he drew up alongside her.

She indicated that she was, and he jumped down to lift her trunk and bags into the back of the conveyance and then helped her into her seat beside him. He was a tall, thin young man with dark curly hair and an attractive smile. Sophie felt at ease with him as they set off on the last part of her long journey. He introduced himself as Harry Coates and told her he worked in the stables at Clayden House. He added that it wasn't far to go, and they should arrive within the hour. Sophie was eager to see her new home.

They eventually arrived at the village of Clayden. Passing by some white, thatched cottages on either side of the road, Harry turned into a lane to the left, taking them up a steep hill until they came to a wall with an archway. Harry drove the trap through into a cobbled courtyard and finally came to a halt. He tethered the horse and helped Sophie alight. She looked round in a puzzled way, wondering which way she should go.

"I'll take you round to the front, miss," Harry said.

She followed him along a path through an arched doorway that led to a sweeping gravel driveway in front of a handsome Georgian-style house. Sophie looked up as they approached the front and observed two rows of windows and four small skylights jutting out of the tiled roof above them. Ivy scrambled up the walls, covering most of the facade.

She mounted the three curved stone steps up to a shiny black front door with a scallop-shell window above it. Just below, the words "CLAYDEN HOUSE" were written in yellow on the glass. Here, Harry left her as she rang the bell to announce her arrival.

The door opened and a maid appeared.

"Would you be so kind as to inform your master that Miss Anderson has arrived?" Sophie asked as confidently as she could.

"Yes, miss. Please come in."

Sophie was led into the hall and left standing on a black-and-white-tiled marble floor in front of a wide, sweeping staircase. It was dark and cool inside, and she shivered slightly. She had expected the maid to return, but instead a short, plump lady in a smart black dress came to greet her.

"How do you do, Miss Anderson. I am Mrs. Arnold, Mr. Wilmott-Smith's housekeeper. I trust you had a good journey?"

"Yes, thank you, Mrs. Arnold," Sophie said. "It went very well, but I am glad to be here at last."

"Welcome to Clayden House. I trust you will be happy with us," the housekeeper replied without a smile. "Please come this way."

Sophie followed her up the stairs to a landing and then up another flight of stairs, less grand than the first one. Mrs. Arnold selected a key from the bunch hanging from her loose belt and unlocked a door on the right, standing to one side to let Sophie through.

Sophie was disappointed by what she saw. The room looked less comfortable than the one at her uncle's house. It was furnished very simply with a single bed, a chest of drawers, a small bedside table and a chair. The pictureless walls were painted white, and there was a fire grate and one window with internal shutters.

"This is your room," Mrs. Arnold told her, and without further explanation, she handed her a key.

Sophie wondered where she would be able to prepare her lessons. Mrs. Arnold had clearly anticipated her question, adding that the schoolroom was next door, and she was to work in there. She then led Sophie into a large room further along the corridor that had once been a nursery. It contained two child-sized desks and a larger one with a chair in front. The room was cluttered with old toys and furniture, which had been cleared to one side. By the window was a large round table and four chairs. On it, Sophie saw a tray covered with a white cloth and guessed it was her supper.

"I'll leave you to settle in then," said Mrs. Arnold. "I have rather a lot to do. I believe the master wants to see you tomorrow morning in the library at ten o'clock. Your supper is on the table and your breakfast will be served in here at eight. There will be a jug of hot water left for you at the bottom of the stairs at the end of this corridor. The servants don't have time to bring it all the way up here."

Mrs. Arnold walked off briskly, leaving Sophie wondering why she had not been welcomed more warmly. Perhaps there had been trouble with the last governess, as she guessed she was not the first to be employed, given the two boys' ages.

She returned to her own room to look round. It was very small, but that might not matter—hopefully she would be spending time with the family downstairs in the evenings.

Hearing a bump behind her, she turned. Harry had brought up her trunk, and she would be able to unpack straight away.

He was about to leave but stopped in the doorway and said, "Welcome to Clayden House, miss. Just watch out for those two boys. They can be little monkeys."

Sophie stared at him, alarmed.

Quickly he added, "What I mean, miss, is that they can be a bit naughty."

"Thank you, Harry. I will bear that in mind," she replied.

His remark had unsettled her. She knew she might have a problem with discipline, so she needed to command respect from the start.

The next morning, Sophie rose early. She was surprised to find she had slept well despite her new surroundings. There was a jug and a large bowl on the chest of drawers, along with two white towels and a bar of soap, and she fetched her hot water and got herself ready for the day ahead. Brushing her long dark hair into a neat coil and putting on a white blouse and smart dark skirt, she studied herself in the mirror. She fastened a cameo brooch to her collar and, satisfied with her appearance, went through to the schoolroom.

It was some time before eight o'clock, so she looked round to see what was there. In a cupboard, she found pens, ink and paper and some exercise books, together with other stationery items and some art materials. On the shelves above were several schoolbooks, including a dictionary, grammars, a globe and large atlas. She was pleased to find the room reasonably well equipped.

The door opened and the maid brought in her breakfast. Sophie welcomed a quiet moment to herself, drinking her tea and enjoying a boiled egg. She felt excited and anxious at the same time and hoped she would have enough material to cover all aspects of the curriculum she would be expected to teach. She needed to find out what the boys had studied already and decided to ask Mr. Wilmott-Smith when she saw him later that morning. She would also need to find out about routines and domestic arrangements from Mrs. Arnold, who would no doubt guide her on these matters.

With breakfast over, Sophie returned to her room, where she made her bed and tidied up. She took out her curriculum folios and began to sort out what she thought would be suitable for her new pupils to begin with. If she needed extra material, she hoped she could make use of the library.

At five minutes to ten, a maid came to her door to tell her that Mr. Wilmott-Smith was ready to see her. She led Sophie downstairs to the library, where Sophie knocked on the door and waited to be summoned inside. When she entered, Mr. Wilmott-Smith was standing by a table with an unsmiling woman sitting beside him.

"Good morning, Miss Anderson. I am Mr. Wilmott-Smith, and this is my wife."

"How do you do, sir, ma'am," Sophie answered.

He did not invite her to be seated.

"You're very young," Mrs. Wilmott-Smith observed, looking her up and down.

"I'm nearly nineteen years old, ma'am," replied Sophie.

Mrs. Wilmott-Smith smiled, pursed her lips and was then silent for the rest of the interview. Mr. Wilmott-Smith began to tell Sophie about her pupils.

"My two sons are lively boys, and they need firm discipline. The eldest, Philip, tends to be lazy when it comes to his lessons and will need to be made to work. He will be taking his entrance exams for his school next year, and he is far from ready. He has a tutor who comes twice a week to instruct him in Latin, but all other subjects must be taught by you. My younger son—we call him Kit—does not appear to be academically minded, but it is early days."

Mrs. Wilmott-Smith smiled indulgently at this remark.

Her husband continued. "Your teaching duties are from nine until two o'clock every weekday, with half an hour for luncheon, and from ten to twelve o'clock on Saturdays. Sundays are free, but you will attend house prayers in the library at eleven. Music is not required. I do not consider it to be a necessary requirement for boys. You will, however, need to teach them the rudimentary elements of drawing."

He picked up a large leatherbound volume from the table and handed it to her.

"This is the schoolroom logbook. You will write a daily account of your lessons in there."

Sophie took it. “Would it be possible for me to make use of your library, sir?”

“Yes, of course, but ask Mrs. Arnold first. Do you have any other questions about your teaching duties?”

“I would like to know about the requirements of Master Philip’s entrance exam, please,” she said.

“That can be arranged,” he told her. “You will also be required to assist Mrs. Arnold in some household duties occasionally if the boys are away or ill,” he added. “These will not be arduous, however.”

Sophie was surprised to hear this. “I was not expecting to undertake domestic tasks,” she replied boldly. “I shall need some of the holidays to prepare future lessons, sir.”

She clasped her hands tightly behind her back, wondering what his response would be.

“As I said, Miss Anderson, they would only be light duties.”

He looked straight at her, and feeling intimidated, Sophie decided to say no more. She would certainly object if they were not.

“Is there anything else, Miss Anderson?”

“Not at present, thank you,” she replied, looking straight back at him.

“Very well. Mrs. Arnold will inform you about any other matters. The boys are away visiting their grandmother at present but will have returned by the time lessons begin on Monday morning. I leave you to continue with your preparations, then.”

Sophie was surprised at this short meeting and Mr. Wilmott-Smith’s abrupt manner. Her employers appeared none too friendly towards her, and she realised she was probably not going to be accepted as one of the family.

She returned to the schoolroom and began to get it ready. Some of the furniture needed moving round so the boys faced into the room, and she placed their two desks apart and hers in front. Bringing in all her folios from her room, she began rearranging the shelves. She was so busy she did not notice Mrs. Arnold enter. Duster in hand, she climbed down from where she was standing on a chair when she saw her.

“I hope this is all right,” she said.

“It’s your domain, Miss Anderson. You have it how you please.”

The housekeeper began to describe Sophie's routines and other duties. She was to have her meals in the schoolroom. Breakfast was to be brought in each morning, and she would share it with the two young masters together with the nursery maid. Luncheon would be the same arrangement. She was to collect her afternoon tea from the kitchen at three and then her evening meal at seven and would be required to return her dishes using the back stairs, which Mrs. Arnold would show her. She was to keep her own room clean and change her own bedding, then mark her dirty linen and take it to the laundry room weekly. She also had to empty any dirty vessels in the sluice room.

Sophie was surprised at the extent of these expectations, as her uncle's servants had always attended to these tasks. It seemed that the servants here were not doing anything for her.

Mrs. Arnold took her on a tour of the house, indicating the rooms that were private. She showed her the kitchen, the laundry room and the servants' hall. She instructed Sophie to always leave the house via the back door, which led to the stable yard where she had arrived. She was only allowed in the private gardens if she had the boys with her. Sophie felt like she was being treated more like a servant, not a lady who was to teach Mr. Wilmott-Smith's two sons.

She began her first week with good intentions. The schoolroom logbook had been helpful in showing her what the boys had been doing with their previous governess, so now all that was left was for her to meet her new pupils.

They were already having breakfast with the maid when Sophie arrived in the schoolroom at eight o'clock on Monday morning. She greeted them and introduced herself. They looked self-conscious and grinned at each other, but the maid, who said her name was Annie, welcomed her and asked if she would like some tea. Sophie thanked her, then looked directly at the two boys.

"I believe it is customary for young gentlemen to rise when a lady comes into a room, and to wish her good morning."

The boys stood up and said good morning to their new governess. Philip was tall for his age and avoided eye contact, glancing at his brother for reassurance, it seemed. Although Kit was younger, he looked more at ease. Sophie saw he had an engaging smile, which she thought he knew how to use. Together with what she had learned from their father, she was beginning to see that much was expected of Philip but that Kit, being younger, was probably rather indulged.

When they had finished, the maid cleared away the breakfast, and Sophie asked the boys to sit at their desks. She handed them their timetables and told them they would be required to get their books ready every day, as shown. Then began the first lesson, which was English grammar.

There was a chalkboard on an easel in the schoolroom, which Sophie used to outline the lesson, and then she gave them their individual tasks. The logbook had given her little indication as to their ability, so she chose to work with Kit first.

Shortly after they had begun, the boys' father arrived. They stood promptly when he entered, and Sophie straightened up. Immediately, an atmosphere of unease spread through the room.

"Good morning, Miss Anderson. Have we made a promising start?"

Sophie assured him they had, and the boys looked relieved. Mr. Wilmott-Smith indicated that they should continue their work, then moved around behind them and looked over each boy's shoulder. When he got to Philip, he bent down and tapped the page with his finger.

Philip winced and hunched his shoulders, leaning in closer to his work.

"This boy's handwriting is atrocious," Mr. Wilmott-Smith said. "I will expect to see a marked improvement next time I come."

With that, he left, and everyone relaxed.

Sophie had noticed that Philip was left-handed. He had real trouble writing along the page, and his writing frequently smudged. "Don't worry, Master Philip," she said. "We'll work on that."

Philip looked a little happier, and Sophie showed him how to hold his pen another way.

The morning continued without further incident, the large schoolroom clock ticking steadily away, and finally it was pens down and lunchtime. The boys were to have their luncheon with their grandmother downstairs—she had returned with them and was to stay a few more days. Sophie was relieved to have her meal alone, as the morning had been a strain and she felt exhausted.

At twelve thirty, the boys returned for another one and a half hours of tuition, which Sophie ended early, as she wanted to read to them. In her belongings were a few volumes for her own recreation, and she happened to have a copy of the popular novel *Treasure Island*, which she thought they would enjoy. She told Kit to ask if he didn't understand anything and then proceeded to read the first chapter.

This seemed to be a new experience for the boys. They fidgeted for a while but then settled down. Both boys appeared relaxed, and Philip's concentrated expression showed he was enjoying the book and found it exciting. He sat upright looking straight at Sophie, who turned each page as the story unfolded. Kit lounged on his desk, his arm supporting his head on one side. Sophie was glad they were enjoying it and would pause to explain words or events she thought Kit would not understand. Afterwards she explained that if she was pleased with their work, at the end of each day they could have another chapter.

The boys were dismissed. Sophie thought her first day had gone well, and she was relieved. After marking the exercises they had completed and preparing work for the following day, she went down for her tea tray and took it to her own room for a change of scene.

As she sipped her cup of tea, she remembered that she needed to send a letter to her uncle. She found pen and paper and began to write that she had arrived safely and went on to describe some of her duties. She hoped he would be pleased to know she had settled in well and made a good beginning, and she was looking forward to his reply.

The following afternoon, she took her letter down to the village. She asked someone for directions to the sub postmaster's house but was told that they did not have one. She could, however, leave her letter at the Two Foxes Inn and collect any post from there. As she handed it, along with a penny, over to the innkeeper, she noticed several old men seated inside staring at her. She acknowledged them with a smile, and they nodded back, glancing at each other with knowing looks. News of her arrival had travelled fast.

In the middle of the village stood a church with a rectory nearby. Some of the cottages were painted white and were thatched, with attractive front gardens full of flowers. Sophie strolled back along the lane past some of them and stopped by a small patch of grass. There, several village boys were kicking a ball around, watched by some girls wearing white pinafores.

They must be waiting to return home for their tea at the end of the afternoon, Sophie thought. It all looked charming, but she knew that poverty was probably not far away.

She walked back up the hill to Clayden House and took her tea to her room again. She was beginning to feel more settled. It didn't worry her that there were no shops in the village, as she had little money left from her journey, and she needed to save the guineas her uncle had given her.

Sophie spent most of her spare time in the schoolroom. Determined to do well, she prepared her lessons carefully. One afternoon, she knocked on Mrs. Arnold's door and asked permission to see the library. Mrs. Arnold escorted her down the stairs and told her she could look round. Sophie surveyed the shelves, which were full of brown leather books with embossed gold titles. Mrs. Arnold warned her to be careful when examining them, as some were very valuable. Sophie saw nothing that was appropriate for her teaching and decided she must ask for some suitable books to be ordered.

For a while, everything went well. Sophie worked with Philip on his handwriting and helped Kit with his reading, encouraging him to read aloud to her every day. After a few weeks, however, she noticed a change in the older boy's attitude. He was becoming uncooperative and difficult. She knew there was pressure on him to prepare for his school entrance exam, and she knew he was behind in his studies. His father's frequent visits to the schoolroom did not help matters.

Philip would be going away to boarding school the following September, and his father wanted him to be ready. Mr. Wilmott-Smith was always critical when he came to examine his son's work and never gave him any praise. He largely ignored Kit but always picked on Philip. Sophie tried to defend him, telling his father that he had made progress, but Mr. Wilmott-Smith was relentless.

Philip was obviously unhappy and worried about going away to school. There was little she could do except encourage him to work harder and catch up. She was reluctant to put pressure on him, however, and would have to give it some thought.

CHAPTER THREE

STORM CLOUDS

TWO MONTHS HAD GONE BY, and October was chilly, with mists in the early mornings. Sophie felt isolated and alone. She was never invited to join the other members of the family, and the boys' mother did not appear to involve herself in her sons' education.

It concerned Sophie that Mr. Wilmott-Smith had such high expectations, and given his unyielding pressure on Philip to improve, his presence in the schoolroom was never welcomed by any of them. Occasionally, he would come to inspect Sophie's lesson plans. She disliked the way he towered over her in a domineering way and how he was often critical of her methods. She soon stopped trying to defend herself and simply said she would attend to his comments.

In addition to these concerns, none of the servants ever came near her, except the nursery maid, Annie, who spoke to her at breakfast. She told Sophie that the two boys were fond of their grandmama and looked forward to their visits with her.

A fire was now lit daily in the schoolroom, and as Sophie did not want to sit in there all the time, she asked Mrs. Arnold about having one in her own room in the afternoons. The housekeeper informed her that she would have to set it up herself, as none of the servants had time, and told her where to find a bucket of coal and some kindling.

Sophie first had to clean out the grate before she could lay the fire, and she then struggled to light it, ending up in tears. She went down the back stairs to find some more newspaper, and it occurred to her that

Harry the groom might be able to help. She had often greeted him as she left the house through the stable yard on her walks to the village, and he was always friendly.

She found him in the stables, busy polishing a harness. He looked up and smiled with surprise when she entered.

"Hello, Miss Anderson! What can I do for you?"

"I need your help, Harry. I am trying to light a fire in my room, and I have not been very successful so far."

"Well, I'm sure I can fix that." He got up and followed Sophie back to her room.

Sophie was surprised by how tall he was.

When he saw her efforts, he laughed. "I'm not surprised it wouldn't light. You need to layer it. Here, I'll show you."

Sophie watched as he quickly emptied the grate and began again, placing the paper in first, then the kindling, and finally small pieces of coal, which he placed carefully on top with the tongs. He lit it, and soon a fire was burning in the grate and the room gradually warmed up.

"Thank you so much, Harry. I think I could manage that again now that I have seen what to do."

Harry stood up. "If you have any more problems, you know where to find me," he said cheerily. He then left quickly. To be found in a woman's bedroom would get him into trouble.

Sophie had success lighting her fire from then on. *How domesticated I am becoming*, she thought to herself. She cleaned her room every Saturday and changed her bed linen when necessary. She had arranged at the beginning of her employment to pay to have her laundry done and didn't mind the other chores, as they gave her something to do.

Her weekends were usually very quiet. Every Saturday, when the weather permitted, Sophie walked down to the village. The lane she took had steep sides and several bends. Once or twice, she would meet a horse and cart struggling towards her and flatten herself against the bank to allow it to pass, receiving a wave and nod from the driver. The villagers were always friendly towards her, and she wished she could get to know them better.

On Sundays, she hardly spoke to anyone. She would like to have attended the service at the church in the village, but Mr. Wilmott-Smith insisted that the whole household, family and servants alike, attend morning prayers in the library. No hymns were sung, but there was a Bible reading, some prayers and a short address. Apart from a few polite good mornings, nobody said much to her, and the servants quickly returned to their duties afterwards. Sophie would go back to her room and spend the rest of the day on her own.

She still had not heard from her uncle. She thought perhaps he wanted no more to do with her, but then she remembered he had asked her to write. He and her cousins were the only relatives she had, as she had no contact with any of her mother's family. She wrote another letter asking if it was possible to spend Christmas with him, but still no answer came.

One Saturday when she returned from her walk, she was shocked to find that her room had been ransacked. She stood wide-eyed in the doorway, surveying the scene in disbelief. Her bedding had been pulled off the bed, her clothes were strewn across the floor and all her belongings were scattered about. She decided she must report it, so she went straight to find Mrs. Arnold.

She knocked on the housekeeper's door, and when she opened it, Sophie said in a wavering voice, "Mrs. Arnold, I am sorry to trouble you, but I have just returned from my walk and found that my room has been ransacked."

Mrs. Arnold's face showed little reaction to this. In fact, she stiffened slightly. "I hope you do not think any of my staff are involved, Miss Anderson."

"No, of course not," Sophie hastened to assure her. "I just thought it should be reported."

"Well, you've done that," the housekeeper said. "I can't say I can do anything about it. I think we both know who is probably responsible for this. If I were you, I would just tidy up and say no more about it. The master will not want to be bothered about such things."

There was little Sophie could do. She wondered why Mrs. Arnold was so reluctant to get involved. Perhaps she thought Mr. Wilmott-Smith would blame the servants?

Sophie returned to her room and began to pick up her things from the floor. She looked round anxiously to see if anything had been taken.

She kept her money in a tin, which was hidden in the back of a chest of drawers. Fortunately, she found it was still there, and no damage appeared to have been done to any items.

As she remade her bed and tidied her clothes away, she struggled with the possibility that Philip might have done this. The thought that he could do such a thing to her after all the help she had given him was hurtful. She recalled what Harry had said when she arrived at Clayden House.

Sophie thought she had better follow Mrs. Arnold's advice and let sleeping dogs lie. If she reported this incident to Mr. Wilmott-Smith, she knew there might be severe repercussions, and that would not help the situation in the schoolroom. But how had someone managed to get into her room? She had locked her door on going out, and it had still been locked on her return. If it was Philip, he had obviously had a key, and this worried her.

There were, however, no more serious incidents, and at the beginning of December, Mrs. Arnold came to speak to Sophie. "Miss Anderson, may I ask what your plans are for the Christmas holidays?"

Sophie had been worrying about this. "I have been trying to contact my uncle," she replied, "but I have unfortunately not heard back from him. If I am unable to visit him, then I'm afraid I have nowhere else to go."

"Well, that shouldn't be a problem," the housekeeper replied in a friendlier tone. "You can stay here, but you must be prepared to do some extra duties. The family is going away on Boxing Day for two weeks. There will be plenty to do before they return."

"Thank you. It is a great relief for me to know I can stay."

Mrs. Arnold managed a smile, and Sophie could see she would probably welcome some company at this time as well as extra help with her work.

The following day, just as Sophie was dismissing the boys at the end of the morning's lessons, Annie came to the schoolroom and informed her that the master wanted to see her immediately. As Sophie followed her out, she noticed Kit and Philip exchange looks. Unperturbed, she went and knocked on Mr. Wilmott-Smith's study door.

"Enter!" a voice called from within.

She was surprised to hear such a sudden command. Surely he knew it was her? When she entered, he was standing behind his desk.

In his hand was a small brass carriage clock. He held it up for her to see. "Miss Anderson, yesterday a valuable item was found to be missing from my drawing room. I immediately ordered a search of all the servants' rooms, including yours, and I must tell you it was found hidden in your chest of drawers."

He narrowed his eyes.

"I honestly have no idea how that got there, Mr. Wilmott-Smith," Sophie said, perplexed.

"You always lock your room, I presume?"

"Yes, always."

"Then can you explain how someone else could have gotten in? I have had servants and other members of staff steal from me before. It is not uncommon, and I make no exceptions. This always results in instant dismissal, without pay."

Sophie thought she was going to faint. She shook her head. "Sir, I would never steal from you."

"I must say, Miss Anderson, I am very disappointed in you."

Sophie began crying. "Please, please believe me, sir. I have not done this. I cannot explain it. I think someone must have a key to my room."

"That is highly unlikely. Mrs. Arnold has charge of all the keys in this house, and she has reported none missing."

"Sir, I am pleading with you to believe me. I am telling the truth, I swear I am."

"I think the evidence speaks for itself, don't you? You are very fortunate I am not sending for the local constable. Go and pack your things. I will arrange for your trunk to be taken down. You are to leave immediately."

Sophie saw how resolute he was and that there was little she could do to convince him. It occurred to her that she should mention her room had been ransacked. Perhaps he would wonder why she had not reported it before. He might deduce that she had taken the clock as some kind of revenge. She knew she could not accuse his sons outright, as she had no way of backing it up.

"Mr. Wilmott-Smith, why would I want to steal from you? I have been here only a short while, and I would in no way do anything to make you want to dismiss me. Please find out who has done this. I swear to God it was not me. I have no idea how the clock got to be in my room. Please don't send me away."

"I have had several members of my household stand in front of me in the past pleading their innocence," he replied. "They all left my employ once it was proven they were guilty of theft. As I said before, the evidence is clear. Who could get into your room without a key but yourself?"

It had been such a shock to be accused of stealing, and she felt numb and unable to think. She packed her belongings as if in a trance, then put on her hat and coat and began to make her way down the stairs.

Harry had been sent to collect her trunk and bags from her room, and as he passed her, he said, "Miss, I am sorry he has sent you away. I'll keep your things in the stables until you know where to send them. What will you do?"

"I don't know, Harry. I don't know," she replied. She could hear her own voice, but it felt like someone else was saying the words. She could not bring herself to look at him.

"Have heart, miss. I wish I could help."

She nodded and continued down the stairs, out of the side entrance, past the stables and through the arch into the lane. She had no idea what to do with herself. Somehow, she must try and get back to her uncle's house. She was thankful she still had the five guineas he had given her and hoped it would be enough to pay for her journey. As she walked down the lane, she had a thought. She would go and see the rector. He would surely help her.

She walked to the rectory and rang the bell pull, by this time sick with worry. She told the maid who opened the door she needed to see the rector, saying it was important.

The maid gave her a look and asked her to step inside. "He is having luncheon at present," she informed Sophie, tossing her head. Her manner was disdainful, and Sophie felt she was being put in her place. "I'll ask if he will see you when he's finished. You may have to wait a while." The maid marched away.

Sophie sat down and looked round. She was in a hallway, and opposite her was a mirror above a large stand full of coats, hats and walking sticks. She could hear the faint voices of people talking in a distant room, interrupted by occasional laughter. As she sat there clutching her bag, she wondered what to say to the rector. Would he believe she was innocent? What could he do to help her? She still hadn't quite taken in what had happened that morning. It had all been so sudden and unexpected.

When she had been sitting there for about an hour, the maid reappeared.

"He will see you now," she said and showed Sophie into his study.

The rector stood up as she entered. He was an imposing man, clean-shaven but with long side whiskers and a balding head.

"How do you do, sir," Sophie began nervously. "Thank you for seeing me. My name is Sophie Anderson, and I am—was—the governess at Clayden House."

The rector nodded. A friend of Mr. Wilmott-Smith's, he had been a frequent visitor to the house and knew who she was.

"What can I do for you?" he asked.

"This morning, sir, I was accused of stealing a valuable clock, which was found in my room after a search. Consequently, I have been instantly dismissed," she told him. "I am entirely innocent, and I have no idea how it got to be in my room. I am not a thief, and I cannot persuade Mr. Wilmott-Smith to believe me." By now, tears were streaming down her face, but she tried hard to keep her composure.

The rector appeared to be considering what she had told him. "Miss Anderson, what can I do? You must understand that I cannot be judge and jury in such a matter. I happen to know that Mr. Wilmott-Smith has had staff steal from him before and takes a very dim view of the matter."

"I have not stolen anything, sir. Please believe me. If you were to speak up on my behalf, I am sure Mr. Wilmott-Smith would take me back."

"I cannot do that, as I do not know the facts, young woman," he snapped, obviously annoyed by her request. "Furthermore, I am reluctant to interfere with Mr. Wilmott-Smith's domestic matters."

Sophie could see that he was unprepared to believe her.

"I cannot give you money," he continued. "If I gave money to everyone who came to my door, I would have half the parish turning up."

"I don't want any money," she answered, her voice almost a whisper.

The rector got out his pocket watch and looked at it.

"You just have time to walk to Kingsbridge before nightfall. Go to the vicarage there and they will tell you where you can get a night's lodging and some charitable help."

Sophie was astonished that he was not prepared to do more. "Thank you. I will take my leave now," she said and turned quickly to go.

Outside, it had started to rain. It was cold, so she ran towards the church to shelter on the porch and consider what to do. The drops began beating down heavily on the roof tiles when she got there, and as she looked out on the bleak churchyard, she felt like giving up. She pulled her coat round her, lay down on the bench and drew her feet under herself. Exhausted, she closed her eyes.

She had been dozing for only a short while when she woke to voices shouting.

"She's over here!"

Looking up, she saw Harry bending down in front of her, his curly hair framing his kind eyes.

"Oh, Harry!" she said, stretching out her hand.

He took hold of it and raised her up. "Master said we were to find you and bring you back. They've found out who did it."

Sophie looked at him in disbelief. "Thank God I can return! What happened?" She felt very confused and clung to Harry's arm.

"One of the boys," he replied. "Master Philip, and Master is very angry with him. He sent us to find you straight away."

Harry and his companion escorted her back to the house, Harry carrying her bag and supporting her as they walked. The rain had come to an end, and Sophie noticed the wet grass glistening in the sun round the gravestones. She found it hard to believe this was happening to her.

When they arrived, she was immediately shown into Mr. Wilmott-Smith's study. She stood in front of him, her face wet with tears and her hair in disarray.

"Ah, Miss Anderson! I am so glad you hadn't gone far. You will be pleased to learn that the culprit has been found and will be punished. You can return to your room and recover. The maid will bring some tea."

There was no apology.

Sophie stood before her employer in disbelief. "Am I not to know who it was, sir?" she asked.

"It is a private family matter, and you can be assured that I am dealing with it appropriately." He did not look up, and Sophie knew she was required to leave the room.

She felt utter disdain for this man, seeing he was not prepared to admit he was in the wrong and obviously had no compassion for her. She went upstairs, where she found a tray with sandwiches, cake, and a pot of tea. She was surprisingly hungry and glad to see it. She took off her coat and, as she sat down on the bed, began crying uncontrollably with relief.

At that moment, Harry arrived with her trunk. "Oh, miss, don't take on so," he said. "Master knows you're innocent now, and that's all that matters."

Sophie wiped her eyes and regarded the tall, lean young man in front of her. He wasn't handsome, but he had a kind, earnest face and a grin that made him attractive. "Thank you, Harry, for your kindness today."

He smiled, seeming pleased he had been able help her.

"Harry, you are the only real friend I have here. Can you tell me why the other servants are so unfriendly towards me?"

"Well, miss, it could be that the last governess used to report on them to Mrs. Arnold. They're not a bad lot here. It's just that the master doesn't know how to appreciate them." He set down her trunk. "Here, miss, I'll do your fire for you. Won't take a jiffy."

Sophie observed him as he went about setting up the wood. What a fine young man he was. He had a fire burning in the grate in no time, and after he left, Sophie enjoyed her tea and relaxed. She knew who the culprit was and wondered what she should do about it. Why had Philip done this? She reasoned that he wanted to get rid of her, as this might delay him taking the entrance exams for his school.

When Monday morning came, Sophie decided the best plan was to carry on as usual and keep the boy guessing. This would give her the advantage. She commenced lessons as usual, but as the afternoon session neared, she carried on instead of reading to them. She had finished *Treasure Island* and had begun to read *Moby Dick*, which the boys had been enjoying.

Sophie noticed that Philip appeared uncomfortable and kept looking at his brother. Kit asked if they were to have a story, and when Sophie replied that she had a good reason not to read to them that day, Philip put his head down and carried on with his work.

The following day, Sophie dismissed Kit at the end of the morning but asked Philip to stay behind. She could see he looked apprehensive.

"Philip, I think you are worried about starting your new school. Am I right?" she asked.

He looked at the floor and nodded in apparent relief.

"My father says I am not ready and will fail the exams," he replied.

"Let me tell you something, Master Philip. Things are often not as bad as we think they are going to be. When we are afraid, we tend to exaggerate in our minds what might happen, but it rarely turns out to be like that. I don't think you should be too worried about those exams. With just a little more work, I think you will pass."

Philip remained silent but appeared to be listening to her.

"Your father may think your studies are behind, but I can tell you that you have been catching up well. There is nothing to stop you achieving more, as you are an intelligent boy. Have you spoken to your mother or father about this?"

"No. My father gets angry with me all the time."

"What about your mama?"

"She's not interested in my schoolwork."

"Why don't you talk to your grandmama next time you go to stay with her?" suggested Sophie.

Despite what Philip had done to hurt her, she felt some compassion for the young boy as he sat before her with his head drooping down.

"I am here to help you, and I think you might enjoy your new school. You will meet boys of your same age and make friends."

With this, she thought she had said enough, so she allowed him to go.

As he left, he said, "Thank you, Miss Anderson."

It was Christmas Day, and after morning prayers, the few remaining staff returned to their duties and Sophie went back upstairs. She had collected some evergreen branches during her walks and had placed them round her room. She lit the fire and some candles, and it began to feel warm and festive. Among her belongings she had a hymn book, and she began singing some of her favourite carols quietly to herself.

At midday, all the staff were to gather downstairs for gifts to be distributed. Sophie put on her best dress for this occasion and looked forward to meeting everyone.

She went down the front stairs to the family dining room. There was a tall Christmas tree in one corner, and she spent some time admiring the shining glass balls that adorned it. The large dining table was covered with a white cloth, and on it there were several silver platters piled high with mince pies. At the end was a large tureen of mulled wine. Garlands of ivy entwined with red ribbons decorated the sides of the table, and Sophie thought it looked wonderfully attractive. Nobody spoke to her, but Mrs. Arnold gave her a smile from across the table.

The servants were helping themselves to the wine, ladling it out into small glass tumblers, when she saw Harry. He came over and wished her the compliments of the season. "Can I get you a drink?" he asked politely.

Sophie was relieved to have someone to talk to. "Yes please, Harry. That would be very kind of you."

They stood together enjoying their wine and mince pies. She asked him what he would be doing for Christmas.

"I have to drive the family to the station tomorrow," he said. "Then I can go home for a few days. I live with my mother in the village."

Suddenly, as the time came for the presents to be given out, there was an air of cheerful anticipation in the room. Everyone lined up round the sides and clapped as Mr. and Mrs. Wilmott-Smith entered, followed by Philip and Kit, both smiling broadly. Sophie was called up first, and Mrs. Wilmott-Smith handed her a simply wrapped parcel with her name on a label. She curtsied slightly, thanked her, and wished the mistress a happy Christmas. The lady of the house smiled broadly and picked up the next parcel.

Sophie withdrew and watched as all the others came forward to receive their gifts. Mr. Wilmott-Smith then gave a short speech of thanks to everyone for their hard work throughout the last year and wished them all a very happy Christmas.

After the festivities were over, Sophie returned to her room, where she opened her present. It was some stockings and a plain blue woollen shawl. Although practical, she had no need for these items, as she already had an adequate wardrobe. Christmas dinner was to be served at three o'clock, so she had a wait before going down for her tray. She decided to use the time to write down some memories of Christmas at home to remind herself of happier times.

On Boxing Day, the family left, and the remaining servants returned to their homes and families for the holidays. Mrs. Arnold never went away—like Sophie, her home was Clayden House. She and Sophie carried out various tasks throughout the house, including dusting, polishing and general tidying up. *What comfortable lives these people have*, thought Sophie as she moved round the rooms. As they worked, they chatted, and Mrs. Arnold told her that Mr. Wilmott-Smith was a partner in a bank in Kingsbridge. Sophie knew the family was well off. She had seen there were some fine pieces of furniture and beautiful pieces of chinaware in cabinets round the house.

On one of the mornings, they had to change the bed linen in the family's bedrooms. They started in the master's room and then moved on to the mistress's. Sophie was surprised they had different bedrooms, but she knew this was the custom in some households. When they entered Philip's room, Mrs. Arnold suddenly looked round, telling Sophie she thought she had left her keys in the mistress's room. Sophie waited for a minute while the housekeeper went back to look for them, then remembered that a key to her own room was still missing.

Convinced Philip must still have it, she glanced at the open door, then moved across to the chest of drawers beside the bed. She opened the top one but saw nothing of interest, so she moved on to the second drawer. Inside was a key that looked remarkably like her own. She took it out quickly and slipped it into her pocket, meaning to try it in her door later. A few moments later, Mrs. Arnold returned with her bunch of keys, none the wiser. Sophie felt elated. Now she could relax, knowing her room was safe from intrusion.

CHAPTER FOUR

A MEETING

AFTER THE CHRISTMAS HOLIDAYS, SOPHIE resumed her lessons in the schoolroom at Clayden House. She continued to read *Moby Dick* to the boys each day and was pleased to see they always packed away their books quickly and settled down to listen, obviously enjoying it. Sophie wondered if Philip had noticed the key in his bedside drawer was missing. His manner had been different towards her since he had returned after the holidays. He seemed relaxed and was friendly and more willing to work. She wondered if he had spoken to his grandmother.

Sophie had heard nothing from her uncle since she had begun her employment. It puzzled her, and she had even asked Mr. Wilmott-Smith if any letters had come for her. He assured her that she would have received any correspondence and seemed surprised she had enquired. She did not share her concern with him, as she considered him to be an unpleasant man and wanted as little to do with him as possible.

She was still desperately lonely. The boys and Annie provided a degree of companionship, but she longed to have some real friends. Maybe she should get to know some of the villagers, but she had little opportunity to walk there in January, as the weather was cold and frosty.

February came, and she decided to venture out even though the ground was still frozen. She walked through the stable yard into the lane. It was slippery, so she decided to try the other lane that branched off to the left, hoping it wasn't as steep. She had never walked that way before, thinking it just led to a farm.

Sophie followed the path down the hill. It curved round a bend, and she was surprised to come across two buildings on the lefthand side. One appeared to be a forge set back from the lane, and next to it, a little further on, was a cottage. Both were thatched, and there was an extended roof in front of the forge, supported by wooden pillars. Outside was a horse trough and a large chestnut tree, and underneath its spreading boughs was a wooden seat. She continued to follow the lane until it brought her to the far side of the village. Although it was a longer way round, she decided to walk that way in the future, as it was less of a steep climb back.

A few days later, when lessons had finished, Sophie looked out of the window and saw that the sun was shining brightly. It was late February, and she wanted to pick some snowdrops to put in her room. She had seen clumps of them growing up the banks on her walk past the blacksmith's forge and cottage, so she dressed warmly and set off down the lane, picking a few flowers here and there.

When she turned the corner, she saw there was a large Shire horse standing outside the forge. The blacksmith was bending down, hammering a shoe onto one of its hind hooves. The farmer, or a farmer's hand, was holding the horse's halter. Although it was cold, the blacksmith had the sleeves of his shirt rolled up, and he wore a large leather apron. Sophie stopped, interested to see what he would do next. She loved horses and would often stroke the warm soft muzzles of the ones in the stable yard.

The blacksmith hammered away, and when he had finished, released the horse's leg gently. He then stood up, and as he did so, he looked straight over to where Sophie was standing. Their eyes met, and he gave her a broad smile, held her gaze and then nodded in greeting. Sophie felt awkward, but she bowed her head slightly in acknowledgment and continued to walk on.

Really! she thought to herself. *These villagers can be very familiar.*

She knew his look had been one of admiration. He was a young man, and up until then she had had little experience making acquaintances with any young men, except Harry, who was so friendly that she felt at ease with him. Embarrassed, Sophie decided to take the steeper lane on her way back. Later, in her room, she kept thinking about her experience. She was curious to see the young blacksmith again and decided she would go that way next time.

She decided to wait a while before venturing down the lane again. A few days later, when the weather was bright and cold, she decided she needed some fresh air. It was towards the end of the afternoon, and rays of sunlight slanted through the trees along the side of the lane. As she approached the forge, she saw two fine-looking bay horses tethered outside. She could see they were not farm horses, and the blacksmith was talking to a groom. It seemed that he had just finished shoeing the horses, and the young man was paying him. The groom then led them round so they were facing up the lane, and Sophie saw it was Harry. He greeted her with a cheerful look on his face, and as Sophie approached, they stopped to talk.

"Hello, miss," he said cheerfully. "It's a bit chilly for a walk."

"Hello, Harry," she replied. "I am not going far today." She stroked one of the horse's necks. "What beautiful creatures these are."

"These are Mr. Wilmott-Smith's carriage horses," explained Harry. "He likes to keep them well shod."

Sophie continued to make a fuss of them but was conscious of the blacksmith looking at her intently.

"Ben, this here is Miss Anderson, from the house," said Harry, turning towards the other man.

"How do you do," she said, then reminded herself that village folk did not use that form of greeting.

Ben smiled at her.

"And how do you do to you," he replied. Was he making slight fun of her?

He is very handsome, despite looking rather grubby, Sophie thought to herself.

Ben had light ginger hair, a beard, and a pleasant open face. She noticed that he had broad shoulders and strong arms, and he looked warm after his exertions. Sophie moved to the side as Harry began to lead the horses round and back up the lane.

"Good day, miss," he said to her. "I need to get back."

As she watched them walking away, Sophie felt awkward standing alone with the blacksmith and decided to make conversation. "It must be very hard work shoeing all these horses," she said.

"It's my living," Ben replied. "But I do get to do other jobs like mending tools and farm machinery, which get broken quite often."

Sophie was tongue-tied. She knew nothing about his work and was unable to think what to say next.

"Wait there a minute." Ben went inside the forge and returned with a small shiny horseshoe. "There you are, Miss Anderson," he said, giving it to her. "This is for you."

Sophie held it in her hand.

"It's not for a foal," he added hastily. "They don't need them. It's for one of those miniature ponies. You know, the ones that pull dainty carriages for ladies like yourself."

Was he making fun of her again?

"Hang it up and it will bring you good luck one day, but only a bit, as it's so small."

This nonsense made Sophie smile. "Thank you…Mr. Browne," she said, looking up at a painted sign above the door which read, "William Browne, Blacksmith."

"Oh, that's my father's name up there," he said. "I've never got round to changing it, but please call me Ben."

"Thank you, Ben," she responded. "It's kind of you to give it to me."

She began to feel more relaxed, but as the sun was sinking lower, it was time for her to return to the house. "I must be going," she said. "It will soon be getting dark."

He nodded and stepped back to allow her to pass. She began to walk up the lane.

"Come again and tell me about your bit of good luck," he called after her, and she looked round and nodded.

My bit of good luck has just begun, she thought.

Unfortunately for Sophie, the weather took a turn for the worse, and the rain made it impossible for her to return to the forge for several days. She wanted to see the handsome young blacksmith again, as she hadn't been able to stop thinking about him.

Spring was well on the way by the time Sophie was able to resume her walks. She felt excited at the prospect of seeing Ben, but when she approached the forge, she saw him talking to two men. She thought it best not to go over, so she waved as she passed. He waved back, and the men looked at her curiously. What must they think about her familiarity towards him? She felt strangely excited inside at his response to her greeting. When she came back from the village, there was no one outside the forge, and she had to return home disappointed.

The following Saturday, on her way down, she was relieved to see him outside once more.

"Hello again, Miss Anderson," he called out in a friendly manner. "Have you had any luck yet?"

"Good day, Ben." Sophie smiled. "I think it might take a little while."

"You seem to like your walks."

"Yes, I love going for walks, especially at this time of year."

There was a moment's silence.

"Would you like to join me and my family for a walk come Easter Sunday?" he asked.

It hadn't occurred to Sophie that he might be married and have a family. She knew he had looked at her in an admiring way, and he had no business doing that if he had a wife. She would have to put her feelings aside if she was to meet them. It had been her wish to make friends with the villagers, after all.

She waited before she answered, "That would be lovely, Ben. Thank you for asking."

"We usually set off about two o'clock. We'll meet you here," he said.

Sophie returned home feeling elated. She had not expected this invitation. It felt wonderful to have something to look forward to at the weekend.

Easter was at the end of March that year, and the Wilmott-Smiths were going to the Lake District for the holiday, so when Easter Sunday arrived, there were no prayers. The morning seemed endless, and Sophie lost count of the times she went to the window to see what the weather was doing. At ten minutes to two, she left the house and walked down the lane, feeling pleasantly excited. The clouds had gone now, and she said a silent prayer of thanks as she walked past the grassy banks full of spring flowers.

As she approached the forge, she saw Ben waiting outside, looking quite different from usual. He was wearing a light jacket, a white shirt with a red neck scarf and beige trousers. Beside him stood a young woman with fair flyaway hair that she had attempted to pin up. She had the same pleasant, open face as Ben but was shorter and obviously younger. Sophie's heart sank at the thought of meeting his wife. Hiding behind the woman's skirt was a small boy who kept peeping round to catch a glimpse of their visitor.

"Miss Anderson, you came!" Ben said, looking pleased. "We are just about to set off. This is my sister Millie, and this"—Ben took hold of the small boy's arm and coaxed him out from behind the woman—"is the other member of our family, little Billy."

Billy wriggled free and dived back behind Millie.

Sophie laughed, relieved to learn Ben wasn't married. "Hello, Millie, how nice to meet you."

Millie seemed a little shy, but her smile was warm as she looked at Sophie.

Ben picked up a canvas bag, which he slung over his shoulder, and they set off down the lane towards the village. Millie picked up Billy and carried him, walking behind Ben and Sophie. They were both silent for a while, not knowing what to say to each other. Sophie hoped they were not heading for the village. She did not want any gossip if she was seen walking out with the blacksmith and his family.

Thankfully, at the bottom of the lane, just before the village, they turned and took a path beside a stream. Millie put Billy down, and he ran ahead on his little legs, full of glee.

"Have you been this way before?" asked Ben.

"No," replied Sophie. "I always keep to the lanes."

The stream was on their right, flowing between steep banks and overhung by trees. It felt mysterious and magical walking by the water as it bubbled over the moss-covered rocks. Soon, the path turned and came to a fence along the side of a field with a stile beside a gate.

"You go first, Millie," said Ben.

Sophie stood to one side while Millie hitched up her skirt to climb over. Ben passed Billy to her, then followed. He turned to Sophie and reached out to help her, holding her hand firmly as she scrambled over the stile. Their eyes met for a moment as she swung her legs over as elegantly as she could, and Ben helped her down. She thanked him but quickly withdrew her hand.

They walked across the field until they came to small spinney. The bank on the edge was covered in primroses. Sophie and Ben didn't have much opportunity to talk, as they had to walk in single file along the narrow path, and Ben had to carry Billy from time to time. They stopped when they got to the trees and sat down on the grass, glad for the rest. The sun peeked out from behind the clouds occasionally, and there was a fresh breeze. Ben took a shawl from his bag and insisted that Sophie sit on it. He then went off with Billy to explore while Millie and Sophie chatted.

Suddenly, Millie said, "I want to tell you that Billy's my son." She watched Sophie to see her reaction.

Sophie had suspected as much. "He's a lovely little boy," she said. "You must be very proud of him."

Millie smiled and nodded. "He's a bit of a handful at times, but Ben is very good with him." She turned to see where her son and brother were.

They were among the trees, foraging about, and she called them over. Ben walked back holding his nephew's hand and sat down next to Sophie. Billy ran off to play, and Ben lay down and closed his eyes.

Sophie studied him. *Poor man*, she thought, *he must get tired doing all that hard work at the forge*. She then looked over and saw Millie and Billy running around together. What a lovely little family they were.

Suddenly Billy ran over and jumped on top of Ben, who then tried to grab him. He darted away, and Ben jumped up and chased after him. Billy shrieked with excitement and ran as fast as he could but fell over in the grass, and Ben was able to grab him. Sophie and Millie laughed at their antics as Ben returned with Billy tucked under his arm, wriggling to get free. He put him down and picked up his bag and got out a glass bottle and three cups. He filled each one carefully and handed them round, giving Sophie hers first.

"We made this last year from some of our blackcurrants," he said. "I hope you like it."

Sophie took a sip. "It's delicious," she said and smiled at him.

Ben then got out some homemade cakes. Billy ran over to get himself one and then shared his mother's drink, sitting still for a while. It felt wonderful to be with these new friends, and Sophie had not felt so happy for a long time and was grateful to them for including her on their day out.

The whole afternoon passed pleasantly. She insisted that they call her Sophie, not Miss Anderson. She felt convinced that her decision to get to know the villagers was the right one. She realised she would have to adjust her behaviour and become more relaxed. She had been brought up to be politely formal and not overly familiar when meeting new acquaintances, and it did worry her that her friendliness might be misconstrued, especially by a young man.

As they sat together, Sophie told Ben about coming to Clayden House after her father died. She did not go into details, but simply said his business had failed and she had no alternative. She explained that she had an uncle and two cousins but no other relatives she was in contact with. Ben revealed that he was apprenticed to be a blacksmith to his father when he was thirteen years old and had taken over the forge when he died three years ago. Sophie then mentioned that Millie had told her Billy was her son, and Ben nodded, but he made no comment.

When they returned to the forge at the end of the afternoon, Sophie thanked them for an enjoyable time. Ben looked pleased and asked her to join them again for a walk the following Sunday, an offer she accepted enthusiastically. When she got back to her room, she looked at the little horseshoe hanging on the end of her bed and smiled. She felt happier now that she had two friends, and she would certainly look forward to her walks with them each week.

CHAPTER FIVE

FORBIDDEN FRUIT

WITH THE FAMILY AWAY FOR the Easter holidays, Sophie had again been required to carry out extra duties, but she worked through her tasks cheerfully, humming away and even making Mrs. Arnold comment that she appeared very happy in her work. Sophie had decided not to go to the village on Saturdays anymore, instead using the time to prepare her lessons. That way, she would be free for her walks each Sunday, which she hoped would continue. She felt excited at the thought of seeing Ben again the following Sunday and was disappointed when it rained heavily.

Two weeks later the weather had improved, and she made her way down to the forge, hoping that Ben and Millie were planning to go out that afternoon. Sure enough, they were there waiting for her. This time, they continued further along the path by the stream, and Sophie was impressed by Ben's knowledge of flowers and trees. They walked until they came to a meadow with a few small grassy mounds, which Billy had great fun climbing up and jumping off.

They sat down on some fallen logs, as the grass was still wet, and Ben shared out refreshments again. The day wasn't warm, so once they had eaten, they continued their walk to the end of the meadow until they reached a gate, where they admired the view. Across the woods and undulating fields, they could see the estuary spreading out unevenly, filling the valley, and it occurred to Sophie that she could sketch this vista on their next walk.

The months of April and May provided opportunities for several more walks, and Sophie's sketchbook soon filled with drawings of the places they visited. Ben was impressed by her talent and often sat beside her, watching her as she sketched. On those Sundays when it was not possible to go out because of the weather, Sophie would remain in her room, feeling disappointed.

She wondered if anyone at the house would comment on her walks with the blacksmith's family. She and Ben were becoming very friendly and more relaxed with one another, and Sophie really enjoyed being with her new friends. Millie was more reserved and was often busy seeing to Billy, so Sophie had many opportunities to talk to Ben. He was very easy going, and she felt drawn to him. She studied his face and thought that he had kind eyes. When she was away from him, she would experience feelings of longing to be with him again. She wondered if this developing friendship was unusual and perhaps something she shouldn't be engaging in. She convinced herself there was nothing objectionable about her new friends, and their social class should not matter.

Sophie loved the month of June, when everything in the countryside was fresh and new. On her walks, she would admire the tall foxgloves leaning out from the banks and the honeysuckle and briar roses growing in the hedgerows. One Sunday, towards the end of the month, Sophie had a surprise when she went to meet Ben and his family. As she turned the corner, she saw a horse and trap waiting outside the forge. She immediately thought they had a visitor and perhaps would not be going out that day, but then Ben came outside with Billy and waved at her.

Billy ran up to her and exclaimed, "We're going for a *wide*!"

Ben smiled. "No, it's *ride,* Billy." He turned to Sophie. "We're going a bit further, as it's such a fine day."

"That sounds like a wonderful idea. What a pleasant surprise," she said, giving Billy a hug. She could see he was excited.

Millie came out of the cottage carrying two bulky canvas bags, and they climbed into the trap. Ben drove, and the girls sat behind with Billy between them. The boy chattered on, his eyes shining as he told Sophie that they were going on a picnic and pointed at the bags on Millie's lap.

The trap bounced along, jogging Sophie and Millie up and down over the ruts and bumps in the lane, and there was a lot of laughter and squeals. Ben finally drew up by the side of the estuary, where there was a small stony beach overhung by oak trees, their low outstretched branches forming a mossy canopy along the bank.

Billy jumped down and made for the edge of the water. He chased the rippling waves backwards and forwards until they caught him and then jumped up and down with delight. While Ben attended to the pony, Millie emptied one of the bags, producing two rugs, a little bucket and wooden spade for Billy and a small cushion, which she gave to Sophie.

"Ben said this was for you to sit on when you are sketching," she said.

Sophie was touched by his consideration and thanked him when he joined them. She then began sketching Millie and Billy playing by the water's edge.

"Are you going to do me next?" Ben asked.

"I may do," she replied, looking at him with a smile.

He had positioned himself next to her, rather closely, and leant over her shoulder to see what she had drawn. "May I see?" he asked as he gently brushed some strands of her hair out of the way.

At his touch, Sophie was overcome with feelings she had never experienced before and stopped drawing. Just then, Billy came and poured some water down Ben's neck, making him jump.

Millie laughed, seeming to enjoy her little boy getting the better of her brother.

"The little…!" exclaimed Ben, getting up to chase him.

Sophie watched as he came back and sat down next to her. He dabbed his neck with his scarf, and Sophie helped dry him off. She liked feeling him so nearby. She had never been so close to a young man before and felt very drawn to him. He thanked her, but she thought he looked slightly embarrassed, and shortly afterwards he got up to pack up the bags.

On the way home, Millie offered to drive the trap and Ben and Sophie sat together in the back. Billy sat between them and was soon fast asleep. Sophie felt comfortable sitting next to Ben. She longed for him to hold her hand, but instead he sat clutching the two bags all the way home. Sophie would always remember the events of that afternoon when she realised how much she wanted to be closer to Ben.

The knowledge that she had fallen in love made Sophie feel awkward and diffident about seeing Ben again. What were his feelings towards her? How could she show him how much she cared about him?

On their next walk, Millie said she had to stay behind as Billy wasn't feeling well. This put Sophie in a dilemma. Was it appropriate for her to be seen walking out alone with a young man? She agreed to walk with Ben but hoped they would not be seen. He took her along the track towards the farm and showed her where Millie worked in the dairy. They then passed by the duck pond, and the path narrowed. Ben took her hand, and they continued their walk past hedgerows along the edges of fields, chatting quietly together. Sophie relaxed as she strolled along, and she had never felt so happy. When they returned to the forge, they sat under the tree outside for a while.

Ben was the first to speak. "I'm glad you agreed to come on our walks, Sophie. Millie and I are getting very fond of you."

Getting fond of me? thought Sophie. She wondered what he really meant. "I was grateful to be asked," she replied. "I have no friends at Clayden House, except perhaps Harry."

"Ah, yes, Harry." He held her hand a little more tightly. "I…I do value your friendship, very much. I never believed that a lady such as yourself would ever want to walk out with me."

"You've made me very happy, Ben."

He put his arm round her, and she leant against him. The sun shone through the leaves of the huge chestnut tree above them and made patterns with the shadows on the ground. All was peaceful as she sat there, quietly contemplating her love for Ben.

A few days later, Sophie had dismissed the boys from their morning lessons and was tidying her desk when Annie came into the schoolroom and informed her that the master wanted to see her at once. Sophie felt uneasy, remembering the last time she had been summoned. He usually came to the schoolroom to discuss anything to do with the boys. Perhaps he was dissatisfied with her work, or it might have something to do with Philip's exams. She gave a tentative knock on the door of his study and heard him call out, "Enter!"

As soon as she went in, she saw that he looked annoyed.

"Miss Anderson, it has been brought to my attention that you have been seen walking out with a most unsuitable person from the village."

Sophie had known this would be noticed at some point, and she was resolved to stand by her right to have her own friends, so she remained silent.

Unable to elicit a response from her, Mr. Wilmott-Smith went on. "Whatever were you thinking, Miss Anderson? Don't you know that a lady such as yourself should not be associating with such a character? You have disgraced yourself and my good name. You must not see this man again while you are in my employ, and if you choose to disregard me, you will be instantly dismissed. Do you understand?" His voice was stern as he leant over his desk towards her. "I know all about this man," he went on. "You are probably unaware he has a bad reputation in the village for getting into fights, and you have been extremely unwise to befriend him."

Sophie felt affronted by the way she was being spoken to and the interference into her personal life. He must be exaggerating. She could not imagine Ben getting into fights—he was so kind and gentle. She was surprised by Mr. Wilmott-Smith's anger towards her. Why was he speaking to her in such a way? She was, however, afraid to confront him.

Without attempting to justify her actions, she simply said, "Very well. May I go now?"

"Yes, and I hope you will attend to what I have said," he replied, giving her a hard look.

As she left, Sophie tried to control her feelings. She returned to her room and kept repeating, "How dare he!" under her breath, thinking he had no right to try and control her life. But what was she to do? She put on her shoes to go and see Ben. She hurried to the forge, feeling angry and frustrated at the way Mr. Wilmott-Smith had spoken to her and how he had treated her, now and in the past.

When she arrived, there was no one in the yard, but she could see the fire glowing and two figures inside. A man she did not know was working the bellows, and Ben was hammering the anvil. He looked up, and when he saw Sophie, he put down his hammer, said something to the other man and then wiped his hands on a cloth and came out. Sophie stood in front of him, trembling.

"Sophie, what's the matter?" he asked, putting his arm round her to calm her.

She began crying, so he led her to the bench, and they sat down together. Between sobs, she managed to tell him what had happened.

"Mr. Wilmott-Smith says that I am to be dismissed if I am ever seen with you again. He…he has no right! I have so enjoyed our walks together, Ben, and…and I cannot bear the thought of never seeing you again."

"Do you want me to sort him out?" he asked.

She could see he was angry.

"I mean it," Ben went on. "Nothing would give me greater pleasure than to give that man a good thumping."

Sophie shook her head, not wanting any violence.

Ben drew her closer, and she put her head on his shoulder.

"He's a menace and a bully. I'm not having him threaten you like this. Sophie, I really care for you. I don't want you to continue working at that place."

Sophie wiped her eyes. "I must stay, Ben. I have no other means of support."

"I can offer you a home," he said, looking intently at her.

Sophie was surprised. What did he mean? "That's very kind of you, Ben, but I wouldn't want to impose on you."

"I'm asking you to marry me!"

She raised her head and stared at him in utter disbelief.

"Don't answer now. Think about it. There's a lot to think about," he added.

Stunned by his proposal of marriage, she looked straight at him. "I-I don't need to think about it. The answer is yes!"

They regarded each other in astonishment for a moment. Ben drew her towards him and hugged her. "Thank you!" was all he could say.

He pulled back, and they looked at each other and laughed. Sophie had never felt so joyful in her whole life.

Ben shook his head. "I didn't expect you to say yes," he said.

"I didn't expect you to ask!"

"You must have known how much I love you?"

Sophie laid her head on his shoulder again, and he took hold of her hand. He told her that he had never thought she would want him. "You know what I am, Sophie. I don't have much to offer you. I just know that I want you to be my wife."

"I have grown to love you, Ben," replied Sophie, "and I want to be with you."

"I gave you that little horseshoe hoping you would come back."

"You had already made me notice you. I remember the first time I saw you looking at me with those blue eyes!"

"You put your nose in the air and walked on past."

Sophie knew she was being teased. "You were staring at me, if I recall."

Presently, Ben glanced across at the forge and said, "Look, I must get back. Let me think…we need a plan." He thought for a few moments, leaning forward looking at the ground, then sat up. "When do you get paid, Sophie?"

She told him it was on the first day of August.

"Just a few weeks. Now this is what we'll do. Carry on as normal until then. We must not contact each other during that time. We cannot give that man any excuse to dismiss you."

"Can I write to you?" she asked.

"No," he said quickly. "Don't even write. If you want to contact me, send a message by Harry. He is a friend of mine. The day before you get paid, pack your trunk, and I will arrange for Harry to collect it and hide it in the stables. The next day, pack your bag, collect your money, and then walk out and come straight here."

Sophie nodded enthusiastically, relieved that he was taking control of everything. He then kissed her, holding her tight. Sophie thought how wonderful it was to be loved and felt as if she could stay there forever in his arms.

As they parted, Ben said, "You're not to worry. I'll miss you."

"I love you, Ben," she replied.

As she left him, Sophie's thoughts were in turmoil. She had just received a proposal of marriage and experienced her first kiss from the man she had grown to love so intently. She would no longer be alone and could now leave Clayden House and the unpleasant Mr. Wilmott-

Smith. She lingered outside the forge and watched Ben as he returned to his work. When she turned to go, she heard his friend taunting him.

"I didn't know you were acquainted with a *lady*."

She did not hear Ben's reply.

CHAPTER SIX

LEAVING

Sophie woke up suddenly. She lay in bed listening to the pigeons outside her bedroom window, and her first thought was that it was the first of August and she was leaving Clayden House forever that day. A wave of relief washed over her. The weeks of waiting had passed, and now, at last, she could see Ben again. She still found it hard to believe that she was getting married.

What did it matter if he was a humble blacksmith? He was a kind and gentle man who had shown he cared for his sister and her child. Sophie knew they would never have much in the way of riches, but she preferred that to life at Clayden House. She had dealt with her doubt as to whether she was marrying to get away from her present situation. She knew she loved Ben and wanted to be his wife. What her life would be like hereafter, she did not know. She wondered if he still felt the same about her and worried he would tell her he didn't think it would work if they married, that she wouldn't like the sort of life he could offer.

The time since he had proposed had given her an opportunity to reflect. She had tried to visualise life with Ben, and although she loved him deeply, she was concerned that wouldn't be enough when he expected a meal on the table after his day's work. Sophie knew she would be required to plan meals and procure the ingredients, but she had never cooked a meal in her life. She had been brought up in a comfortable home where there were servants. Perhaps Ben would become disenchanted with her if she couldn't run the home, so she had a lot to learn.

During her last few days in the schoolroom, her feelings had been mixed. Philip had made better progress since Christmas, and she thought he was ready for his school entrance exams. She knew she had done all she could for him and had wished him well at his new school. She had grown fond of Kit and thought he would probably do better without the influence of his brother. Thankfully, Mr. Wilmott-Smith hadn't bothered her too much lately. She detested the man and had only spoken to his wife a few times. At the end of her last day, after removing her belongings, she had closed and locked the door of the schoolroom with the greatest relief.

In her mind, she went over what she must do. She would pack her bag, collect her money and then leave, just as Ben had told her. She got up and prepared for the day ahead, and Annie brought her breakfast tray to her room, as the boys were having their breakfast downstairs. Sophie expressed her appreciation for the maid's service over the last year and gave her a small gift of money. Annie looked pleased, if a little embarrassed, and thanked her before leaving. Sophie had grown to like this young woman with whom she had shared her breakfast each day. The boys had never been good conversationalists.

She waited patiently until it was time to go downstairs to collect her salary. Harry had collected her trunk and bags the evening before and had given his congratulations. Ben must have told him they were to be married. Sophie sat on the bed with her satchel on her lap, hoping no one would come into her room and wonder why it was so empty. She had not told anyone she would be leaving.

Her door was slightly open, and she could hear the clock in the hall chiming ten. At last, it was time to go. She descended the stairs and made her way to the library, where she had been told to collect her money. Inside, two men were sitting behind a table, one with a large ledger in front of him and the other with a cash box. She did not recognise them and decided they were probably from the bank.

Without looking up, one of them said, "Name?"

"Miss Anderson."

His finger moved down the page of the ledger. "Thirty pounds less two pounds twelve shillings for laundry. Twenty-seven pounds and eight shillings."

He turned to look at the other man, who put his hand into the cash-box and counted out her money. Sophie picked up the gold sovereigns and shiny shillings that he placed on the table. They felt so good in the palm of her hand—the first money she had earned herself. Placing all the coins carefully in her purse, she signed the ledger, thanked both men and withdrew.

She walked back upstairs, across the landing, up the next flight of stairs and down the back stairs to the door that led out into the stable yard. There was no one about, so she continued through the arch towards her new life and freedom.

She hurried down the lane, feeling nervous, her hands shaking. As soon as she turned the corner, she saw Ben, Millie and Billy waving to welcome her. Ben came over and embraced her and gave her a kiss. She then turned to Millie and Billy and hugged them both.

"It is wonderful seeing you all again! I feel I have been released from prison. I hope nobody comes looking for me," she said, looking anxiously behind her.

"They won't send anyone after you," said Ben. "If they do, they won't be coming again."

The horse and trap were waiting outside the forge, and Ben explained that he had arranged for Sophie to lodge with a lady in the village. "You'll like her," he said. "She was a friend of my mother's, and I've known her a long time. She will look after you well."

Sophie was disappointed he had not invited her to go into the cottage and see where she was to live. Seeing her glance towards the cottage, Ben added quickly, "It's best you don't live here until we're wed, Sophie, and you'll want to be away from Clayden House."

Sophie knew that, as a gentlewoman, she had her reputation to think of, and she was relieved that she would be away from her place of employment. She climbed into the trap, and Millie and Billy, who were also coming for the ride, got into the back. Ben drove them down the hill and to the far end of the village, to a cottage surrounded by a picket fence. The door opened, and a smiling lady with white hair tied in a bun came out to welcome them.

"This is Mrs. Chambers," said Ben.

She greeted Sophie warmly. "Hello, my dear. I have been so looking forward to meeting you."

They all went inside, Millie holding Billy's hand tightly in case he ran around. The cottage was as neat and tidy as its owner, and Sophie thought she would be happy living there. Ben saw her settled in, then excused himself. He said they needed to return to the forge as he might have some customers waiting and that he had some errands to attend to. He added that he would collect Sophie's trunk and bags from the stables and return them to her later that day.

Once the others had left, Mrs. Chambers took Sophie round her home and explained the routines. "I hope this will be acceptable to you, Miss Anderson."

Sophie assured her that it was all perfect. She had been shown into a charming little bedroom that contained a bed, a small chest of drawers and a chair. On one side of the fireplace was a narrow cupboard and on the other side some bookshelves. There was a flowered coverlet on the bed and matching curtains at the window. The walls were decorated with a pastel blue patterned wallpaper and hung with some attractive pictures. It was all very welcoming.

Mrs. Chambers had prepared some salad from her garden for their midday meal and some strawberries for after. Sophie welcomed this light lunch, feeling nervous and excited. Afterwards, she excused herself and went to rest in her new bedroom. She hadn't slept well the night before, and the morning had been emotionally exhausting.

She fell into a gentle sleep and was woken a little later by a knock on the door. Ben had arrived with her trunk. There was hardly room to put it down, but he eased it in and then sat on the bed and began kissing her.

"We'd better go downstairs," said Sophie after some moments, drawing back from his passionate embrace. Ben laughed and followed her.

Mrs. Chambers laid tea on the table in the sitting room and left after inviting Ben and Sophie to help themselves. They talked about their wedding, and Ben explained that he had arranged for their banns to be read in church the following Sunday. These notices had to be read out to the congregation for three consecutive weeks, announcing their intention to marry, before they could be wed. They would be expected to attend church every Sunday to hear them. This meant they could get married at the beginning of September.

"Ben, can you ask Millie if she would be my bridesmaid?" Sophie asked.

"She will like that," he replied. "Thank you."

Ben told her that they he would take them both into Kingsbridge the following Saturday to purchase "wedding stuff," as he called it. He would ask Mrs. Chambers to watch Billy for the day so Millie could come.

Sophie thought about her purse of sovereigns and how she could now buy things. This reminded her that she should be paying some rent while staying at the cottage, so she asked Ben how much it would be.

"Don't worry about that," he said. "It is all taken care of."

Sophie realised that Ben was there to love and take care of her now. It was kind of him to pay for her lodgings until they got married.

Millie and Billy joined him when he came over the next day, and they discussed wedding clothes. Mrs. Chambers recommended a dressmaker in Kingsbridge, and it was decided that Ben's suit would be ordered at the tailors.

"I would like to help out with the expenses," Sophie told Ben. "My uncle gave me five guineas when I left, and I think this would be just the thing to spend them on."

Ben did not disagree, and Sophie thought she detected some relief in his expression. Perhaps he was not that well off.

During the next few days, Sophie relaxed and insisted on helping in the house and garden. At first Mrs. Chambers protested, but Sophie confided in her that she needed to learn about household management.

"My mother wanted me to concentrate on my education, so she did not involve me in anything to do with the running of the house. When she was ill, our governess helped her with this."

"How old were you when you lost your mother, my dear?" asked Mrs. Chambers.

"Just fifteen. It took me a long time to get over. My father helped me and encouraged me to continue my studies. I do wish that they were both here to see me get married."

"You will feel they are with you on the day," said Mrs. Chambers, patting Sophie's hand.

Sophie wondered what her parents would have made of her choice. Ben was a man who had to work hard for his living. She would never enjoy the conveniences and comforts that a middle-class marriage would have given her. These thoughts were a little disturbing. Was she doing the right thing?

Mrs. Chambers was very motherly and a good teacher, and she ran her home very efficiently. She gave Sophie cookery lessons and showed her how to preserve food, bake bread and grow vegetables and herbs in the garden. Sophie learned how to launder clothes and how to clean the house. She had never enjoyed herself so much. When shopping in Kingsbridge, Sophie had bought two notebooks, and she would copy recipes in one and make notes on household management in the other. She enjoyed working alongside Mrs. Chambers in her kitchen every morning, and in the afternoons, she would go for a walk or read. Sophie preferred this domestic way of life to that of a governess, but she knew she would have to work hard as a blacksmith's wife.

In the evenings, Ben and Sophie sat in Mrs. Chambers's garden, talking together.

Sophie spoke more about her father's death. "My father and I were very close after my mother died, and I was hoping to help him in his business. He imported wines and, unknown to me, he was in debt. He had borrowed a substantial amount of money from his brother, the uncle I told you about, and it was never paid back. My father took his own life because of these financial difficulties, obviously unable to see his way out of it all."

Ben put his arm round her. "I am so sorry. It must have been dreadful for you."

"I was summoned out of school and told by my uncle that I had to support myself from now on. That is how I came to be a governess at Clayden House."

"Didn't your uncle offer you a home?"

"No. I suppose I should have asked him why I couldn't stay, but he wasn't well at the time, and I was embarrassed that my father had left such a large unpaid debt. Despite writing several letters, I have never heard another word from him."

"Don't you have any other relatives?"

"My mother was an only child, but I think she had some cousins. I don't know where they live, however. What about you?"

"I did not want to be a blacksmith, but I had no choice. My mother died when I was sixteen and Father took to drink. It was a difficult time, especially for Millie."

"Did she have Billy then?"

"No, thank goodness. Father had died just before it all happened."

Sophie was still curious about the circumstances of Millie's pregnancy, but she felt it wasn't right to probe. No mention had been made to who the father was. She admired Ben for looking after his sister and her child.

As if reading her thoughts, Ben said, "I hope you don't mind Millie staying with us after we marry. I could not expect her to leave."

"Of course she must stay," answered Sophie adamantly. "We are all one family."

Ben smiled and hugged her. "Billy is like a son to me," he said.

The following Saturday morning, Ben and Millie arrived with Billy outside Mrs. Chambers's cottage in the horse and trap. They left Billy with dire warnings to "be good" and set off for Kingsbridge. It was market day, and the whole town was busy and bustling with people.

Ben left the trap tethered at the top of High Street and went to collect some items for Mrs. Chambers while Sophie and Millie visited the dressmaker. They discussed patterns, and after being measured, they made their way down the hill to purchase the lengths of fabric they would need. The market was busy, and they had to push through the crowd to reach the stall selling material. They pulled out several rolls before making their choice and then moved on to the haberdashers to select the trimmings. Sophie had chosen a cream material with embossed flowers, and Millie was to have a lilac patterned dress. These purchases were to be delivered to the dressmaker on their way home that day, and they were to return to her in two weeks' time for a final fitting.

After they were done at the market, they all met up at the Harbour Inn for lunch, then wandered around the shops and found a tailor for Ben, where he ordered his wedding suit. They then sat by the estuary for a while, watching the ships and the general bustle on the quayside.

"This is where I collect my coal and the iron rods I need for the horseshoes," Ben told Sophie. "I have an account with a merchant, so I get regular supplies."

Sophie realised she would have to acquaint herself with the running of the forge. It would be their only means of livelihood.

On the way back, she and Millie were both excited and chatted happily about their wedding dresses and flowers until Ben told them to "give way, for goodness sake!" The two of them broke into giggles. Sophie had lost a lot of her initial reserve when conversing with Millie, finding her easy to get along with.

At Mrs. Chambers's cottage, Billy was duly returned to his mother with assurances that he had been well-behaved, but Millie confided in Sophie that she suspected he had been spoiled with treats.

Once Millie and Ben had left, Sophie thought about her day. The dressmaker's attentions had made her realise that she really was to be married and that it would be her special day. She recalled how she and Millie had left the shop together and walked down the hill excitedly, exchanging ideas as to what their dresses would be like. The market had been alive with Saturday-morning shoppers, and they had jostled among them, looking at all the stalls and pointing out items they would like to buy. In the afternoon they had sat by the quayside watching the men unloading the goods and piling them into carts to take up the hill. Then they themselves walked back up to the horse and trap. It had been a wonderful day.

CHAPTER SEVEN

AN INVITATION

SOPHIE WAS PICKING SALAD FROM the garden when Mrs. Chambers came and handed her a letter. She thought it was at last a reply from her uncle, but then she saw it was a hand-delivered note. It was from Mrs. Hunter, the rector's wife, inviting her to tea the following afternoon. Sophie had never met Mrs. Hunter and could only think it must have something to do with her wedding. She didn't mention it to Ben that evening, as it occurred to her it might be about him.

The next day, she arrived at the rectory and was shown in. Mrs. Hunter was sitting in an elegantly furnished room, waiting to greet her. She was a middle-aged woman with pink cheeks and smiling eyes. Her dark green dress was gathered in at the waist and had full sleeves, and several gold chains adorned her ample bosom.

"Miss Anderson, how do you do. I am so glad you could come. Please do be seated."

"How do you do, Mrs. Hunter," replied Sophie. "It is very kind of you to invite me."

As Sophie sat, Mrs. Hunter pulled the bell rope to order tea, giving Sophie a bright smile as she did so. Sophie was apprehensive, suspecting that the woman must know about her sudden exit from Clayden House. She remembered the rector telling her Mr. Wilmott-Smith was a friend.

The maid entered with a tray, placing it on the table between them. Mrs. Hunter picked up the silver teapot. "You'll take some tea, my dear?" she asked.

"Thank you, yes."

She handed Sophie a cup and poured herself one, then offered her a plate of sliced cake. While they sipped their tea, they talked for a while about the weather, and at any other time Sophie would have enjoyed their conversation, but she felt wary.

Eventually, Mrs. Hunter put down her cup and regarded Sophie. "My husband tells me that you have recently terminated your position as governess at Clayden House and you are intending to marry?"

"Yes, ma'am."

"I am also told this person you wish to marry is not of your social standing?"

"No."

"My dear, are you sure you know what you are doing?"

So, Sophie had been right in her suspicions. She had no intention of justifying her decision to marry Ben and so did not reply.

Undeterred, Mrs. Hunter went on. "I think you need to think about this very carefully, Miss Anderson. It is just not done for a woman of your position, marrying beneath herself like this."

Sophie remembered being treated as a servant at Clayden House, not as a middle-class young lady.

"This man you are hoping to marry, do you know anything about him?" Without waiting for an answer, Mrs. Hunter continued. "I know the family. He is a most unsuitable character and will bring you nothing but trouble. You really must break off this engagement. It is pure folly."

She appeared to be waiting for a reaction, but Sophie still said nothing.

"You will be ruined if you marry this man," Mrs. Hunter pressed. "I *implore* you to think again. I cannot make myself any plainer."

Sophie was puzzled. She was curious to know why this woman was so adamant she should not marry Ben. The rector's wife had never taken any interest in her before, and Sophie was sure the rector would have told her about the time she had knocked on their door in a destitute state.

"May I ask why I would be ruined, ma'am?"

Looking away, Mrs. Hunter shifted uncomfortably in her chair. "I have my reasons," she replied. "I know matters about him which I cannot discuss with you, but believe me, it is in your best interest not to marry him. You are an educated young lady. You could do much better. Why on earth are you intent on marrying him?"

Sophie had no desire to discuss the matter, so she said as politely as she could, "You have given me a lot to think about, Mrs. Hunter. Thank you for inviting me to tea. I shall take my leave now, and I think I shall do the right thing."

This seemed to satisfy the rector's wife, and she rang the bell again. Sophie rose to go and was shown out, glad to step outside and breathe in the fresh summer air. The rectory was not far from Mrs. Chambers's cottage, but she needed to walk for a while. She felt very affronted by Mrs. Hunter's interference and did not fully understand it. Both she and Mr. Wilmott-Smith had denigrated Ben without giving any real reason as to why. Sophie felt concerned and wanted to know what it was they held against him.

Doubts and questions arose in her mind as she walked down the lane, although she tried hard to dispel them. She wanted nothing to spoil her wedding and her future with Ben. He was a kind man who had shown he loved her and wanted to be with her. Perhaps she should not tell him about her meeting with Mrs. Hunter. It might make him angry, and they needed the rector to marry them. She would ask Mrs. Chambers about it, who had known Ben's family for some time. It was something she did not really want to confront. A dark cloud had appeared, threatening to destroy her happiness.

The following Sunday, they had to attend church to hear their banns read. Ben had arranged to meet Sophie outside and led her to a pew at the back. Mrs. Chambers sat with her friends in her usual place, and the service began. Sophie hadn't been to church for quite a while, but she had enjoyed singing hymns as a young girl and joined in the service enthusiastically. Ben seemed unsettled and fidgeted through most of it. Sophie saw members of the congregation looking at them both with interested glances.

At the end of the service, Ben led her straight out before the rector reached the porch to bid farewell to his flock. She was relieved not to have to acknowledge Mrs. Hunter with Ben holding her arm. They walked back to Mrs. Chambers's cottage, where they sat in the garden.

"I want to tell you something," Ben began.

That made her nervous. Whatever could it be?

"When Millie was fifteen, she was seduced by the rector's son, Jonathan. He is the father of Billy. When I found out, I went to see the rector and that woman, his wife, to tell them and ask what they intended to do about it. They flatly refused to believe it was their precious son to blame and accused Millie of lying to extort money from them. I was furious, but there was nothing I could do. I bided my time and waited for Jonathan one night when he was returning to the rectory. He too denied all knowledge of his crime, so I dealt with him."

Sophie was shocked at what she was hearing. "Oh, Ben! Whatever did you do?"

"I beat him up."

Hearing him admit to violence astounded and upset her.

"He was laid up for a while, then bundled off somewhere. Nothing was done. The father didn't want any scandal. I think he must be living elsewhere now, but I believe he visits his parents from time to time."

Sophie stared at Ben, wanting to disbelieve what she had heard. "How could you do such a dreadful thing?" she asked.

"I was angry, Sophie. Millie was very young, and that traitor seduced her, then abandoned her, hiding behind his parents' respectability."

"Poor Millie," said Sophie, her eyes full of sorrow. "To be treated in such a way."

Sophie didn't know what to think. She knew that Ben loved his sister and obviously hated her getting hurt. It was now obvious why the rector's wife held Ben in such low regard.

"Ben," she said, "his father is going to marry us."

"Yes, he'll have to do that."

Sophie then told him about her visit to Mrs. Hunter.

"That man and his wife are the worst kind, no more Christian than my boot!" He kicked his foot hard against the grass. "I suppose you think I did the wrong thing, Sophie, but you have no idea how angry I was."

"Thank you for telling me all this. Poor little Billy, not knowing his father."

He took her hand, and she realised he wanted reassurance. "Ben, I love you, and I hope you would not want to do anything like that again."

He said nothing and still looked angry at the memory of it all.

Mrs. Chambers arrived home from church and invited them all to luncheon, so Ben returned home to collect his sister and nephew. Sophie went to her room and took off her hat. She had a lot to think about.

At the back of her mind, she was still wondering whether all would be well if she were to marry Ben. She kept remembering Mrs. Hunter saying, "He'll bring you nothing but trouble." Was Ben a violent man? She could see he was a strong man. He had to be for his work.

Sophie decided to bring up the subject with Mrs. Chambers. Every afternoon, they would share a pot of tea, and the next time they sat down together, Sophie expressed her concerns.

Mrs. Chambers listened quietly, then proceeded to tell her a little about the family. "Ben's father was a tough man. As a blacksmith, he had to be, and often folk couldn't pay him. There was a lot of poverty in those days, and they were very hard up at times. Ben's mother was a lovely woman, and she handled her husband well, but after she died, he went a bit off the rails, preferring the company at the village inn. He was hard on Ben, making him miss school and work in the forge, and he didn't give him any choice in the matter.

"Ben is a kind man. Yes, he has fallen out with some folk if they have crossed him, but he has been good to me, and he has helped others in the village. He does it quietly, and not many people realise. He will make you a good husband, Sophie, but not a perfect one. You may have to be firm and put your foot down from time to time, and sometimes you will just have to look the other way. You know men will be men. You are an intelligent and perceptive young woman, and you will know what to do."

Sophie hoped she would. Arrangements were going ahead for the wedding, and the day was fast approaching.

CHAPTER EIGHT

THE WEDDING

All Sophie's concerns were forgotten on the morning of the wedding. She and Millie were snuggled up together under the bed covers, looking forward to the day ahead. Millie had come to stay with Sophie while Billy stayed with his uncle at Forge Cottage. The girls wondered how Ben was coping with getting him ready.

Sophie felt sad at the thought of leaving Mrs. Chambers's comfortable home. She had learned so much from her, but she was looking forward to running her own household. She could see that Millie was pleased that she was coming to live with them. Sophie would be there to help with the cooking and housework. Millie asked if she minded her increasing her hours at the farm dairy.

"No, of course not," replied Sophie good-naturedly.

At this, Millie looked very pleased and added, "I wondered if you would care for Billy so I would not have to take him with me. He does have a habit of running about and getting in the way when I'm milking."

Sophie readily agreed, realising that Millie needed to have a break from caring for her son.

After breakfast, Millie helped Sophie put on her wedding dress. It had a fitted bodice with puff sleeves, and there were satin-covered buttons down the front and on each cuff. The skirt draped down in soft folds and was a little longer at the back. She did not have a veil. Instead, some jasmine flowers were entwined in her hair, and she had a bouquet of flowers from Mrs. Chambers's garden with trails of ivy hanging down. Attached to the bouquet was the little horseshoe Ben had given her.

Millie put on her bridesmaid's dress, which was printed with small lilac flowers and trimmed with cream lace, and she wore lace gloves. Mrs. Chambers fussed round them both, making sure the dresses fit perfectly.

"You both look a real picture!" she exclaimed, handing Sophie her bouquet. "Now, I think all is ready for us to go!"

Mrs. Chambers put on her hat and gloves and ushered them out of the door. They walked together through the lych-gate and up the path past the ancient yew tree to the church porch. Sophie stepped carefully and held up the hem of her dress slightly. Millie followed, holding her posy of flowers. Outside the church, Sophie could hear the soft sounds of the organ playing within, and when she entered, she was surprised to see that the church was full of village folk. Everyone, it seemed, wanted to see Ben's bride. The village had been buzzing with talk ever since the banns had been read announcing the blacksmith was to marry the lady teacher up at the house. Sophie wondered what the villagers would make of her once she was Ben's wife.

Ben had asked a friend, Thomas, to give Sophie away. The elderly man had been delighted, and he was now waiting for her just inside the door. He took her arm, and he, Sophie and Millie processed down the aisle towards the formidable figure of the rector, who stood in front of the altar waiting to conduct the service.

When Sophie reached him, Ben turned towards his bride and smiled his charming smile, and she remembered when she had walked down the lane for the first time and seen him outside the forge. She now realised she must have begun to fall in love with him that very day.

The service progressed as words were spoken, promises made and hymns sung, and Sophie felt she was in a dream. The rector's haughty face did not change throughout the ceremony. Afterward, Ben led her out, holding her arm and smiling proudly. They bent their heads slightly as handfuls of flower petals were thrown over them by the cheering group of villagers and then climbed into the waiting horse and trap, which Mille had decorated with ribbons and flowers. Harry drove along the lane back to Forge Cottage, followed by the wedding guests.

The wedding breakfast had been laid in the orchard in Ben's cottage garden for the family and a few close friends. An awning was hung between the trees for shade, and tables had been placed together underneath, covered in a white cloth. Two silver candelabras with white candles and two vases of pinks stood at each end of the table, between strands of ivy. Sophie was enchanted by the scene.

"Oh, Ben, this is wonderful!"

"Millie helped. We wanted to give you the best we could," he replied.

The guests were seated, and the wedding breakfast commenced.

Harry stood up, cleared his throat, and prepared to deliver his speech. "I would like to begin by saying I am glad that my good friend Ben has found himself such a fine wife as Sophie. He is a lucky man!"

There were murmurings of agreement and smiling nods from the guests.

"I first met Sophie when I collected her from Kingsbridge to bring her to Clayden House just over a year ago. Never in my mind did I think I would be standing here now as Ben's best man, but I am proud to do so. Ben is a hardworking and good man, and he has gained himself a prize by winning the hand of Sophie." He then turned towards her. "I just hope she can manage those bellows."

Everyone joined in the laughter that followed, and Sophie took on a look of pretended shock and shook her head at Ben.

Harry held up his glass. "Please join me in a toast to the happy couple. To the bride and groom!"

The guests raised their glasses, wishing the newly married couple long and lasting happiness.

Sophie looked at Ben. Their eyes met, and she knew she loved him dearly.

At three o'clock, friends and acquaintances from the village arrived, bringing more plates of food. Sophie went round greeting everyone, trying to remember names. She wanted them to think she was friendly and would be a good wife to Ben. She looked over to the far side of the orchard where Ben was standing, talking to friends. He looked confident and happy, and she could see he was proud to be married to her. It was at that moment Sophie convinced herself she had done the right thing in becoming his wife.

The day moved to evening as the sun set behind the trees. All the guests had gone, and Ben and Sophie were left sitting by themselves under the trees while Millie took Billy away to bed. Ben took hold of his wife's hand.

"Well, my love, we are now married. I hope I can make you happy and provide a comfortable home. I know you are used to a better life than I can provide, but I will make sure you will always have the best I can give you."

"And I hope I will make you a good wife," Sophie replied. "Whatever the future, we shall be together."

After they had been talking for a while, it began to feel chilly, so Ben suggested Sophie go inside while he cleared up a bit. Sophie went into the cottage for the first time, breathing in its sweet, old-fashioned smell. As she entered the small kitchen, she noticed the wedding meal clutter and food on the table and knew it would need to be attended to in the morning.

She went up the narrow wooden stairs to a small landing and into her new bedroom. It had a low ceiling and a small casement window looking out towards the forge. There was a large double bed with a brass bedstead that almost filled the room. It was covered with a quilted bedspread, and Millie had put some flowers on the pillows. As Sophie got undressed, she imagined Ben sleeping in this room, and his parents before him and perhaps his grandparents also. Now she had joined the family.

What a wonderful day it has been, she thought as she went over the events in her mind. Ben and Millie had worked so hard, and she must show them her appreciation. Billy had behaved well and had spent much of the day chasing round the garden with some of the village boys. He would be tired tomorrow.

Eventually Ben arrived, and he looked over at her as she lay in the bed, bending over to kiss her. "Are you ready for some joyful loving?" he asked.

Sophie held out her hand towards him, and he took it in his. "I love you so much," she replied.

"It's just us now, Sophie. It's been an exciting day, the best day of my life, but we have had to share it with everyone. Now we can be alone." He wrapped his arms round her and held her close.

The next morning, Sophie was woken by Millie bringing in a jug of hot water. Ben had risen earlier, and Millie told her they had cleaned all the plates and dishes and were now returning them to Mrs. Chambers in the horse and cart. When they returned, they would all have breakfast together. Billy was sleeping in.

After she had washed, Sophie went over to her trunk and looked for some suitable clothes to wear. She knew there was work to be done. Mrs. Chambers had thoughtfully given her two large pinafores, and once she was dressed, she put one on and descended the stairs.

She was dismayed by what she saw. The kitchen was quite shabby and required a thorough cleaning. The floor was dirty, and the table in the middle of the room needed a good scrub. The kitchen range had been lit, and there was a kettle steaming away on top. By the fire was an old Windsor chair with rather grubby cushions, and on the floor were rag mats that had seen better days. There was a dresser displaying an assortment of china plates and jugs, plus a fitted cupboard with some shelves in the corner. The back of the kitchen led into a small scullery with a sink, a tap and a pantry. Sophie peeped inside and saw that too needed to be cleared out.

She sat down and sighed. How was she going to tackle all this and cook a meal in one day? She knew she couldn't live with all this muddle and dirt and wondered what to do about it.

Millie came in as Ben was stabling the horse and greeted Sophie brightly. She then picked up the kettle and made a pot of tea, placing a milk jug, cups and saucers, plates, a loaf of bread, butter, jam and honey on the table. It was all simple country fare, and Sophie was looking forward to it. Ben came in and looked at her, but Sophie spoke before he had time to say anything. "Thank you for all your hard work yesterday. It was a perfect wedding, and I am very grateful to you both."

They smiled and appeared pleased. Sophie looked at them, brother and sister together, and thought, *They are my family now*. She forgot the state of the kitchen for the time being and got up and hugged them. Ben cut the bread, and Sophie complimented Millie on it.

"Oh, I didn't make it," she said. "I got it from the farm."

Ben went on to explain that they got a lot of produce from the farm, such as eggs, butter, milk, and vegetables. It was a relief to Sophie to know that at least these basics were provided for.

He then apologised. "I'm sorry the kitchen is a bit of a mess, Sophie. I've been so busy lately." He scanned her face, obviously waiting for her reaction.

"Well, I'll set to today and see if I can tidy up a bit," she replied.

Millie looked at her. "If we are going to do it, we might as well do it properly and have a good clear-out and clean."

Sophie could see that Ben was relieved.

"I think we could do it in one day," he said. "If you take everything outside and clean, I can whitewash the walls."

He looked at Sophie, eyebrows raised, and she smiled back at him. And so she spent the first day of her married life with her apron on and her hair tied up in a cloth, sweeping all the cobwebs and dirt out of the kitchen. Millie had to attend to Billy, and she gave him his breakfast in the garden, which he thought was great fun. Afterwards he ran round, getting in the way and chasing the spiders that Sophie's cleaning had disturbed.

To make up the whitewash, Ben went to the outhouse, where he kept a sack of lime, and crushed some up in an old tin bath. He then added the water, stirring until it had the right consistency. The lime reacted with it, causing it to heat up. Care had to be taken at this stage when dealing with the mixture, but Ben knew what he was doing, having watched his father make up bucketloads for the stables and cottage walls in the past.

By this time, the girls had cleared the room of furniture and he could begin to limewash the kitchen walls. Sophie turned her attention to the pantry, where there were preserves in pots that had obviously been there a long time. Ben told her that his mother had made some of them. She took them outside and decided to ditch the contents but keep the pots, as she could refill them at some other time. The previous day, some of the villagers had brought wedding gifts of preserves and pickles, and these she put into her clean new pantry.

She carefully washed all the kitchen utensils and china and left them outside on the grass to dry. She made a mental note of items that needed replacing, which she would purchase next time they went shopping in Kingsbridge. Her purse of sovereigns was getting depleted, and she had really wanted to put the remainder aside for emergencies. However, now that she had seen the state of the cottage, she decided to spend her money buying the things they needed.

At lunchtime, they stopped to have bread and cheese and a mug of cider, and they all agreed that they were making good progress. Billy was munching on a piece of bread.

"I saw a big spider," he announced.

"Did it chase you?" asked his uncle.

"No, I chased HIM!"

"You were very brave, Billy," said Sophie. "Your aunt Sophie does not like big spiders."

"It won't be the only one," added Ben. "There'll be a mite few more about—this cottage is very old—and then, of course, there's the thatch…"

Millie put her hand to her mouth, laughing.

"Oh, stop it, all of you!" Sophie shuddered. She had come across a few that morning when cleaning.

"Don't worry," said Ben. "The limewash will keep them at bay for a while."

At the end of the afternoon, they were ready to put the furniture back into the clean white kitchen. Sophie enjoyed arranging the cleanly washed china on the dresser shelves. She stood with Millie, surveying the results of their hard work. All the grime and dust had gone, and even the range had been given a new coat of blacking by Ben.

"My grandfather put that in," he had told them. "Before that, my grandmother had to cook over an open fire."

Mrs. Chambers appeared at the door with a basket covered with a white cloth. She had brought them a pie for supper but declined their offer to stay, leaving them to enjoy it. Sophie was so grateful and called her an angel. Mrs. Chambers had rightly guessed that Sophie's first day would be challenging, but she seemed amazed at what they had achieved.

That evening, they were sitting together in their clean kitchen, pleased with what they had done in a day. When Billy went to bed, Sophie went up with him to read him a story. He was delighted and wanted another, but she told him he would have to wait until tomorrow, making up her mind to buy him a few more picture books. When she came downstairs, Ben was sitting in his fireside chair, so she drew up a little stool and sat beside him, leaning her head against him. He put his arm round her and said, "Beauty and the beast."

"You are not a beast," she protested, "and I am no beauty."

"You are to me," he replied, bending down to kiss the top of her head.

"I shall call you my 'old bear.'" Sophie laughed.

Millie was sitting at the table sewing and looked up.

"What's all this lovers' talk?" she asked.

"Listen and learn, my girl!" answered Ben.

"I don't have to listen to all that stuff," she said. "I'm not interested in sweethearts. I shall never get married."

Her reply concerned Sophie, and she thought she should talk to her about it. Millie had been rejected and hurt once, and it seemed to influence her thinking. She was eighteen years old, but looked younger, and should be enjoying the attentions of young men. Sophie had noticed one or two chatting to Millie at the wedding. Sophie had grown very fond of her sister-in-law and made a promise to herself to try to get her to change her mind. She had enjoyed working together with her that day.

What a strange turn her life had taken, and how good it felt.

CHAPTER NINE

MARRIED LIFE

SOPHIE EXPLORED HER NEW HOME and garden to see what else needed to be done. Ben had opened the forge, and she welcomed the time to be alone and settle in. Millie went to the farm first thing every morning, and for the first week, she took Billy with her, pulling him along in a little cart on wheels that Ben had made.

Downstairs in the cottage was the kitchen and a small parlour, which were separated by a staircase, and there were two bedrooms upstairs. The parlour was dark and the furniture old-fashioned, but Sophie knew she couldn't make too many demands to replace it. Instead, she decided to give it a good clean and concentrate on the bedroom.

She sat at the kitchen table working out her meals for the week and trying to figure what she would need. She had seen the kitchen garden. It was neglected, and there was not much to be had. She noticed that the orchard was full of apples, pears and plums, so she would be busy picking those.

After a week, Millie asked if Billy could stay behind when she went to work. She had to rise early and get Billy ready, so it would be easier if Sophie could look after him. Sophie agreed, but at first, she found that looking after Billy and trying to do her work at the same time was often difficult. She established a routine with Billy and realised that he needed more toys to occupy him. He liked working alongside her, and if she was working dough or making pastry, she would give him a small piece to roll out and make little cake shapes. Likewise, she would give him a small bowl of soapy water to play with if she was washing clothes.

There was a lot to learn about daily routines at the cottage. Ben would get up first and light the fires in the kitchen and the forge. Sophie would rise and get Billy his breakfast, and Ben would come in to join them. Despite how much there was to do, she was enjoying her new life. She managed to cook some successful suppers, and Ben was very appreciative.

One evening, about two weeks after the wedding, Sophie was sitting at the table reading and Millie was upstairs putting Billy to bed.

Ben was sitting in his chair deep in thought, and he suddenly announced, “There's something you should know. I cannot read or write very well.”

Sophie put down her book. She was unsure how to react to his statement. She realised it had been hard for him to admit to this inability, especially to her. She saw that he felt awkward. He was staring at the fire and frowning.

“Is it something you would like to improve?” she asked.

Ben's face relaxed, and he looked up at her. “Yes, but I need your help.”

“I can certainly plan some lessons for you, so we could begin next week. You will need to do a short session every day and lots of practice.”

“I'm sure I could do that. I have little else to do after work.”

It hadn't escaped Sophie's attention that she had never seen Ben read or write anything, and she wasn't at all surprised when he admitted that he struggled with it. She spent the next few evenings preparing spelling exercises and lists of words for him to learn. The following Saturday, she asked Ben to take her into Kingsbridge to purchase exercise books, pencils and a simple reader. She also bought Billy a few toys and some picture books.

Ben was true to his word and worked hard at his lessons. He had some basic skills but lacked fluency, so Sophie had acquired a small child's slate and some chalk so he could practice his spellings. This he did every evening after his day's work. Ben would often return to the cottage tired, but he persevered with his studies. Sophie would then test him and praise his progress. She realised her life as a teacher had not been entirely left behind.

"I didn't realise this would be so hard," Ben said one evening. "My memory isn't as good as it was."

"You are making good progress," Sophie replied reassuringly. She came and put her arm round his hunched shoulders. "You just need lots of repetition practising your spellings."

Ben looked up at her, his eyes showing that he trusted her to help him overcome his doubts.

Sophie was more than happy to be helping her husband with his literacy skills, or rather, lack of them, but something else concerned her more. She was beginning to wonder why there wasn't more money coming in, seeing as he worked so hard. She knew she had to address the problem and risk upsetting Ben by making him feel he wasn't pulling his weight.

An opportunity came when he needed to pick up and pay for a delivery of coal in Kingsbridge. He asked Sophie for some of her money, as he did not have enough. She responded willingly and counted it out from her purse.

"Ben, how do you manage about money—I mean the payments and bills?" she asked.

"Well, folk usually pay me when I shoe a horse or do a job for them. They put money into a tin box, and I bring it in here and put it in the jar." He indicated the large stone jar on the dresser.

"What about those who don't pay straight away?"

"Some promise to drop it in later, or they give payment in kind."

"Do you always get the money?"

"Not always. I think there's some that never pay up."

"What about 'payment in kind'?" she asked. "What exactly does that mean?"

"Some folk give me some eggs or a side of ham, perhaps some vegetables, or even a cake. We have always had this kind of arrangement with the farmer. That's why Millie brings home a lot of the items from the farm. It was always like that in my father's time, and it has just carried on."

Sophie looked dismayed. "Ben, that shouldn't be happening in this day and age. People pay with cash now."

"Some of them are unable to pay me, Sophie," he answered. "Poor old Thomas for instance. I repaired his kettle, and he mended my garden gate. Made a good job of it, too."

"Well, that's an exception. The farmer should pay you, Ben. You must do a lot of work for him, and other people should pay too. You must make that clear from now on. No more owing and no more payment in kind."

Ben sighed but said he knew he had to agree.

"Honestly, Ben, the farmer wouldn't go to market to buy a pig and offer a pound of butter and a cabbage for it."

"What should I do?" he asked. "I know things have got to change."

They discussed some strategies and finally decided that if his customers had no money, they would be given a bill. Sophie told him they could get some invoices printed and purchase a receipt book and a ledger for bookkeeping. Ben would need to charge more for his work. She was sure he would be confident dealing with the paperwork now that he was having reading and writing lessons.

"We can also get a poster printed with all your new prices on it," said Sophie. "If people don't or won't pay you, then you refuse them next time they come."

After they had put the new arrangements into action, Ben told her that, surprisingly, most people accepted the new conditions without much opposition. The farmer had agreed reluctantly. He knew he had been underpaying Ben for his services. He also agreed that Millie's work should be paid for in cash.

It wasn't long before Sophie noticed more money coming in. She had agreed to use her bookkeeping skills and keep an eye on their income. Perhaps now she could begin to improve the rooms in the cottage. After spending one evening closely examining the accounts, she put down her pen and spoke to Ben.

"I think we are breaking even at last. The money coming in has increased and will more than cover our outgoings."

Ben was sitting in his chair by the range reading a simple storybook Sophie had given him, his finger moving slowly from word to word on the page. He closed the book and turned his attention to what Sophie had said.

"That's very good news. We'll be making a profit next!"

"If we do," said Sophie, cautiously, "I would like to refurbish the parlour."

"You don't like my grandparents' taste in furniture then?" Ben had a mischievous glint in his eyes and waited to see his wife's reaction.

"It's so heavy and dark."

"If you can make us some extra money, my love, you may spend it however you like."

Sophie's eyes shone with pleasure. She hadn't expected Ben to be so compliant.

She was pleased when he came in one day and announced that there was to be an auction at a nearby farm of all effects. He took her there on the day, and they returned with the cart loaded with some smarter items of furniture, including a settle, a gateleg table, chairs and a chest of drawers. They also managed to get a clock, a mirror and some attractive pictures and other items. Sophie paid for these and was pleased to see the back of the old furniture.

Harry sometimes came to see them. Sophie welcomed his visits, as he brought news from the village and, more intriguingly, also from Clayden House. He had told her the servants had been buzzing when they heard that she had walked out, and that Mr. Wilmott-Smith had been furious. Philip had passed his entrance exams and had now been sent off to school. The tutor who had come weekly for him was now teaching Kit. Apparently, Mr. Wilmott-Smith was refusing to appoint any more governesses.

How Harry had come to learn all this was a mystery to Sophie, but he told her that the servants always knew what went on. She wondered about her friend Annie, who had been the only one to make her feel welcome, apart from Harry. It was strange having the House so near, as she never saw anybody from there. The family never came to the village, and Harry had told her the men servants were forbidden to frequent the inn. He was the only one who lived in the village, and he refused to obey such a rule.

The year progressed, and it was soon time to prepare for Christmas. Sophie remembered the last one she had endured at Clayden House and how lonely she had felt. She was happy when she thought how different it would be this year. She decorated the cottage with holly and fir branches, and Ben brought home a small tree, which they decorated with pinecones and red ribbons. Millie collected a goose from the farm, which the farmer's wife prepared, as Sophie could not face cleaning it. They shared their Christmas dinner with Harry and his mother Mildred, who Millie had befriended when her own mother died. Mrs. Chambers also came, together with old Thomas.

Once everyone had arrived, they all sat round the table in the parlour and Ben set to carving the bird. Sophie and Millie added the trimmings, piling up everyone's plates with potatoes and vegetables. Sophie had devised a few parlour games and quizzes for the afternoon, and Forge Cottage had not seen such festivities and laughter for many years.

Ben and Sophie exchanged their small gifts. Sophie opened hers first and was thrilled to find that Ben had given her a small cameo brooch. It had belonged to his mother. She had decided to give Ben the fountain pen that Robert had given her. She thought it would look impressive when he wrote out his invoices, and she'd included a small bottle of ink. Both had given and received recycled gifts, as money was so tight.

Billy was thrilled with the toys and books that Sophie had given him. Ben had made him a small hobbyhorse with a wheel at the back, and Billy went round and round the table, riding it until he was dizzy.

"Time to stop now," said Mille firmly, coming into the kitchen and seeing her son was getting overexcited. She had thrown the shawl that Sophie had given her over her shoulders and had been admiring herself in the new mirror in the parlour. Sophie had never worn the shawl presented to her last Christmas by Mrs. Wilmott-Smith and was glad that Millie liked it.

"You'll turn a few heads when you go out in that," Sophie said to her, hoping it might include a young man. "We need to get you a new dress to go with it."

Millie glanced at her. She knew exactly what her sister-in-law was hinting at. "And what would I want to get all dressed up for?" she asked.

"I don't know yet. I'm sure there will be an opportunity for us to put on our glad rags."

Millie shrugged and went to take her son up for his rest. He had tired himself out.

Ben laughed when she had gone. "That went well," he said. "Full marks for trying."

At the end of the day, Ben took Mrs. Chambers and old Thomas home while Sophie and Millie cleared up. It was surprising how quickly the small kitchen became cluttered. Once they were done, they snuggled up together in the parlour, waiting for Ben to come in. The log fire glowed in the grate as they drank glasses of mulled wine.

"Sophie," said Millie quietly, "I'm glad you married Ben."

CHAPTER TEN

BILLY'S BIRTHDAY

After Christmas, the weather got colder. Snow fell and lay on the ground for several days. Ben was not called on to do much work at the forge, so he set about decorating the bedroom. Sophie had chosen the paper and was busy making new curtains, and as the winter sun shone brightly through the small window, it looked light and fresh instead of dark and dingy. Ben had whitewashed the walls in the other rooms, giving the cottage a new lease on life.

February came, and the weather grew milder. Millie had told Billy it would soon be his birthday and had tried to explain how long he had to wait. Every day was the same—he played, had his meals and went to bed. He stayed indoors if the weather was cold or wet, but he was allowed outside most days. He played his imaginary games in the garden until it was time to go back inside the warm kitchen, which often smelled of his aunt's newly baked bread.

When Sophie was looking after him, she knew the one place he longed to explore was the forge, which of course was forbidden. He had been round there a few times with his mother, holding her hand. Sophie had caught him once or twice peeking round the side of the cottage, looking over the gate at the horses standing outside the forge. He'd seen that a fire glowed inside, and Ben had told him a dragon lived there.

At last, Billy's birthday arrived, and he was to have his presents later that day. It was breakfast as usual and then playtime. He was told that he was to have a treat later. After lunch, he was put to bed for a short rest while Sophie and Millie cleared away and prepared the tea things. When they got him up, they took him to the outhouse where the apples were stored and picked out some. Billy asked if that was his treat. His mother laughed and said, "Wait and see."

They returned to the cottage, and after a while Ben appeared at the door. "Billy, would you like to come round to the forge?"

Would he! Billy jumped up and down with obvious joy.

Millie and Sophie put on their woollen shawls, and Millie took him by the hand. Sophie picked up the basket of apples, and they went round to the forge. When they walked round the corner, they saw a large Shire horse tethered to the post outside.

The forge was open at the front and faced the lane. The workshop within was dark except for the fire burning in a raised container at the back. This had a hood over it leading to a brick chimney, and there was a handle attached to a pair of leather bellows to the side of the fire. Along the wooden beams above were rows of horseshoes hung on large nail pegs in order of size. The blacksmith's tools were lined up round the sides of the walls and around the firebox. Beside this, in the middle of the floor, was the anvil, set on a large piece of tree trunk. Billy was not allowed to go inside. Instead, he was led towards the horse, which was held by a man. He smiled at Billy.

"Hello, young man," he said. "This here is Bolton. He's just had his shoes done. Would ye like a ride?"

Billy had never been so close to such a big horse before. He managed an eager nod, and Ben lifted him up onto the horse's back.

"Hold on with both hands, Billy," he said. "Hold tight!"

Billy held on to the horse's rough, wiry mane as instructed.

"Now we are going to walk slowly down the lane," said Ben, and he and the other man, one each side, steered Bolton round and led him slowly across the piece of rough ground towards the lane. The huge beast moved slowly, undulating from side to side as he went along. They walked down the lane to the bend and then turned to come back. Millie and Sophie waved, but Billy did not wave back, as he was holding on firmly. They continued to go up and down the lane a few more times, and then finally Bolton halted outside the forge and Ben lifted Billy down. Billy's legs wobbled slightly as he tried to stand on firm ground again.

"Now we must give Bolton a reward for giving you such a lovely ride," said Millie and took an apple from the basket Sophie was holding. Billy was led round to the horse's head, and Bolton looked at him with his large round brown eyes.

"Hold your hand very flat," said Millie. "Bolton will pick it up with his lips. He won't bite you."

Billy did what he had been told, and Bolton scooped up the apple. "He tickled me!" Billy laughed and took another apple from the basket. He gave Bolton a few more, and then Ben said that Bolton had work to do and had to go. Billy patted his muzzle, and the man led Bolton away down the lane. Billy waved avidly.

"Bye-bye, Bolton!" he called as the enormous horse walked away, swaying slightly from side to side.

"Did you enjoy your ride?" asked Sophie.

Billy nodded vigorously. "Will he come back one day?" he asked.

"Yes, he will," answered Ben. "I shall have to give him some new shoes."

Billy and his mother walked slowly back to the cottage, leaving Ben to lock up. Sophie had gone ahead and placed Billy's birthday cake in the middle of the tea table and lit his four candles. When Billy came in, he was overjoyed at what he saw and clapped his little hands together.

"Oh, what a lovely cake!"

Millie helped him to climb up onto a chair.

"How many candles are there?" asked his aunt.

Billy leant forward and counted, "One, two three, four!"

Ben had taken off his apron and come in. They sang "Happy Birthday," and Billy blew all his candles out, then opened his presents. Milly had given him a small wooden train, Ben a ball and skittles that he had carved himself, and from Sophie he got a slate and some coloured chalk. Billy was excited, not knowing which to play with first.

"What do you say, Billy?" asked Ben, raising his eyebrows.

Billy looked round at everyone. "Thank you!" he said, his eyes shining with happiness.

CHAPTER ELEVEN

LOSS

Now that Sophie was happier with the cottage, she turned her attention to the kitchen garden. Because of the arrangement with the farm, Ben hadn't bothered to cultivate it, and Sophie was having to do some hard digging and weeding to get it ready for spring sowing. They would now grow their own vegetables, as the farmer was paying Ben cash for his work. More money was coming in since they had sorted out Ben's finances, and Millie was able to contribute to the housekeeping from the wage she earned at the farm.

In April it was Ben's birthday and the anniversary of his and Sophie's first walk together on Easter Sunday. He was making steady progress with his reading and writing, so Sophie had bought him some simple books and a dictionary. He unwrapped the package and carefully opened the pages of one of the books.

"Thank you, Sophie. You have great faith in my reading progress. This looks quite challenging!"

Sophie gave him a kiss. "We can read it together to begin with."

He looked at her kindly. "I'll enjoy that."

Millie handed him some money. "Here you are, Ben. You can put this towards some carpentry tools. Then you can make Billy lots of toys."

Ben nodded. "If I find some spare time from work and reading lessons!"

It was young Billy's turn, and he presented his uncle with his drawings of dragons. Ben took them from him and studied them carefully.

"They're very scary, Billy, you've drawn them well. I shall put these up in the forge so that the dragon who lives there can see them."

"Yes. Then he might run away," Billy said.

"I hope not. My fire will go out, and I will never be able to light it again."

Billy opened his mouth and looked shocked at hearing this.

Millie frowned. "I wish you wouldn't fill his head with such nonsense."

Ben chuckled and winked at his nephew. "Uncle's only joking," he said.

While Millie was putting Billy to bed that evening, Sophie went over to where Ben sat in his chair by the fire. "Have you had a good birthday?" she asked.

"Yes, thank you. It was the best birthday I've had because I shared it with you." He put his arm round her.

"You haven't had all your presents yet. There is one more to come."

Ben looked intrigued. Sophie took hold of his hand and placed it on her stomach. It took him a moment or two to understand, then he exclaimed, "Really?"

She nodded and laughed.

He jumped up and pulled her to him, embracing her tightly. "Oh, Sophie, I can't believe it! My clever girl!"

Just then, Millie came in and demanded to know what all the fuss was about.

"Sophie and I are going to have a baby!"

She was delighted, and the evening was spent discussing names and making plans.

Ben was adamant his son was not going to be a blacksmith. "He'll have some proper schooling," he stated.

Nothing Sophie or Millie said could persuade him that it might be a girl.

Throughout the spring, Sophie continued in the garden and managed to sow a few seeds. She had found some packets in a drawer in the kitchen, but Ben thought they might be too old to germinate.

One morning, after she came back into the house, she felt a sharp pain. She clasped herself and sat on a chair. "Millie!" she called out. "Millie, be quick!"

Millie was tidying her bedroom and rushed downstairs when she heard Sophie's cries. Billy arrived first and stood in the doorway with his finger in his mouth, looking concerned. Millie, seeing Sophie holding her belly, immediately knew what was wrong and told Billy to run and get Ben. He sped out, and they soon returned.

Billy was told to go and play in the garden, and they closed the door behind him. Sophie was relieved that they were there and allowed herself to be helped to lie on the stone floor of the kitchen. She knew she was about to lose the baby, and there was little they could do to prevent it. When it was over, she held onto Ben as he carried her upstairs.

As he laid her gently on the bed, she began sobbing. "I'm so sorry Ben. I'm so sorry."

He held her and did his best to comfort her.

"It's all my fault. I shouldn't have been digging," she said. "Oh, I am so sorry."

"No," said Ben adamantly. "No, it's my fault. I should have taken better care of you and not expected you to do all this work. You're not made for it, Sophie. The village women are used to it, having done it since they were born, but you're not. You don't have to prove anything. In the future, you will do less, and we will do more. You are to rest now until you are fully recovered, and then we will sort out an easier time for you."

She nodded and closed her eyes. She knew Ben was right—she could not carry on like this and bear a child. Perhaps he could help take care of Billy, as she was finding the young boy more of a handful now that he was getting older. She would ask in the village for someone to help with the laundry. They did have a little more money coming in now that would pay for it. Her worries gradually subsided, and she fell asleep.

When she woke, Ben brought her a cup of tea, and as she was sipping it, he sat down on the bed and put his arm round her. "I have been thinking about Billy. I can have him every morning. He is old enough to know of the dangers inside the forge. He can play outside most days. Sometimes there are village children about who come to see the horses."

Sophie nodded in agreement. "As long as Millie doesn't mind."

"I've already discussed it with her, and she is quite happy for me to have him. I have also found a woman in the village to do the laundry."

Sophie closed her eyes in relief. She was devastated to have lost their child and was determined that she would carry the next one to term.

Sophie needed to take it easy for a while, and she found it was much better not to have Billy to care for each day. She was feeling very weak and tired. She knew the garden had proved to be too much work and realised that Harry would make a much better job of it, so she decided to ask him if he would take it on. She spent the next two weeks resting and doing light jobs. Mrs. Chambers came round a few times and brought some provisions with her. She was very motherly towards Sophie and gave her some comforting advice. Although Sophie began to feel better physically, she still felt very low and often wept.

When she began to recover, Ben took her to the seaside. It was a little further away than the estuary, and he drove her to a spot he knew on top of the cliffs that had sweeping views. She sat beside him with the wind blowing through her hair and over her face and looked out across the wide expanse of the sea.

After a while, Ben took hold of her hands and looked into her eyes. "We must look forward now, not back," he said.

CHAPTER TWELVE

A SURPRISE VISIT

HARRY DID A GOOD JOB cultivating the kitchen garden after his work each day, and Sophie was looking forward to harvesting the produce. She would sometimes sit outside and talk to him as he worked. Ben would do his writing exercises and, if there was time, come out to join her.

The sorrow of losing their child had brought them closer together, and Ben was very protective of Sophie, always making sure she had some leisure time. He continued to take her out in the horse and trap every weekend to show her some of the local sights.

It was the beginning of July, and Sophie had been making bread at the kitchen table and had just put it into the tins to rise when there was a knock at the door. It was always open in the summer months, so she looked up and was surprised to see who it was.

"Cousin Robert! This is unexpected!"

"Ah, Sophie! I have found you. I called at Clayden House, and they told me you had married…the blacksmith?" As he spoke, he looked round in the direction of the forge.

"Yes, that's right," she replied.

"You mean to say you have left your position as governess to marry a blacksmith? How did that happen?" he asked.

Sophie told him to come in and she would explain. He entered the small kitchen, looking round, and Sophie wondered what he must be thinking of her modest home.

"I was very unhappy at Clayden House, Robert. They treated me very badly, and I was lonely. I met Ben on my walks, and we fell in love. It's as simple as that. I know what you are thinking, but we are very happy."

"Well, I am very glad to hear it, Sophie, and my congratulations to you both! I do hope you will excuse this sudden visit."

"Yes, of course. It's lovely to see you. How is my uncle?" she asked.

"I'm sorry to tell you he died last March. He had been ill for some time."

Sophie felt a jolt of sorrow. Her poor uncle!

"I am so sorry. I'd known he was unwell. I wrote several times and wondered why he had not replied."

"I apologise for not informing you, Sophie. He became worse shortly after you left. I think the shock of your father's death affected him, and he too had money troubles. It was only as I was going through his papers recently that I came across where you had gone."

At that moment, Ben came to the door and said, "Do your horses need attending to, sir?"

Sophie introduced him to her cousin.

"How do you do," said Robert, offering to shake Ben's rather grubby hand.

"How do you do, sir," he replied.

There was an awkward silence, and Robert was the first to speak.

"I have Frank in the carriage," he said. "Before he comes in, I need to tell you that last year he had a bad riding accident, and as a result of his injuries, he is now a cripple."

Sophie was shocked. She had no fond memories of Frank, but it was awful that this had happened to him.

Robert turned to Ben. "Will you help me bring him in?" he asked.

The two men went out and then returned, Ben assisting Frank, who was dragging one leg badly. He helped him into the chair by the range. Sophie looked at her cousin, who appeared shattered after his journey and not well. He smiled weakly at her as she introduced him to Ben.

"Hello, Sophie, and good day to you, Ben." He looked round. "What a snug little place you have here."

Robert spoke again. "The thing is, Sophie, Frank and I have come to ask you a huge favour. I am on my way to the Channel Islands to get married. I was hoping to take him with me as my best man, but as you can see, he is in no fit state to travel further."

"We were intending to come and see you as we were travelling this way," added Frank. "We wanted to know how you were getting on. I didn't expect you would be married."

"I must ask you if you would consider looking after my brother for a short while until I return," Robert continued.

Sophie was confused. "The cottage is very small," she replied, hesitantly. "We don't really have much room."

Before she could go on, Ben said, "Let the fellow stay, Sophie. I am sure we can fit him in." He turned to Frank. "You don't take up much room, do you?"

Robert looked relieved.

"You are very welcome to stay, Frank," said Sophie. "As Ben says, we'll find room for you somewhere."

Frank expressed his thanks and asked Ben to fetch his luggage. Sophie hoped he wouldn't expect them to be his servants. She wouldn't have time for that, but she realised he would need some help. "Can I offer you both some refreshment?" she asked.

Robert declined, as he said he had a boat to catch. Before he left, he put a small purse on the table, saying it was for "expenses." He then said his farewells and promised to write as soon as he arrived in Jersey.

"My very best wishes to the bride," said Frank. "I hope we shall meet one day."

After Robert had driven away, Sophie came back inside and asked Frank if he would like some tea. He nodded and said, "He won't be back very soon, Sophie. I know for a fact that his wife doesn't want to live here."

Sophie felt annoyed that Robert had left Frank with them if that was the case.

As if reading her thoughts, Frank went on. "He's been a good brother to me since my accident. I couldn't have had better care."

Sophie gave him his tea.

"And Sophie," Frank went on, "I'm sorry I was rude to you."

She nodded, remembering how he had spoken to her when she was living with them. "Thank you, Frank. As far as Ben and I are concerned, you are very welcome to stay with us for as long as you like."

All this time, Billy had been watching and listening intently. They had few visitors, and he seemed intrigued. A little shyly, he went up to Frank and stood in front of him.

Sophie thought she ought to introduce him, so she said, "Billy, this is, um, your Uncle Frank."

Billy continued to stare, then asked, "Will you play with me?"

Ben, who had just come back in from closing the forge, said, "Be careful what you promise, Frank!"

"I'm afraid I can't play with you Billy," replied Frank, smiling kindly at the boy.

"Why?"

"Because I have a poorly leg."

"Why?"

"My horse threw me and landed on top of me."

Billy's eyes opened wide. "He was a naughty horse," he observed.

"He wasn't really a naughty horse. I think I was riding him too fast," Frank said.

This seemed to satisfy Billy, and he went away to find his ball. He had managed to extract more information from Frank than Sophie and Ben had got from Robert.

Sophie suggested that Frank might like to rest. He looked relieved and agreed, so Ben helped him up the narrow stairs, and he laid down on their bed.

When Ben came downstairs, he and Sophie talked about what to do and where to put Frank. Ben suggested that he go over to Mrs. Chambers's and ask to borrow a bed.

"And some bedding," added Sophie.

Ben went to hitch up the horse and cart, and when he returned a little later, he had a bedstead and feather mattress, bedding, and pillows in the back. "She said we could have them for as long as we like," he told Sophie.

Now they had to decide where to put Frank. The parlour was the only room that could offer some privacy. Ben suggested that they move the settle across to the other side of the fireplace at a right angle to the wall so that it partitioned off a small space for the bed. They rearranged the room and decided that it worked very well. They did not use the parlour much in the summer months, but they could still sit in there until Frank wanted to retire.

Later that afternoon, Ben helped Frank downstairs and they showed him the arrangement. He seemed very content, but obviously needed a lot of help moving around. By this time, Millie had returned, and Sophie thought she saw Frank cast her an admiring glance when they were introduced. Millie said a quick hello and went upstairs.

Later that night, Ben revealed to Sophie that when he helped Frank get ready for bed, he'd seen that he was wearing an iron brace. "I need to examine his leg," he said. "Do you think he will let me?"

Sophie knew that over the years Ben had become very experienced with horses that were lame or injured. He was often successful at getting them better. He had told her that the government was aware that many farriers were doing this work and was trying to discourage them, preferring to have veterinary practitioners deal with horses' ailments. Ben had continued to treat any lame horses brought to him, as there were no veterinary surgeons where they lived.

The next morning, Sophie asked Frank if he would let Ben look at his damaged leg. She explained that he was used to working with horses' leg problems.

Frank laughed. "Am I going to get shod?" he joked but then agreed.

Sophie watched as Ben examined his leg carefully.

"You shouldn't be wearing that thing," he said, pointing to the brace. "Your muscle will waste away and there will be no getting it back. As it is, we can work on it and build it up. You must try and use your leg until it aches, then stop."

"How can I do that?" asked Frank, perplexed.

"I'll think of something," said Ben. "Meanwhile, I'll have this." He took the leg iron away to his forge.

A few days later, Ben produced from his workshop an adapted chair on wheels that he had made. He placed it on the kitchen floor and asked Frank to sit in it. "You'll have to push it along by your legs and use your good one to steer it. It will give you some mobility and exercise your legs and strengthen them."

Ben had put on castors that made the chair very manoeuvrable. Frank did as Ben had instructed and made a short circuit round the kitchen table. He looked thrilled.

"What can I say? Thank you so much, Ben. You are a genius!"

Billy was watching intently. "I want a moving chair too!" he demanded.

"You don't need one," stated Ben. "You have two good legs. Uncle Frank has only one."

Billy pouted and looked sullen. Frank put his arm out and helped him up onto his lap.

"Come on, young fellow. We can have lots of rides together!"

Millie was watching as Frank took Billy round the kitchen. "Thank you, Frank. You're very kind."

They exchanged looks, and Sophie could see that they were also forming a friendship. Later that evening in the parlour, Frank was showing Millie some card tricks. They then commenced a game, and Millie suddenly called out, "You're cheating Frank! I saw that!"

Frank laughed at her and told her he hadn't.

"Yes, you have. I'm not stupid. You swapped cards. I saw you!"

Frank continued to laugh heartily while Millie became more indignant, and finally he gave in. "OK, you saw me cheat, but I meant you to."

Millie gave him a playful slap on the arm and told him to behave. As Sophie watched them having fun, she could sense an attraction growing. They certainly got on well together. She was glad that Frank had settled into their family life, and he seemed to be at ease living with them and was certainly a lot more cheerful than when he'd arrived.

Ben continued to work on Frank's leg, rubbing it with balm and massaging the muscle. He had said he couldn't cure his lameness, but he could improve it. He told Sophie he was going to "toughen Frank up a bit."

CHAPTER THIRTEEN

THE FIGHT

The summer days passed, and soon it was harvest time. Ben was busy repairing agricultural machinery that the local farmers brought him this time of year, as parts were often breaking. It was relentless since every job was different and had to be done quickly. When Billy saw the machines arriving, pulled by the big Shire horses, he would get very excited and jump up and down. Whenever Bolton came, Billy would run into the cottage and ask Sophie for apples for him.

Sophie would sometimes invite Harry into the cottage for some refreshment after his gardening. She valued his friendship and help. One evening when Ben was working late in the forge, Harry was with Sophie in the kitchen, and as he left, he bent over and gave her a gentle kiss goodbye on the cheek. They were in the doorway, and at that moment, Ben came along. He gave Harry a hard look and then walked straight past him into the cottage. Harry left quickly, and Sophie went back inside.

"What was all that about?" demanded Ben.

Sophie was surprised to hear anger in his voice. "Whatever do you mean?" she asked.

"Well, it seems to me that Harry is getting a mite fond of you, and you don't exactly discourage him."

"Harry is a good and kind friend," she replied. "That's all it is."

"It looked a bit more than that to me. Do you let him kiss you like that often?"

"I don't know what you mean, 'like that.'"

"He's always been sweet on you, you know. When we used to go drinking, he was always talking about you. 'Sophie this' and 'Sophie that.' I heard all about you before we ever met."

"I didn't know that. I had no idea that Harry was discussing me with you."

"And another thing," Ben went on. "When you were told to leave, it was Harry who got that older boy to confess and took him straight to his father."

Sophie sat down, astonished. She'd never known about Harry's actions. "How did he do that?" she asked.

"Oh, he knew some of his past misdemeanours and threatened to tell his father all about them."

"That was kind of him to help me," she said quietly.

"So now he thinks he can kiss you, and you seemed to enjoy it."

This last remark made Sophie angry, and she stood up. "How could you think such a thing!" she exclaimed.

Marching out of the kitchen, she went into the garden and sat down under the trees, taking in all that Ben had told her. Did he really think she would encourage Harry's advances? He obviously saw her as the kind of woman who would do that sort of thing. The more she thought about it, the angrier she felt. She had no idea if Harry had feelings for her, but she realised he was a lonely young man. He didn't appear to have a sweetheart, and perhaps she should be careful of her friendship with him.

As she thought this, she felt two strong arms round her and heard Ben softly say her name. She turned and looked at him, and he came and sat next to her.

"I shouldn't have said all that to you, Sophie. I am very sorry."

She looked at him and relented, gently tugging his hair. "You're a silly old bear!" she said.

"I shouldn't have treated Harry like that," Ben said. "I'll take him out for a drink and apologise."

Ben had not been out with his friend very often since his marriage, and the following Friday evening, he had gone to meet Harry at the Two Foxes. Sophie had retired early but was suddenly woken by the sound of the door banging open and a lot of noise in the kitchen. Startled, she threw a shawl round her shoulders and went downstairs cautiously. When she got to the kitchen, Harry was helping Ben into his chair. Alarmed, she saw that Ben's face was covered in blood.

"I'm sorry, miss. He's been in a bit of a fight. He'll be all right once he sleeps it off," said Harry, who then beat a hasty retreat.

Sophie was appalled as she stood there staring at Ben, who was groaning away in his chair. At that moment, Millie came downstairs. She looked at her brother and said, "Oh no, not again!"

This stunned Sophie even more. She felt helpless and let Millie take charge of the situation. Frank had hobbled to the doorway of the parlour, as he too had been woken up by all the noise.

"Oh dear!" he said.

Millie rekindled the fire and put the kettle on for hot water. She sent Sophie to get some clean rags, and they set to cleaning Ben up. He had suffered a black eye, cuts to his face and bruises to his body.

"We'll leave him down here for tonight," said Millie. "He'll be all right."

By now Ben, obviously full of ale, was sinking into a deep sleep. They all went back to bed, but Sophie could not settle. How could he do this, whatever had happened? She knew Ben had been prone to using his fists, but she had thought those days were behind him. She could not condone such behaviour. How could he be a good husband or father if he reacted this way?

The next morning, Sophie got dressed as quickly as she could and went downstairs. Ben was still in his chair by the fire, dozing peacefully. She left him to sleep and busied herself getting the breakfast ready. The chinking of the cups woke him, and he looked round with evident chagrin, but Sophie ignored him, continuing to lay the table.

Millie came down with Billy, who was told not to disturb his uncle. Once she had helped Frank get dressed, they all sat down at the table, except Ben, who remained in his chair. Millie poured him a cup of tea, and he sat up and groaned. Sophie could not bring herself to speak to him.

Suddenly, he said, "I think I'll close the forge today." He looked over at Sophie, who sighed and looked away.

After breakfast, Ben shuffled out, saying he would do some gardening. Sophie still had not spoken a word to him.

Millie looked at her. "They can be a rough lot at the inn, Sophie. I'm sure it wasn't entirely Ben's fault."

Sophie continued her dignified silence.

"What's the matter with Uncle Ben?" asked Billy as he tucked into his bowl of bread and milk.

"He got into a fight, but he's all right," said his mother.

"We're going out for a ride today, Billy. Had you remembered?" asked Frank.

Frank appeared to want no part of Sophie and Ben's differences, and he and Millie got up to go as soon as breakfast was finished. It was Saturday, and Millie had arranged to take the trap and go into Kingsbridge. She was quite capable of hitching up the horse, so they both went to the stable, taking Billy. Frank's mobility was improving, and he could now get about using a stick.

Sophie continued to work in the kitchen, but she was interrupted a little later by a loud rap on the door. She looked up and saw a man standing there. He was smartly dressed in a brown tweed suit, so she knew he wasn't a farm worker or groom. "I'm sorry, the forge is closed today," she said.

"I don't want the forge," he replied abruptly. "I wish to speak to Mr. Browne—Mr. Ben Browne. The name's Blake."

Sophie felt a surge of anxiety, knowing this must have something to do with Ben's fight. She asked the man in to wait and went down to the garden to find Ben. He was sitting by the vegetable plot, resting. His hoe was leaning against a tree, and she could see he hadn't done much weeding.

"Ben," she called. "There's a man named Blake to see you."

He looked up. "Thank you, Sophie. I know who he is."

Sophie's anger had gone. She felt anxious for Ben and sensed trouble. Taking his arm, she slowly walked back inside with him.

"Hello, Blake," said Ben, giving him a withering look. "What do you want?"

Blake seemed unperturbed. "I understand you were involved in a fight last night," he said. "As a result of this, one of my workers will have to be laid off for three weeks, which means loss of earnings for him and his family. I'll have to hire someone for that time, so that'll be thirty shillings in all. I expect this money by three o'clock tomorrow, otherwise I'll take you to court."

Ben said nothing, just gave a short laugh. Once Blake had left, Sophie looked at him. She had no idea how they would find thirty shillings.

"Don't worry," said Ben. "I've no intention of paying him anything. The money will go straight into his pocket, I'll be bound. I'll ask Harry to find out if it really is true. If it is, I'll give any money to the family, not to Blake. I don't trust that man." He told Sophie that the man was steward to a local landowner, and he knew all about him.

Sophie saw that her husband looked worn out, so she insisted that he rest. Settling him in his chair, she put her arm round him and kissed him.

When Millie and Frank got back, they seemed relieved to see that Ben and Sophie were talking again. After Billy had gone to bed, Ben told them about the visit. "That Blake's a nasty piece of work," he said. "He has a reputation as a gambler and isn't liked. I'll go over tomorrow and see him."

Frank's brow creased. "No, don't, Ben. You're in no fit state to go, and you'll only make things worse. Let me go—I'll sort it out." He turned to Millie. "If you'll drive me over."

Millie nodded in agreement.

Then Sophie said, "I think you should let them go, Ben."

Ben shrugged his shoulders and agreed. Later that night, as they were lying together in bed, Sophie spoke. "Ben, promise me you won't ever do this again."

There was a moment's silence before he answered. "I promise."

Frank and Millie set off the next day and returned about three hours later. They looked very pleased with themselves.

"It's all been settled. No payment needed," Frank told Ben. "He won't be taking you to court."

Ben looked surprised. "However did you do it?"

"Oh," said Frank, nonchalantly, "when you said he was a gambler, I thought I would show him some card tricks, and we had a few good games of cards!"

Sophie knew exactly what that meant. “Oh, Frank, you haven’t taught him to cheat at cards!”

“They all cheat at these games—believe me,” he replied.

“What if he doesn’t keep his word?” she asked.

“I’ll put it round that he cheats at cards!” Frank laughed.

Ben said he would ask Harry to go round to his assailant’s family to see if they would be suffering financially. Then he turned to Frank and said, “Thank you for that. You are a true brother!”

Millie’s eyes opened wide, and she rushed over to Ben and flung her arms round him. “Really?” she exclaimed.

Ben nodded, and she went over to Frank and hugged him.

“I know you two are dying to get wed,” said Ben. “You’d better get on with it.”

As Millie was still a minor, she had to have her brother’s permission to marry. When she and Ben were alone, Sophie voiced her doubts. “I want Millie to be happy,” she said, “but I’m not sure it’s a good match. I think she could do better.”

“That could have been said of you when we married. What exactly is your objection?”

Sophie explained that she thought Frank was not steady. “I don’t know what they will live on,” she said.

Ben said he would have a “man-to-man” with Frank and ascertain his ability to support himself and Millie.

Sophie left the two men in the parlour after supper the following evening. Afterwards, Ben said that Frank had told him he had inherited some money when his father died and he and Millie were making plans, which they would discuss with them later.

After supper the next day, Ben went to the dresser shelf and took down the purse Robert had left. They had not used any of the money. He went over to Millie and placed it in her hands. “For your wedding,” he said.

Millie burst into a smile, especially when she opened it and found it came to ten sovereigns. Sophie was glad that Millie had some money to spend. She was beginning to feel happier about the engagement.

“So, it’s off to the dressmakers again.” Ben laughed. “Frank can take you this time.”

Millie explained to Billy about Frank being his new papa. Up until then he had called him "uncle with stick." They had a good relationship, and it was obvious Frank was very fond of the little boy who had wanted to play with him from the time he'd arrived.

The wedding was to happen before Christmas, and Sophie and Millie were busy making the arrangements. Millie had decided to have a cloak with a fur hood made for her ride from the church. The wedding breakfast was to be in the cottage with a few guests. They thought they could accommodate about fifteen.

"If they don't move around too much," said Ben.

He had been working long days and often returned home late. He ate his meal in silence and said he was too tired to do his reading. He sometimes answered Sophie abruptly, looking annoyed at her questions about his day. Sophie wondered what was bothering him. One evening, Ben came in after a hard week of work. Many of the jobs had been urgent, and he had worked late on the Friday. Sophie and Millie filled the big tin bath with some hot soapy water for him.

As Sophie was washing his back, he turned to her and said, "I've had enough of blacksmithing, Sophie."

Sophie instantly stopped what she was doing. "Oh, Ben!" was all she could say.

"I never wanted to do it in the first place, and now I'm trapped, as I have no other means of supporting you."

"I'm sure there's an answer to this, Ben—a way out," Sophie told him. "Have you any idea what you might like to do instead?"

"I've always wanted to work with horses, a bit like Harry's job," he said.

"Whatever you decide to do, I shall support you."

They left the subject there for the time being, as they needed to concentrate on the wedding. Sophie was still concerned for Millie's future. She and Ben were alone one evening, with Millie and Frank sitting outside in the garden. "

"When do you think we will find out about these plans Frank told you about?" Sophie began. "Where will they be living? I think we ought to know before the wedding."

Ben agreed. "I'll ask them when they come in," he said.

Shortly afterwards, the door opened, and Frank and Millie came into the kitchen, arm in arm. Both were smiling broadly. Ben greeted them.

"Ah, the happy couple returns! Sophie and I were just wondering what these plans of yours were."

Frank glanced at Millie, and she gave a slight nod.

"Funnily enough, we were just discussing them before we came in," he replied.

He sat down at the table, and Millie went into the parlour and brought back a bottle and some glasses. She passed them round and filled each one. Frank picked his up and raised it to Sophie and Ben.

"Firstly, I would like to say how much I have enjoyed living here. Sophie, you have been more than generous after the way I treated you when you were living with us, especially as your father had just died under such sad circumstances. And Ben, what a man! Treated me like a horse and got my somewhat unsteady legs going. Thank you, both of you, and I am sorry I shall be taking Millie and Billy away from you."

Thoughts rushed through Sophie's head, among them what life would be like without Frank and Millie. They had been a happy family, and she was sorry they would be going. But where were they going?

Frank continued, "We are going to buy a property in Salcombe and use it to board holiday visitors. Millie will look after the rooms, and I will cook the meals."

Sophie and Ben looked at each other. Salcombe was not so very far away.

"We shall have to stable visitors' horses and our own," Frank continued.

Ben leant forward, looking interested.

"Now, we have something to ask you." Frank looked steadily at them both. "We want to know if you would come and help set all this up. Perhaps for a few weeks, or even a few months. I don't know what problems this will cause for the forge," he added. "Perhaps you can get someone to take it on for a short while."

This seemed like an answer to Ben's wish. "What you say is very appealing, Frank. It might be just the thing for us to do, but we need to think about it. I do know of an Albert Betts not so far from here. He is coming to the end of his apprenticeship and will be wanting a forge of his own to run."

He looked at Sophie, who knew she had to say something. "I don't know how useful I will be," she told them. "I think I'm pregnant again."

The announcement was met with a joyful response, and Ben welled up as he hugged her. "You must take it easy, then," he said. "If we do this, it will be light duties for you only."

"I imagine Sophie could take on the paperwork and accounts," said Millie. "She is the clever one."

A lot of discussion followed, and Frank and Millie were eager to find a suitable property as soon as possible. Sophie was enthusiastic but wanted the option to return to Forge Cottage whenever they thought it time to do so. She realised what a wonderful opportunity this would be for Ben.

The following day, Ben told Frank that he and Sophie would accept their offer.

CHAPTER FOURTEEN

NEW OPPORTUNITIES

FRANK AND MILLIE SPENT THE next few weeks looking for their new home while Sophie prepared for their move. Ben went to see Albert and arranged for him to take over the forge from New Year until Easter. He told Ben that he preferred to travel over each day and continue to live at home.

Harry came to help tidy up the garden, and he and Sophie were collecting leftover autumn fruit lingering on the trees when she asked him a question. "The fight, Harry, can you tell me about it?"

It had been some weeks since it had happened, but it was still on Sophie's mind.

Harry put down his basket and looked uneasy. "We were having our drink, and some of Blake's men came in. They don't usually come to our inn, and they were looking for trouble. They think it's all a bit of fun, and they'd got wind that Ben had married a schoolteacher. They were taunting him, and then one of them made an unpleasant remark about how the likes of him had managed to get a lady to go with him, if you know what I mean, miss. Then Ben went for him."

This made Sophie think about the fight differently. She realised why Ben had not wanted to tell her the reason for it. "Thank you, Harry. I now understand, and I can hardly blame Ben for what he did," she said.

"I wish he'd have told you himself, miss."

She looked at him. "Harry, I also want to thank you for something you did for me when I was a governess, the time I was dismissed."

Harry looked up at her, then quickly looked back down.

Sophie took that to mean he knew what she meant. "You were a good and kind friend to me, and Ben and I value your friendship very much."

Harry nodded, bending down to pick up his basket, and they continued gathering the fruit.

Sophie had noticed that Ben was a different man since his decision to give up blacksmithing, at least for the time being. He worked hard at his literacy lessons and was gaining fluency in his reading, and his confidence had improved. Sophie could see that he was excited about the change in their lifestyle and was kept busy writing out a list of instructions for Albert concerning the forge.

At the beginning of November, Frank and Millie returned home one afternoon, looking pleased. Sophie and Ben were impatient to hear their news.

"We have found a place to live," announced Millie excitedly. "It is in Salcombe. It's a beautiful house overlooking the sea. We were lucky to find it."

"The property is part of the Hartwell Manor Estate, and the owner is Sir Ralph Chapman," added Frank. "He and his wife, Lady Chapman, live nearby in Hartwell Hall. We have been told he does want to sell, but he is going away, so we shall be renting to begin with."

Millie was almost jumping up and down. "Wait till you see it, Sophie!" she exclaimed. "It's so beautiful—you will love living there, and it is very suitable for our holiday guests."

Sophie was thrilled. "I am so pleased you have found somewhere," she said, giving Millie a hug. "It sounds just like what you have been wanting. We are going to be so busy getting ready for the move, but first we must prepare for your wedding."

Millie looked worried and said she had concerns about the rector. "I don't think he will be wanting to marry us," she said. "I know Ben told you what happened with his son, and he won't want anything to do with us."

"He cannot refuse," Sophie reassured her. "He will act professionally and leave his feelings towards you and Ben out of it."

Frank said he would arrange to have the banns read, and the following day, he went to see the rector. When he returned, he assured Millie that all had gone well, and the rector had taken down their details without comment.

Throughout November, Frank and Millie attended the church every Sunday to hear their banns read. Sophie went with them for support, but Ben refused. "Seeing that man on the day will be enough for me," he said.

Sophie was determined to make Millie's wedding day special. She remembered what a successful day her own had been and how grateful she was. She insisted on paying for Millie's dress and accessories, and they enjoyed visiting the dressmaker together. Mrs. Chambers had offered to help with the wedding breakfast, and Sophie spent her time baking and cleaning the cottage.

The wedding day was to be at the beginning of December, and the day before, Frank and Billy went to stay with Harry and his mother. Sophie set to decorating the parlour and laying the table. Frank's bed had been removed, and Ben had returned it to Mrs. Chambers. Finally, when she had everything in place, Sophie went out to the stables to see the trap, which Ben had decorated with white ribbons and evergreen branches.

The following morning, Ben rose early to groom the horse and plait his mane and tail. Sophie helped Millie into her dress and arranged her hair. Millie said she felt like a real lady when she saw herself in the full-length mirror. Sophie then handed her posy to her, which Mrs. Chambers had made with ivy and mistletoe, as there were no flowers to be had.

Old Thomas had again been asked to be the escort. He walked Millie down the aisle, and the rector conducted the ceremony as if nothing had happened, but with no smile for the happy couple. Sophie watched as Ben stepped forward with the ring. She noticed that he looked the rector straight in the eye.

At the end of the service, Frank and Millie turned towards the congregation, looking radiant. Sophie had been anxious about Millie's reputation in the village. It was widely known that she had an illegitimate child by the rector's son, but from the affectionate looks Sophie noticed, it seemed that most of them blamed Jonathan and saw Millie as a victim. She could see how much pleasure the marriage had given to the villagers when they all crowded round the couple outside the church. Most of them knew Millie well and had seen her grow up. They surged forward, cheering and waving.

"Best wishes to you!" they cried. "Lots of happiness!"

Millie and Frank acknowledged their congratulations, smiling and waving back as they climbed into the trap.

"Make sure that fine young man takes care of you!" added an older woman as Harry drove them away.

Back at Forge Cottage, all was excitement and anticipation as the wedding guests arrived, having followed on foot, with young Billy running ahead to arrive first. They all crowded into the parlour and stood or sat where they could. Sophie and Mrs. Chambers bustled about with plates of food, and Ben poured drinks. Old Thomas attempted to calm Billy down while Harry helped his mother to a seat. Millie was talking to the farmer and his wife, who were congratulating her and saying they were sorry she was leaving her work at the dairy.

The wedding breakfast was served, and it was Ben's turn to raise a toast. "To my lovely sister and my very good friend!" he announced, raising his glass. He then took the opportunity to tell the gathered company about their plans to move to Salcombe. There were murmurs of surprise and consternation and some bewilderment. He hastily assured them that it would only be a temporary move and that they were not leaving the village permanently.

When their guests had finally departed, Sophie sank into Ben's chair. The excitement of the day had made her tired. She knew she had to be careful during her pregnancy, and now she had to think about Christmas.

Millie and Frank helped with the preparations, and on Christmas Day, they all crowded round the table in the parlour. Mrs. Chambers had been invited, together with old Thomas, Harry and his mother, Mildred. Billy found the silver threepenny piece in his Christmas pudding and crowed with excitement. Sophie had slipped it in there for him when he wasn't looking. She noticed that Harry seemed out of sorts. He looked sad at times and was rather quiet. She was very fond of him, and it worried her. Perhaps it was because his mother had been unwell.

In the new year, Ben and Frank made several journeys ferrying their belongings across to their new home. The lane to Salcombe was steep in places, and Ben often had to alight and lead the horse. The day before they finally left, he cleaned out the stables for the last time and checked all round. Albert had visited several times, and Ben had shown him the forge and introduced him to some of his customers. Frank, Millie, and Billy were already at the new house, and now it was time for Ben and Sophie to join them. Ben was excited, but Sophie knew she would miss the cottage, and she had mixed feelings when Ben closed the door and locked it.

Millie had been right—Sophie did love the house. It was situated on an elevated piece of ground with views of the estuary at the back. It was Georgian in style, and the front was well proportioned, with four tall windows flanking an elegant front door along the lower storey and five windows above. The lower windows and the door were all arched and edged with white stone, and across the back of the house was a narrow iron veranda with a curved roof that covered both levels. Two of the bedrooms, including Ben and Sophie's, opened onto it. The grounds were well maintained with trees and shrubs and sloped downhill.

The four of them began getting the house ready for the season. It was already furnished, and Millie was to prepare the rooms. Frank and Sophie set to equipping the kitchen and purchasing provisions. Sophie had brought her recipe book and was going to teach Frank how to cook. The house was in very good repair, so there was little for Ben to do other than a few painting jobs inside. He busied himself tidying the grounds and going on walks, sometimes taking Billy with him.

Frank and Millie had wanted to begin letting rooms at Easter, but they had a booking before then. A doctor wanted to bring his wife at the beginning of February for her to recuperate after an illness.

A few days after they had settled in, a letter arrived from Lady Lucinda, the wife of Sir Ralph, the estate's owner, inviting them to afternoon tea at the Hall. She explained that her husband was still away shooting in Scotland.

On their arrival, the two couples and Billy were ushered into a smartly furnished room, and Lady Lucinda came to greet them. Sophie looked at the elegant woman standing before her. She was very beautiful and was wearing a low-cut rose-pink dress and an emerald necklace.

She extended a hand to Frank, which he accepted with a bow and a slight kiss. He seemed quite at ease. Ben's stiffness told Sophie he wasn't comfortable, but she was pleased to see he had the sense to copy Frank. The lady gave Sophie and Millie a radiant smile and patted Billy on the head, which he didn't seem to like. Frank formally introduced everyone, and they were invited to sit down on some comfortable sofas by the roaring fire.

Lady Lucinda began the conversation. "How very exciting for you all, starting this new venture!"

Frank went on to explain what they were hoping to do and added that they were very pleased with the house.

She nodded in agreement. "It has lovely views of the estuary. I am sure your guests will appreciate that."

Millie and Ben appeared to be tongue-tied, so Sophie thought she ought to say something. "Devon is a beautiful part of the country, and I believe is becoming very sought after as a holiday destination."

"Yes, indeed. But we don't want all our beauty spots to get too crowded!" replied their hostess with a smile.

The conversation continued in a polite, restrained way, with Frank and Sophie doing most of the talking. Millie looked out of her depth, and Sophie saw Ben looking intently at Lady Lucinda. When she asked him a question, he seemed startled and looked at Sophie for reassurance.

"I understand that you would like to work with horses, Mr. Browne."

Sophie assumed she must have heard this from the estate manager, who had been talking to Frank.

Ben looked nervous. "Yes, ma'am," he replied.

She looked pleased. "Then I have something to put to you. My husband is extending his trip to Scotland, and he has taken our groom with him. Would you be interested in replacing him until their return?"

How wonderful—Ben would now be able to do what he really wanted. Sophie waited to see how he would respond.

"I would be very interested, ma'am," he replied. "I think caring for horses is one of the best jobs a man can have." He reddened slightly, but Lady Lucinda put him at ease.

"I agree!" she replied, her eyes shining. "Now I think it's time for some tea!"

After the visit, everyone expressed their pleasure that Ben had been given this opportunity, and Sophie was especially thankful. Ben told her how impressed he had been with their visit to the Hall and how excited he was at the offer to work with the horses.

The estate manager called round to discuss terms the next day. When he left, Ben told them about his duties. "I'll be looking after Lady Lucinda's hunter," he announced proudly. "There are also Sir Ralph's two carriage horses and some working horses. I think I managed to explain that I have lots of experience with horses."

Sophie had never seen her husband so happy and brimming with confidence.

CHAPTER FOURTEEN

A NEW LIFE

At six o'clock in the morning on the first day of February, Ben set off for work at the Hall. It was a twenty-minute walk through the fields from where they were living. He kissed Sophie goodbye when he left. She wished him well and then rose to get ready for her day's work. She was enjoying being pregnant again and experiencing a feeling of joy and well-being in her new surroundings. The sun shone through the large windows into the expansive bedroom she now inhabited. How different it all felt from her life as a blacksmith's wife at their small cottage.

When Ben returned later that afternoon, he told her that he had found everything at the stables in some disarray and had to work hard to tidy it all. Apart from feeding and watering the horses, he'd needed to clean all the leather and brass in the tack room. He said that Lady Lucinda liked to ride most mornings and would usually go round the grounds by herself. He was required to get her mount ready and to attend to it when she returned. The thoroughbred she rode was called Prince, and he was a large horse.

"I don't mind admitting to you, Sophie, that I didn't fancy riding him. I reckon he's over sixteen hands high. Lady Lucinda hopped up on him, as calm as ever. There is a mounting block, though."

"Your first day went well, then?"

"Yes, I think I will be able to manage. I have some time after feeding the horses in the mornings, so I will be able to come home for some breakfast."

Life at Hartwell Lodge settled into routines for each of them as they settled into their new roles. At dinner each night, everyone wanted to talk about their day. They were finding their new way of life stimulating and exciting.

Sophie would work in the kitchen preparing the evening meal with Frank. They were trying out some tasty recipes, so dinner was always an enjoyable occasion. One evening Sophie told them that Frank had made the pie for their meal, but he had made the pastry far too wet and hadn't been able to get it off his hands. She said it had made her laugh.

"Well, I had never done such a thing before!" he remonstrated.

"How are you two getting on in the kitchen?" asked Millie. "I hope my husband is going to become an expert cook under your teaching, Sophie."

Sophie assured her he was doing very well and then asked Ben how his day had been. He had been going to the stables for just over a week. He looked up suddenly and appeared to have been lost in his thoughts.

"Oh…all went well," he replied. "There's a lot that needs doing."

Ben was sometimes a little late coming into breakfast, as he had to take Prince out for some exercise first thing if Lady Lucinda wasn't riding that morning. He told Sophie he was relieved to find him to be a very responsive, well-trained horse, and he had enjoyed his ride. "I felt like the lord of the manor," he said.

Sophie was pleased at how happy Ben seemed.

At the Lodge, Millie had insisted that they change out of their working clothes and sit at the dining room table each evening. Their visitors would be middle- or upper-class people who would expect certain standards.

After a while, Sophie noticed that Ben seemed unsettled. He became less animated, talked little about his day and was evasive and quiet. She thought he might be finding it hard to adjust to his new life.

Halfway through February, Frank and Millie welcomed their first visitors. The doctor and his wife were very informal and friendly and liked to join the family in the sitting room in the evenings. Ben made sure they had a good fire going in the large fireplace. The doctor's wife would retire to bed early, and the doctor would stay up playing cards with Frank. Sophie saw that Ben tended not to join in the conversations. One evening, she even asked him if he felt unwell.

He sat up suddenly. "No, of course not," he answered, somewhat abruptly.

"Is everything going well at the stables?"

Ben shifted in his chair.

"Why shouldn't it be?"

"You seem unsettled, Ben. I had hoped you would enjoy your new employment. Has anyone said anything to you about your work?"

"No. Lady Lucinda is very pleased with what I have done so far."

"Well, that's good." Sophie said no more but felt that she had not really satisfied her concerns.

The weeks went by, and Sophie was kept busy with meals and domestic arrangements. Ben had insisted that she rest in the afternoons, leaving Millie and Frank to get on with preparing the house. When Ben had time off, he would often go for long walks by himself.

One day, just as he was about to leave, Sophie asked him why he was going out again. "I feel you are avoiding me, Ben. I would like to see more of you and perhaps go on some short walks with you."

"I just need time to unwind after work," he replied.

Sophie was puzzled. He had never needed time to do this before. Why now? "Is it getting too much?" she asked. "You know I will always go back to Forge Cottage if that's what you want to do."

"No. I like working here, Sophie. I don't want to go back." He left to go on his walk.

It was April, and the spring had brought more visitors. Frank and Millie were busy, and Sophie was often called on to look after Billy. She sometimes took him down to the harbour to watch the fishing boats, or else they would explore the coastline together. Billy clamoured to run along the beach and find shells. Once a fisherman had given them a ride in his boat to the mouth of the inlet. Sophie was enjoying her new life much more than she'd thought she would. She was also looking forward to the birth of her child.

At breakfast one morning, Frank had a note delivered at the Lodge. It was from Lady Lucinda. Ben had already left for the stables, so Frank read it and, looking flustered, folded the letter and put it into his pocket quickly.

Millie looked at him. “What was that, Frank? Not bad news, I hope. Another bill perhaps?”

“No, no, it’s from Lady Lucinda.” He looked somewhat mystified. “She writes that she is going away.”

Sophie was helping Billy butter his toast and looked up. “Leaving?” she repeated.

“Yes. All her affairs will be dealt with by her estate manager.”

“What about Ben’s job?”

Frank looked uncomfortable. “His employment is terminated,” he said.

Sophie gasped. “He will be so disappointed. Oh, poor Ben.”

Frank looked over at Millie, who was also taken aback. “I think we had better discuss this this evening,” he suggested. “When Ben and the rest of us are all here.”

When Ben came in later, his face was downcast, and he avoided eye contact with everybody. He also had been informed by the estate manager that his position as groom was to be ended. He told Sophie that it had been arranged for Prince to be looked after by a friend of the family who lived nearby and that he was to take him there. An estate worker would be taking charge of the working horses. The manager had told him to call into the estate office after work that day to be paid.

Sophie was bitterly disappointed. “Oh, Ben,” she said, tears welling up in her eyes. “This is awful news. I am so sorry. Why has Lady Lucinda gone away so suddenly? I don’t understand it.” It was strange that Lady Lucinda had left after giving Ben the job as her groom. Perhaps Sir Ralph was returning at last.

Ben turned away. “I don’t know,” he said shortly. “To hell with them!”

He walked out, and Sophie was left feeling bewildered. She had never seen Ben like this before.

There was now nothing to keep them at Salcombe, as Frank and Millie were managing well. Without Ben’s extra income, he and Sophie would have to return to Forge Cottage. That evening, it was agreed that they should leave the following week. Frank and Millie said they were very sorry to see them go and were full of gratitude for all their help. Ben wrote to let the replacement blacksmith, Albert, know he would have to finish sooner than expected.

When it was time to leave, Ben put their bags into the trap, and he and Sophie said their goodbyes. Millie hugged her sister-in-law and told her to try and have lots of rest. She looked very concerned. "The next time I see you will be when the baby is born," she said.

Billy moped about and appeared sad to see them go. Sophie knew how much he had enjoyed his trips out with her. Frank shook Ben's hand firmly, looking at him intently. Ben then mounted the trap and drew the reins together. The journey home was very restrained, and he did not say much. Sophie knew he must be feeling very disappointed and that he was not looking forward to having to go back to blacksmithing.

When they arrived home, Sophie entered Forge Cottage and put the basket of food Millie had given to her onto the kitchen table. The journey had tired her out. After seeing her in, Ben put the horse away and then came in and sat down beside her. He looked straight at her and said, "Sophie, I have something to tell you."

His face alarmed her—he looked serious and uneasy, and she wondered what it could be.

"Lady Lucinda had to go away because she is expecting a child."

"But whose baby is it?" asked Sophie innocently. "I thought her husband was in Scotland."

Ben looked away. "It's mine," he said, his voice choked.

At this, Sophie went pale and looked shocked. She put her hand to her mouth. "Oh no, Ben, surely not! We have been so happy. It can't be!"

"I can't explain it, Sophie. It was pure folly and weakness on my part. I am so sorry I have hurt you like this. Please, please forgive me. I swear never to hurt you again as long as I live."

He tried to put his arm round her, but she pushed him away. "How could you do this to me?" she demanded. Then, looking down at herself, she added, "To us!"

Ben sat at the table with his head in his hands. Suddenly, he got up and went out, pushing the door shut behind him.

CHAPTER FIFTEEN

HEALING

After Ben suddenly left, Sophie sat at the kitchen table, overwhelmed, and feeling quite sick. The cottage was silent except for the ticking of the clock. She looked round and thought about how quiet it was without Millie and Frank there and little Billy running around. Now things were going to be so different. She felt very alone.

She experienced so many emotions as she took in what Ben had told her. With anger, she remembered how he had accused her of being unfaithful with Harry when all he had done was to give her a kiss goodbye. She also recalled Mrs. Hunter's words about Ben bringing her trouble. *Nothing*, she thought, *could be as bad as this trouble*. She would never let him touch her again. She couldn't understand why he had betrayed her like this if he really loved her. *Why, oh, why had she married him? Why hadn't she heeded the warnings?*

She ran through several scenarios in her mind. What was she to do? Did she want to leave Ben? She could stay with Frank and Millie while things cooled down, but it would hardly be fair on them when they were trying to look after their guests. Should she confront Ben and have a go at him? That would not make things better between them. How had he allowed himself to be seduced by that woman? Mrs. Chambers had told her that "men will be men." Had she meant this sort of behaviour?

At this point, her feelings gave way, and she began sobbing uncontrollably. Her thoughts turned to her unborn child, not far off now. She wanted her baby to be part of a happy family with a mother and father who loved each other. She would have to try and heal things as best she could and face the future. It wouldn't be easy—a lot of damage had been done.

She got up slowly and started to get the meal ready, although she wasn't hungry. She lit the range and put the kettle on. She emptied Millie's basket of provisions and went to the pantry, getting out a jar of preserved plums to go with the clotted cream. She found it comforting to be back in her small kitchen doing normal things.

When the table was laid and the tea made, she began to wonder where Ben was. It was getting dark, and he had been gone some time. She thought he might be at the inn drowning his sorrows or maybe at Harry's unloading his troubles. Had he perhaps left for good?

She wrapped a shawl round her shoulders and went out into the lane to look for him. When she turned the corner, she saw him sitting under the chestnut tree outside the forge, the same place he had proposed to her. He was bent over with his head in his hands. What should she do? She walked over slowly and stood beside him.

"Come on in, Ben. It's getting cold and dark," she said.

He put his arms round her, laying his head against her swollen body, and said softly, "Oh Sophie, what have I done! Whatever have I done to you?"

"Come and have your supper, then we can talk."

As he rose to go in, she took his hand, and they walked back to the cottage. After their meal, Sophie cleared the table and Ben lit the fire and some candles in the parlour, then they sat together on the settle. He clasped both her hands in his.

"Sophie, my darling, what can I say? I am so ashamed of what I have done, and I beg your forgiveness. Never again will I do anything to hurt you. I promise to be a good husband and a good father to our child."

Sophie could see how distraught he was. He was near to tears.

"I know I have messed up our chance of a better life in Salcombe and my own chance to work with horses."

Whatever he said, Sophie continued to feel aggrieved and deeply hurt. She looked away, hardly able to look at him. It was going to take time for her to forgive him, if she ever could, and she would never forget what he had done to her. When she felt emotionally stronger, she would demand he tell her the details of what had happened.

The next few days were difficult. They were like two strangers. Sophie could not bring herself to sleep with her husband and asked him to go into the spare bedroom. She lay in bed alone each night, staring up at the ceiling and trying to make sense of what had happened. She could feel the little one move inside her and hoped he or she would never know what their father had done, how he had betrayed her. The days passed, but it didn't get easier, and she would often find herself weeping at the thought of it all. She decided to write to Millie and ask her to come over to see her.

Ben seemed to be trying to make the best of getting back to his blacksmithing. This was helped by the fact that all his customers said they were glad to see him again. They made comments such as, "That other fellow, the time 'e took to shoe a horse!"

Sophie could see that Ben seemed resigned at getting back to familiar routines, but she was feeling lonely. She worked away in the kitchen, but all the pleasure was now gone for her. She missed having Millie and Frank and Billy there—the cottage felt empty. She hoped she would hear from Millie soon.

She continued to make her preparations for the baby with a heavy heart. Ben had made a cradle, which he placed at the foot of their bed, and Sophie got busy making some clothes and hemming little sheets.

She knew she could not go on like this, so one day she walked over to see Mrs. Chambers. She knew she could confide in her. Her friend was obviously pleased to see her, and this cheered her a little. As Sophie sat down by the fire in Mrs. Chambers's small, comfortable sitting room, she remembered happier days, when Ben had taken her there before they were married.

Mrs. Chambers made a pot of tea and then settled herself down in her chair. Sophie told her that "something had happened" while they were in Salcombe that had meant they had to return. She then related all the bare details.

After listening carefully, Mrs. Chambers told her that this happened often in marriages, but she was surprised it had happened with Ben. She regarded Sophie for a few moments, then said, "You need to reconcile with Ben before your baby is born, my dear. Don't be afraid to show him how hurt you are but allow him to try and heal that hurt. Don't put up a lot of barriers he has to get through."

"Why should I make it easy for him?" asked Sophie bitterly. "Why shouldn't he suffer as well?"

"I think you will find he is suffering, very deeply."

Sophie sat with her hands in her lap, thinking. She knew Mrs. Chambers was right, but she could not forgive Ben that easily.

"You must both look to the future and enjoy the birth of your little child. Ben will make an excellent father. He has cared for his sister in her troubles and been good to little Billy."

This reassured Sophie a little and lifted her spirits. It felt good to share her concerns with someone, and Mrs. Chambers always had sound advice to give. She had knitted some baby clothes, and as Sophie admired them, she suddenly realised that a little person would be filling them soon.

"I think little baby Browne is coming at just the right time," said Mrs. Chambers reassuringly.

As Sophie made her way back home, she decided that she would have to try and forgive Ben. That night, she asked him to come back to their bed. Millie had written to say that she would come over the following weekend, and she arrived on the Saturday morning, knowing Ben worked then. Sophie told her what had happened the day they had left the Lodge and returned home. Sophie asked Millie if she knew about Ben's baby.

"Yes, Frank told me. It was in the letter he received. We had to let Ben tell you himself, Sophie. You realise that."

Sophie nodded. "Oh, Millie, what am I going to do? My world has fallen apart. How could he do this?"

"Frank thinks Lucinda seduced him, but of course, he let himself be seduced."

Sophie imagined Lucinda in her tightly fitted riding habit, asking Ben to help her dismount after her ride, encouraging him to put his arms round her slim waist. She shuddered. How she hated her!

"How long was it going on for?" she asked Millie.

"A few weeks, I think. Frank said Ben had confessed to him and Frank had told him to end it, otherwise he would throw him out. He's very angry about it."

"I do hope it will not damage your business." Sophie sounded concerned. "Sir Ralph is bound to find out."

After Millie left, Sophie thought about what she had been told. Ben had not revealed to her that he had confided in Frank.

Sophie was finding each day tedious, and she was impatient for the baby to be born. She found it difficult to enjoy anything, as her thoughts kept going back to what Ben had done. Sometimes they talked about names but could never quite agree. In the end it was decided that if it was a boy, Ben would choose his name and Sophie would choose the next one, and the other way round if it was a girl.

"But of course, it is going to be a boy!" Ben was adamant.

On the first of May, Sophie and Ben went to the village green to join in the May Day celebrations. They watched the children dancing round the maypole and the crowning of the May queen. Ben seemed to know everyone, but Sophie still hadn't gotten to know many of the villagers. The forge was set back from the rest of the village, and Sophie decided that she would walk there more regularly once she had the baby.

A letter arrived addressed to Ben, and Sophie collected it from the village inn. It had been forwarded from the Lodge. When she got back, she decided to open it before Ben got home, as she knew it had something to do with Lucinda. The address was written in a fine copperplate hand. She saw it was from Lady Lucinda's brother, Reverend William Burrows.

For the attention of Mr. Browne

Confidential

Dear Sir,

I am writing on behalf of my sister, Lady Lucinda Chapman. I understand that she is expecting your child. Having not heard from you, she requested I contact you.

Lady Lucinda is now estranged from her husband and has no means of support at present except me. While I am intending to help my sister, I have, sir, every expectation that you will do likewise. What this support will be is subject to future discussions between the two of us.

Yours sincerely,

Rev. William Burrows

Sophie had tried to put her husband's affair firmly behind her. She had wondered if he had tried to contact Lady Lucinda. She put the letter away in a drawer while she decided what to do about it.

A few days later, Sophie was preparing vegetables in the kitchen when she experienced what felt like a kick inside her and her waters broke. Ben had given her a bell for when this happened, so she went to the door and rang it as loudly as she could. He came running from the forge and helped her upstairs, where she lay down on the bed, moaning and clutching her stomach. Ben tried to calm her.

"I want Millie. Tell Millie to come!" she demanded.

Ben held Sophie's hand while she writhed in pain.

"Get Millie!" she gasped. "This is all your fault, Ben. Go away! I don't want you here. I want Millie!" She was very restless and continued to groan, then saw that Ben was stunned when she told him to go.

"Sophie," he said, gently holding her hand, but she pulled it away.

"Go away!" she said. How she hated him!

She heard him go downstairs. She knew that he had plenty to do and heard him throw some coal on the fire and fill the kettle up. He then had to hurry down to the village to fetch Betty Mears, the village midwife, who in her time had delivered Ben, his sister and Billy. Sophie was relieved when at last Betty entered the bedroom. Millie arrived sometime later, having been fetched by Ben. Mrs. Chambers also came to help out, but after a short while, she went downstairs to see Ben.

Sophie was in pain and discomfort for some time, but when it was all over, Betty held up the baby and said, "It's a fine boy, Mrs. Browne!"

Sophie felt so relieved and knew Ben would be so happy. Strangely, she felt pleased at this. She regretted how she had spoken to him.

Betty cleaned the baby up, and Millie made Sophie comfortable. Then her baby was placed in her arms. What a precious moment that was to her.

"My job's done," said Betty in her matter-of-fact way. She spoke to Sophie briefly about feeding and then went downstairs.

"Tell Ben to come up, please, Millie," said Sophie.

Ben stepped quietly into the bedroom and saw his son cradled in Sophie's arms, and she looked up and smiled broadly. He kissed her gently and then looked at his newborn son. He bent down and kissed him and held his little fingers in his hand. "Oh, Sophie, he's so tiny!" he exclaimed.

Sophie nodded and drew him closer to her, then held him out to Ben. "Here you are, Ben. You hold him."

Ben cradled the small form in his strong arms, not taking his eyes off him. He then looked at his wife. "Thank you, Sophie, thank you!" He gave the child back and turned his attention to her. "I'm sorry you had a time of it, my love."

She smiled weakly. "It's all over now." She squeezed his hand. "I'm sorry I said those things to you. I was frightened."

"Yes, I understand."

Mrs. Chambers was still downstairs, and Sophie asked if she could come up. Mrs. Chambers said she had never seen such a beautiful child, "Good looking, like his parents." Millie then shooed everyone out so she could help Sophie feed the baby.

Millie said she was able to stay for a week. She had arranged for the wife of the estate manager to assist Frank and look after Billy when Sophie had her baby. The following evening, Ben went down to the Two Foxes to "wet the baby's head" by buying all the drinks and promised faithfully that he would come back in one piece.

Sophie had a series of visitors come from the village to see the baby. They brought little gifts—a posy of flowers, a jar of homemade jam, some vegetables or a few cakes. Some of the older women had knitted little jackets or crocheted shawls, and Sophie was overwhelmed by their kindness. Millie and Frank's present was a baby carriage, which would be delivered later.

Despite their loathing of the rector, Sophie and Ben decided to have their son christened. Ben fetched Millie, Frank and Billy on the day, and the little group walked to the church with the baby dressed in a christening robe that Mrs. Chambers had made from Sophie's wedding dress.

The rector took the child in his arms and dipped his finger in the holy water. He made the sign of the cross on his head and said, "I name this child Charles Henry Browne. May God bless him."

From then on, it seemed to Sophie that her whole days were taken up with the baby. He took ages to feed, and she had no sooner put him down to sleep than it was time for his next meal. She felt so tired and overwhelmed, and it worried her when things were left undone. She struggled on, but one day when Ben came in for his lunch, she was sitting at the kitchen table crying.

He sat beside her and put his arm round her. "What is it, Sophie? What can I do?"

"I feel so tired and down," she replied.

"You need help so you can rest more," he said. "I will close the forge for two hours in the afternoons and come and look after little Charles so you can rest. If he gets hungry, he'll just have to wait!"

Sophie nodded gratefully. She had tried so hard to keep going and felt she had failed.

"I'll arrange for the laundry to be done too. I should have thought of all this before," Ben added.

As she improved, she began to feel happier. Ben had done all he could to help her through a difficult time, and it brought them close together. Sophie knew that her husband was unhappy. She knew he disliked blacksmithing more than ever, and he had feelings of failure because he had ruined their chances of a new life.

CHAPTER SIXTEEN

A VISITOR AND A VISIT

Whenever Sophie went to the village, she was surprised to find out how generally well-liked Ben was. It was just as Mrs. Chambers had told her—he and his family did not have the bad name she had been led to believe. The rector, of course, had his own reasons for saying otherwise. The villagers told her they saw Ben as their blacksmith, and he had the reputation of a craftsman who produced good work at fair prices. His services were relied on by all the local villagers and some customers from even further afield. Ben never sent anyone away if he could do the work.

Sophie mentioned her new-found knowledge to her husband at supper one night. He merely shrugged and carried on with his meal. "That doesn't mean I have to like it," he said.

Sophie sighed. There seemed no hope of any change at present, as they needed a regular income.

A few weeks later, Ben was out collecting supplies of coal and iron rods from Kingsbridge quay. That afternoon, Sophie had fed Charles and put him down to rest when she heard a tentative knock on the door. Although it was summer, she kept it closed when Ben was away. She opened it and saw a young man standing there. He was smartly dressed and looked anxious. He had dark hair and an intelligent-looking face. His blue eyes regarded her earnestly, and there was something about him that seemed familiar.

"Could I please speak to Mr. Browne?" he asked.

"I am Mrs. Browne. Can I ask what it is about?"

"I do apologise," he replied politely. "My name is Jonathan, Jonathan Hunter. My father is the rector here."

Immediately, Sophie knew why she recognised him. He had Billy's eyes. He was obviously here to find out about Millie and his son, and she was unsure what to do.

"Please don't turn me away," he pleaded. "All I ask is to have the opportunity to ask Mr. Browne something, and then I will go."

Sophie could see he was emotional, and she felt pity for him. "You'd better come in," she said. "Mr. Browne shouldn't be too long." She offered him a seat at the kitchen table.

Before long, Ben came in, and when he saw who it was, he gave him a hard look. "What's he doing here?" he asked roughly.

"Sit down, Ben," Sophie said. "Jonathan has something to ask you, and I think we should hear him."

"Then can I throw him out?" growled Ben.

Jonathan looked startled but held his resolve and began. "I want to say how deeply I regret the way I behaved towards Millie and you, sir, and how I have neglected my child."

Ben looked uncomfortable but sat down and continued to listen. Jonathan went on to tell them that his father had been extremely angry when he'd heard that Millie was expecting his son's child and had immediately sent him away to live with his aunt until he went up to Oxford. His studies had now finished, and he had taken holy orders. He had just been appointed a curacy in Somerset.

"I didn't stand up to my father as I should have done," he went on. "I have never forgotten Millie and our son. Sometimes, when I came home, I would come up here hoping to catch a glimpse of him. I saw him riding a horse on his birthday last year. All I ask is that I can have some news of him as he grows up, if you could ask Millie, sir. I know she is married, and Billy has a new father, and I don't want to disrupt their family life. My dearest wish is that my son may come to know me and love me as his father one day."

Jonathan appeared to be fighting back tears at this point, then recovered himself. "Before taking up my curacy, I had to speak to my spiritual advisor, and I shared with him what happened. He encouraged me to try to make amends, not just for my sake, but to put to rights the wrong I have done. I hope I can do that one day."

"I think your parents have a lot to answer for, Jonathan," said Ben. "They should have been more charitable and a better example to you. I apologise for the way I treated you. It wasn't the right thing to do."

"Do your parents know you have come here today?" asked Sophie.

"No," replied Jonathan. "We never speak about it."

They all sat in silence for a few moments, then Ben spoke. "What is it you want me to do, Jonathan?"

"Please, would you convey to Millie my deep regrets and ask her if she could find it in her heart to allow me to hear news of Billy from time to time? Perhaps she could write to you if she doesn't want anything to do with me."

Ben agreed, much to Sophie's relief. Jonathan thanked them both for seeing him and gave them his address. He politely bid them good day, and Ben showed him out.

"I think I may have misjudged that young man," he said, almost to himself.

Sophie said she would write to Millie.

"I have my doubts if she will agree," Ben said, "but who am I to try and stop a man wanting to know about his son?"

Sophie looked away, remembering the letter that had come.

The answer from Millie took some time. She explained that she wanted nothing to do with Jonathan but thought that Billy might want to know who his father was in the future, so she agreed to send news of her son. Sophie wrote to Jonathan, promising to forward Millie's letters.

As well as caring for his own son most afternoons, Ben spent each evening sitting in his chair cradling him in his arms. His book lay on the shelf unread, and he and Sophie would quietly talk together about their day. He was now able to make love to her again, and they were beginning to grow close again after a difficult time.

One morning, at breakfast, Ben was looking for some bills and was rifling about in the dresser drawer. He pulled out the letter that Sophie had put away and saw it was addressed to him. He saw that it had been opened.

"When did this come?" he asked, holding it up to show her.

Sophie started and said, "It came a little while ago, before Charles was born."

Ben looked at her. "Were you hiding it?"

"No, I was going to show it to you, I promise."

He sighed and sat down and read it through, holding his head in his hand.

"What are you going to do?" she asked.

Ben looked diffident.

"Do you still love her?"

"No, no, of course not!"

Silence again. Sophie could feel her emotions welling up inside her. The hurt and anger were still there.

"We need to decide what to do," he said.

"*You* have to decide, Ben."

He waited a few moments before he said, "I don't want to abandon the child."

"What are you going to do about it then?" she demanded.

"I think I should go and see her brother. I also want to find out about her husband—William says they are estranged. I would like to be part of the child's upbringing, but that depends on you, Sophie."

She knew she had little choice but to agree. His child was to be born, and as there was no changing that, the child should know his father.

Ben got up to go to work. "Thank you," he said simply. That evening he wrote out his reply, showed it to his wife and posted it the following day.

Sophie tried to carry on as normal. When the sun was shining, she would put Charles out under the trees in the orchard in his baby carriage and he would wave his arms awkwardly at the moving leaves above him. She tried to enjoy her time with her child, showing him every attention.

Ben walked to the Two Foxes each day to see if a letter had arrived, and finally it came. It was an invitation from Reverend William Burrows to visit his home in Somerset. He said he was anxious to meet Ben before his sister's baby was born.

When Ben told Sophie and showed her the letter, she said coldly, "You go if you want to, Ben."

He wrote back to Lucinda's brother to ask him when he could visit, and he did not have long to wait for a reply.

Ben had been into the village and had picked up two letters, one from the reverend and the other from Millie. The letter from Lucinda's brother was concise. He said that Lucinda was well, and they would be pleased to receive a visit from Ben at his own convenience. Millie's letter was also an invitation, and she asked Sophie and Ben to come and stay with them at their house in Salcombe in September. The main holiday season would be finishing at the end of August, and they had taken no more bookings because they wanted a break. They had been working flat out for several months. Millie also sent some news of Billy to send on to his father.

Sophie was pleased at the thought of seeing Millie and Frank again. It was agreed that she and the baby could stay at Salcombe while Ben went to see William. He wrote suggesting he come the second week in September. He hadn't seen Lucinda for about six months.

As William's rectory was in Somerset, it would be quite a long journey. Sophie busied herself getting things ready. She packed Ben's best clothes and made sure he had clean shirts. She was concerned about how he would cope as a guest at the rectory, as she knew the way of life there would be different from what he was used to at home.

She approached the subject one evening. "You need to know what to do when you visit the rectory," she said to Ben.

He put down the book he was reading.

"Life is more formal in such a household," she explained and went on to describe the conventions of middle-class life. Ben looked disconcerted at what he was hearing. He was not used to such a lifestyle and had never experienced it or had to deal with servants. Sophie advised him as best she could.

They made arrangements for Albert Betts to cover at the forge, and a few days later, they arrived at the Lodge in Salcombe. Millie and Frank were delighted to see them. When Sophie entered their bedroom overlooking the sea, memories came back to her. She thought about how, during all that time, her husband was being unfaithful to her. It was not getting any easier for her to get on with her life. How could she put it all behind her with his illegitimate child about to be born?

Sophie was gladdened to see how thrilled Frank looked when she put Charles into his arms. She then let Billy hold him carefully after sitting him down on a sofa. He looked at Sophie and said, "I think he likes me!"

Sophie carefully took her child back and held him close.

Ben swept his young nephew up in the air. "Hello my little man! What do you think of your cousin?"

"He's going to be my friend," announced Billy.

Sophie had brought some presents for them all, and Billy went outside with his uncle to play with his new football. While they were gone, Millie spoke about Ben's visit to Somerset and asked if it was a good idea.

"Billy is well loved, and he is a very happy child. Not having his natural father has not mattered at all," she said. "So why does Ben have to get involved? Lucinda made her choice, and her brother is prepared to give her a home. Why must he go there?"

"I think he feels it is the honourable thing to do," replied Sophie, "and I have agreed."

Millie looked sceptical. "I hope you won't regret it."

"I love Ben," said Sophie. "I have to try and forgive him."

The following day, Ben prepared to leave to catch his train to Somerset. He would travel to Taunton and hire a pony and trap to complete his journey.

"Goodbye," said Sophie, giving him his bag. "I hope it goes well. I shall be thinking of you all the while."

Ben gave her a hug and kissed her goodbye.

CHAPTER SEVENTEEN

REMORSE

When Ben finally arrived back at Salcombe, Sophie was anxious to know about his visit. He reassured her that it had gone well, and he had spoken with Lucinda's brother.

"They made me very welcome," he began. "I had a lovely room and bed. The maid put out all my clothes and tidied up. I managed at the meals, thanks to your instructions. You ought to have seen the range of dishes brought out for breakfast. And we had partridge for dinner!"

Sophie stiffened. All this was of no interest to her. "But what did William say to you?"

"We discussed what role I was to have in the raising of the child. I made it clear I had no money to give but would do what I could for his sister."

Sophie thought Ben was being evasive in not mentioning Lucinda's name.

"He told me Sir Ralph was suing for a divorce on the grounds of adultery and desertion and she would come out of it with nothing. William is prepared to give her a home for the time being."

"That's very good of him."

"He told me she has always been rather spoiled and reckless, and he had warned her not to marry Sir Ralph, but she wanted a title and…"

"I don't want to hear all that," interrupted Sophie.

Ben stopped speaking.

"Let's put this behind us for now and enjoy our time with Frank and Millie and your son."

Ben nodded and tried to put his arm round his wife, but she moved away to attend to her child, who had begun to cry.

Sophie thought Frank looked tired, and he had a slight cough. *No wonder they needed a break,* she thought. She helped with all the meals, and Ben did a few jobs around the house that Frank could not manage.

The day came to return to Forge Cottage, and they packed up the trap and set off for home. This time their return was more congenial.

After they had unpacked and settled in, Sophie told Ben that she had an idea. She suggested that perhaps from now on he could share his work with young Albert, who was still looking for a forge to run. "You could do the farrier work, as you are good with the horses, and Albert could do the heavier work."

"What would I do on the other days?" Ben asked. "I don't want to be a farm labourer. I haven't done six years' apprenticeship to do that."

"We have a horse and trap. Perhaps you could hire yourself out to take people to where they want to go," Sophie suggested. "I'm sure there are folks around here who need transport. We could even get another horse, and if you change some of the outbuildings into stables, we could start up a small livery."

Ben thought her ideas were good. This would give him the opportunity to work with horses again.

"And I would like to take up dressmaking," Sophie continued. "I have a little of my money left, and I could buy one of those sewing machines."

Ben spoke to Albert about taking on some of his work, saying they could begin on a trial basis in case things didn't work out. Albert seemed very keen to accept the proposal. Ben had told Sophie that the role of the blacksmith was changing. He said people were buying factory-made items and replacing them when they became worn out or broken. The farmers were going over to steam engines, and something called "tractors," so they weren't using horses as much, decreasing the need for his services.

The following day, Sophie took Charles out in his baby carriage and walked to the village. She called at the inn for the post, and there was one letter addressed to Ben. Sophie didn't recognise the handwriting. It was not Millie's. It couldn't be Robert's, as there were no foreign frank marks. She suddenly realised that it might be from Lucinda. She knew William's handwriting from his letters, and this was different.

After Ben had finished his work at the forge that afternoon, he had a wash and then sat down at the table. Sophie took the letter off the dresser, where she had placed it, and handed it to him. She saw that he looked startled. He read it quickly and then stuffed it into his pocket.

"Aren't you going to let me read it?" she asked, studying Ben's face carefully.

"Oh, it's nothing, just from Lucinda thanking me for coming."

Sophie did not give up easily. "I would like to see it," she said firmly.

"I told you what it's about."

"I would still like to see it," Sophie said, beginning to show her displeasure.

Ben was silent.

"It's a love letter, isn't it? Can I read it?" she demanded.

"No."

Sophie was getting angry. What was he hiding? "What exactly went on while you were at Somerset?" she asked. "Something must have happened. Have you told me everything? I can't forgive you if you have deceived me." She was convinced Ben was lying to her. She stood before him with her eyes focused intently on him, waiting for an answer.

"Nothing happened," Ben replied, averting his eyes.

"Then why has she written you a love letter?"

"It doesn't matter, Sophie."

"It does matter! You either let me read the letter, or I am leaving!"

Ben did nothing.

"Ben!" She waited. "Right. I want you to take me to Millie's. I can't stay here if you are going to carry on lying to me."

By now Sophie was in tears. She demanded that he go and get the horse and trap ready to take her. Ben pushed his chair back angrily and strode out. Sophie went upstairs to pack some of her own and the baby's things. She began to sob. She angrily pulled out her clothes from the chest of drawers and pushed them into her bag. When she came down, she wrapped the baby up warmly and picked him up. She then went outside and climbed into the back of the trap. She and Ben set off in silence. It wasn't a long journey, but it seemed to take an age. Finally, they arrived, and Ben dropped her outside the Lodge and drove away quickly. Millie was surprised to see her standing at the door.

"Whatever's happened?" she asked.

Sophie stood there crying. "Can I stay here for a while, please, Millie?" she asked.

A little later, Millie asked her what had happened. Sophie told her about Lucinda's letter and Ben's refusal to show it to her. Millie assured her that she could stay "while things cooled down a bit."

"What do you think it said then, Sophie?" asked Millie, wide-eyed.

"It was a love letter—I'm convinced of it," she replied. "Something happened while Ben was staying with them. It seems he is still infatuated with her."

"I expect Ben will come and get you when things have calmed down," Millie said in a soothing tone.

Frank was listening quietly to all this. "Tomorrow I'll go over and see Ben, talk some sense into him."

Sophie sat in her bedroom overlooking the sea. It occurred to her that Lucinda's husband might want Frank and Millie to leave his property now that his wife had left him because she was expecting Ben's child. She realised Ben had no idea the repercussions he had caused by his foolhardy actions. It could mean an end to all of Frank and Millie's hard work and ruin their enterprise.

The following day, she expected Ben to come and fetch her, but he didn't show up. By the third day, she was getting worried. Could she manage if she left him for good? She knew Millie and Frank would give her a home, if they still had one, but it would put them in a difficult position. How would she support herself and her baby? What if leaving had sent him back to Lucinda? What if they were in each other's arms now? She felt so miserable, so downhearted. Why had it happened like this?

Later that afternoon there was a tap on her bedroom door, and Millie poked her head round. "Sophie, Ben's here!"

Sophie felt overjoyed, but she was not going to show it. She hadn't forgiven Ben—the upset was far from over—but she had missed him.

"Do you want to see him?" asked Millie.

Sophie nodded and tried to pull herself together. She dried her eyes and waited. The door opened, and Ben appeared, clutching a bunch of flowers. He gave them to her and bent down to kiss the top of her head.

"Hello, Ben," she said coolly.

"Sophie, my love, I am so very sorry I have hurt you again." He took the letter from his pocket and gave it to her.

Sophie was surprised at this. Without opening it, she slowly tore it in half again and again until it was in tiny pieces, which she dropped onto the floor like confetti.

Ben embraced her warmly. "Let me tell you what happened on my visit. When I left, I kissed Lucinda goodbye. I shouldn't have done, but she ran out of the house just as I was leaving and pleaded for me to come again. She obviously got the wrong idea. I have decided not to go back there at present."

Sophie was content with this. Perhaps she had overreacted, but she knew that in future she was not going to look the other way and bottle up her feelings just to make Ben feel better. She would challenge him and have it out. Ben drove his wife and baby home, and when they arrived, she found he had laid the table for tea and there was a fruit cake from Mrs. Chambers.

"She also allowed me to pick some flowers from her garden," he said.

"I knew they weren't from ours!" Sophie laughed.

They had their tea, and then Ben sat in his chair cradling Charles in his arms. Sophie heard him quietly talking.

"I hope you'll have better sense, my boy, than your father has."

Charles didn't respond. He'd fallen fast asleep.

CHAPTER EIGHTEEN

NEW VENTURES

BEN AND SOPHIE WERE EXCITED about their new plans, and Ben got to work straight away on building the new stables. Albert was slowly gaining popularity at the forge, and Ben's customers seemed content with the arrangements. Ben made enquiries about Sophie's sewing machine and finally found one in Kingsbridge. They went to collect it one afternoon, and Sophie was shown how to use it. She was told it was easy once you got the knack. She could now start getting some orders for her dressmaking.

In November, a letter arrived from William, and Ben let Sophie read it. Lucinda had given birth to a son, Lionel Benjamin. Ben asked Sophie if he could see his child.

"I don't want you to go," she said. "You are my husband, and your son is here. Your place is with us."

Ben looked emotional. "Please, Sophie." His words sounded choked. "I have to see him, just once."

"But you promised me you wouldn't go there again."

Ben looked distraught, and she began to feel a little sorry for him. She wondered if she could ever trust him again. "I don't want you to go alone. Perhaps Frank would go with you this time."

Ben looked relieved. "Yes, I'll ask him."

"I think you should make it a day visit and not stay there. You could put up at an inn nearby." Sophie made it clear these were her terms.

Ben wrote two letters, one to William and one to Frank and Millie. Late in the morning two days later, Sophie heard a trap draw up outside the cottage.

In walked Millie. “Hello Sophie,” she said, without smiling. “I need to talk to you and Ben. Can you fetch him?”

Sophie went round to the forge and told him Millie had arrived.

He came quickly, looking concerned. “Millie, what’s the matter?” he asked.

“It’s Frank,” she answered. “I have to tell you he’s not well. We had it confirmed last week—he has tuberculosis.”

Ben slumped into a chair, visibly shocked.

Sophie put her arms round Millie. “Oh, Millie, we are so very, very sorry.”

“We had a feeling he was not well from the start,” she continued. “When our first guests came, the doctor examined Frank and told us what it might be. He has been struggling for a while now, and that is why we stopped letting rooms. We are not able to carry on, so after Christmas, we shall be leaving the Lodge and moving somewhere smaller. We want to be by the sea. It will be good for Frank, and Billy will love playing on the beach. I want to take Frank away from all the worry of running a business.”

“Have you told Billy about Frank?” asked Sophie.

“Not yet. He loves him like a father, and it will be difficult telling him.”

“Will you be selling up, then?” asked Ben.

“No, we are still renting. With Sir Ralph still away, we haven’t completed the sale.”

Sophie asked Millie to sit down and stay awhile, but Millie said she had to get back.

“We received your letter about the birth of your son, Ben,” said Millie. “I’m afraid Frank is unable to go with you to see him.”

Before she left, Millie brightened up a little and said, “Can you come to us for Christmas? I want it to be the best Christmas ever!”

Ben and Sophie eagerly accepted, and Millie left. When she had gone, Ben said to Sophie, “What can we do?”

"I don't know, Ben. There's nothing much we can do but pray he will get better."

Suddenly, their plans seemed unimportant. Nevertheless, Ben told Sophie that evening that he still wanted to go to see his son.

"I think I will ask Harry to go with me," he said. "While I am there, I will tell them that, as I cannot be a proper father, it will be best if I stay away for the time being. I know they will judge me, but what else can I do?"

Sophie had thought long and hard about Ben's responsibility towards his and Lucinda's child. "I think that will be the best thing," she answered.

There, they let the matter rest. A short time later a letter came from William, welcoming a visit from Ben. Harry had agreed to accompany him, knowing all about Ben's love child. Reluctantly, Sophie waved goodbye to Ben despite her many misgivings about his visit.

They returned late the following day. Ben told Sophie that Lucinda's aunt was there and so he knew Lucinda was being well cared for. Sophie listened patiently, but she felt unhappy as Ben went on to describe how healthy the baby was and how he thought it looked like him. He went on to say that William had told him they still wanted Ben to have a role in the upbringing of his son. Sophie's heart sank, as she could see this had pleased him.

Loaded with food and presents, they travelled to Millie and Frank's on a cold Christmas Eve. Sophie had wanted to go to church that night to sing Christmas carols, but Ben refused. His dislike of the rector had intensified since Jonathan's visit.

When they arrived, they were alarmed at Frank's appearance—he had lost weight since they'd last seen him in September. Sophie was in a reflective mood as she unpacked in their lovely bedroom. She knew she would never stay there again, and she had poignant memories, memories she would rather forget.

Billy showed his excitement, as he knew they had brought presents for him. He was nearly five now, and Sophie had bought him some reading books. Millie had worked hard decorating the house with greenery, red ribbons and candles. In the dining room was a large Christmas tree in the corner with all the presents heaped underneath. At the end of their evening meal, Billy hung up his stocking by the large fireplace and went happily to bed.

"We're going to be grand," said Millie. "The ladies will retire now and leave you men to your port and cigars."

Sophie left Ben leaning back in his chair with his glass of port wine while Frank clipped him a cigar. Later, he told her about his conversation with Frank.

"He is giving us fifty pounds towards our new venture. He insisted, saying that he considers we gave him his life back when he came to live with us and is grateful for our generosity. He also said that he is ashamed of what his father did to you, Sophie. Sending you out into the world to earn your own living. He said he is just putting things to rights. I thanked him and told him he was a kind and generous man and a good friend to me."

This touched Sophie deeply. She remembered how angry Millie had said he'd been about Ben's infidelity.

Almost reading her mind, Ben added, "One more thing. He said he was trusting me to remain faithful to you from now on. He said I was lucky to have such a wonderful wife."

Sophie gave an inward sigh, wondering what the future would bring.

CHAPTER NINETEEN

SADNESS

IN THE NEW YEAR, SOPHIE thought she was pregnant, but she kept the knowledge to herself for the time being. Ben continued converting the outbuildings, and Harry would come over to help when he could. He said he already knew of someone who wanted stabling.

Sophie had placed leaflets in a few shop windows in Kingsbridge, advertising herself as a "seamstress able to make simple garments at competitive prices," and before long, she had a few orders. She practiced at home, and Ben listened to the clickety clack of the machine while he tried to read his book after work.

Ben helped Millie and Frank with their move, as they had found a cottage to rent beside the sea not far from Salcombe. It was simply furnished, and Sophie made new bed covers and curtains for them. Ben made sure they had plenty of coal, as the weather was cold, and he always kept a good store of it at the forge. Sophie also helped with stocking up the pantry and arranged for a local farm to deliver milk and eggs. It was going to be very different for Frank and Millie living in a small cottage after the spacious rooms at the Lodge.

After the move, Sophie decided to tell Ben her good news, but he was rather concerned at hearing it. "I don't think you should visit Frank in your condition," he said. "You could catch the infection. I'll go over to Frank's whenever I can to spend time with him. You must stay here. Millie will understand."

Sophie was upset, as she wanted to see her cousin while she could.

"When the weather gets warmer, you can spend time outside with him," Ben suggested.

Sophie and Ben were asked to care for Billy for the duration of Frank's illness, so Ben went to collect him. When they returned, Sophie told Billy he was to have a little holiday and might even get to ride a horse again. Ben said later that Frank had wept when he was saying goodbye to his little stepson.

It was spring, and the days were lengthening. The stables were ready, and Ben had one horse in livery. The horses were sometimes put out to grass in the orchard under the old fruit trees, and Sophie loved to watch them move slowly about as they grazed. Ben had a few fares to take villagers into Kingsbridge in his horse and trap, but it was still too early in the year for much travel.

He and Sophie had not decided what to do with Frank's money, as they had managed to finance the changes they had made from their own savings. Sophie wrote to Frank telling him about the developments at the forge. She knew he would be pleased to hear about them.

There was a short period of sunny weather, and Sophie and Billy went over with baby Charles to see Frank. They found him sitting on a beach covered by a rug, and he was thrilled to see Billy. Sophie could see that Millie was becoming exhausted. She was devoted to her husband's care, but it was evident that Frank was sinking fast. It was therefore of some relief to Sophie when she had a visitor a few days later.

He called through the kitchen door to her, "Hello, Sophie! It's Robert!"

Sophie had her back to the door and swung round. "Oh, Robert, you're here. Oh, thank goodness you're here!"

Robert told her he had dropped everything to come to see his brother when Millie had written him telling him how seriously ill he was. He had decided to call in to see Sophie first to find out how Frank was.

"He is very unwell, Robert. We are all very concerned."

She had been about to give Charles his meal. Robert studied the child. "And this is young Charles? He's a bonny-looking chap! Do you think he'll have his father's muscles?" He gently squeezed Charles's chubby arm.

Charles was sitting in his highchair, and he looked at Robert in alarm. He began to wave his arms and legs about and make noises. Robert laughed and said he was a rum little fellow.

Ben returned, and when they spoke about Frank's condition, the mood became sombre. Sophie suggested Robert stay the night, as it was getting late, and ride over to see his brother in the morning.

A few days later, Robert returned in the morning to tell Sophie and Ben the sad news. There hadn't been time to summon them, as Frank had died much sooner than expected. They found it hard to believe. Sophie felt stunned.

Now Billy had to be told. They had explained to him that his papa was very ill and might not get well again. Ben said he would do it, and he spoke quietly to Billy, telling him that his papa was so poorly that God had taken pity on him and taken him to heaven.

Billy looked at him earnestly. "Will he get better there?"

"He will get better there," replied Ben, "but he will not be coming back. He loved you very much, Billy, and that will never change. We must be glad that you had such a fine papa."

Billy nodded, but said, "I don't want Papa to go away. I want him to get better here."

"The doctors cannot make him better, Billy."

Billy looked crestfallen. "I shall have to look after Mama then, as Papa has gone away."

"Yes, Billy, we all shall."

"Let's go into the garden and pick some flowers for Ben to take over to Mama," suggested Sophie.

"When can I see Mama?" he asked.

"Very soon, Billy."

Ben rode over with Robert straight away to help Millie with the funeral arrangements. Robert said he would stay as long as was needed, as he was the executor of Frank's will.

When Ben returned, he said that Millie had asked if Billy could stay with them a while longer. "She seems very distant," he told Sophie. "I think she needs some peace and quiet."

The funeral was held at Frank and Millie's church in Salcombe a few days later. Mrs. Chambers looked after Billy and Charles. Sophie was longing to see Millie again to comfort her. She knew how resolute her sister-in-law could be and feared she would retreat into herself and be unable to accept any form of sympathy. *How cruel it is*, she thought, *that these two loving friends were parted so soon when they were happy together and full of plans for their future.*

When they returned, they told Billy that his papa had been laid to rest in a beautiful part of Salcombe overlooking the sea and they would take him there. Later that week, Ben took them over to the cottage to see Millie. It was as Sophie had feared. Millie was very subdued but smiled broadly at the sight of her son.

"Hello, Billy, my darling. Are you all right? We must both be brave and look after each other now Papa has gone."

She hugged him warmly, and Billy did his best to comfort her. "Mama, when am I coming home?"

Millie looked a little confused, not knowing what to say. "I don't know yet, darling, Mama has to sort a lot of things out."

"He can stay with us for as long as you like," said Sophie. "But he does miss you." She hoped Millie would make some sort of decision.

"I wondered if he could stay just a little while longer, please. As I said, I have a lot to do here, then I will give up living here and come back to stay with you and Ben, if you will have us." Millie looked at her son, who had a worried look on his face.

"Of course you can come back," replied Sophie without any hesitation, and Ben nodded in agreement.

"I think it's time he had some schooling," said Millie, putting her arm round Billy. She turned to him. "Would you like Aunt Sophie to start giving you lessons?"

He did not look very enthusiastic and pulled a face.

Sophie laughed. "You're a bright boy and will learn quickly," she said to him.

"He's my future," said Millie.

Billy protested when it was time to leave. It was the first time he had cried since being told about his father's death. It was difficult to persuade him to leave his mama, but Ben shared an idea. "I think it's time we got you a pony and taught you to ride. Then you will be able to ride over with me to see Mama."

Billy's face lit up when he heard this, and he chatted about it all the way back to Forge Cottage. A few days later, Billy was taken to his father's grave to put flowers there and say a prayer. Ben found a pony suitable for him. It was a brown and white colt, and Billy called him Rascal.

Sophie gave Billy his lessons every morning. He was somewhat reluctant at first but gradually began to accept the discipline involved, and Sophie was pleased with his progress. She'd been right—he was quick to learn, and she had to work hard preparing his lessons. In the afternoons, when Charles had his rest, she would read to Billy so that he would develop a love of literature. She found it wasn't always easy teaching Billy and looking after Charles.

After three weeks, Robert left to return home to his wife in the Channel Islands. It had taken time to sort out the will. Millie then moved back in with Sophie and Ben.

One death often heralds another, and shortly afterwards, Sophie heard news that the rector had died suddenly. Billy had only one grandparent now, and this gave her an idea.

After the rector's funeral, she waited for several days, and then one afternoon when Ben was looking after Billy in the forge, she took Charles in his baby carriage and walked over to leave him with Mrs. Chambers. She was not at home, so Sophie had to take him with her to the rectory. She was admitted into the drawing room, where Mrs. Hunter, dressed in black, was sitting on a large sofa by the fire.

"Miss Anderson, we meet again."

Sophie greeted her politely and gave her condolences. The rector's wife gave a slight nod of her head in acknowledgement. "Have you come to show me the blacksmith's son?" she asked, looking at Charles.

Sophie explained that she had hoped to leave him with a friend.

"I see that you didn't heed my advice."

"We are very happily married, thank you ma'am," replied Sophie, silently wondering if she was.

"And you like being a blacksmith's wife?"

"Yes, I do."

Mrs. Hunter had been looking at Charles all this time and smiled at him. "A bonny fellow. He looks very much like you," she said and put out her hand to touch his outstretched arms.

Sophie braced herself. "Mrs. Hunter, Millie's husband died not so long ago. They have been living in Salcombe, but now Billy and his mother are back in the village, living with us. I have come to ask you if you would be willing to meet your grandson?"

There was silence. Mrs. Hunter turned her gaze away from Charles and looked straight at Sophie. "You have come here today to ask me that?" she asked.

"Yes. I know you will have to move away at some point in the future, ma'am, and I wanted to ask you before you go."

Silence. Sophie was regretting that she had come.

"Is it my money you are thinking of, I wonder?" was the next question.

"No, not at all, ma'am. Millie's husband Frank left Billy well provided for."

"I think it is too late for any reconciliations now," murmured Mrs. Hunter.

Sophie felt disappointed for both Billy and Mrs. Hunter, but she knew she had been right in her attempt to bring them together. Before she took her leave, she said, "Billy is grieving, and so are you, Mrs. Hunter. You may both find comfort in getting to know each other."

Mrs. Hunter rang the bell for the maid. "I think you had better leave now, Mrs. Browne. Some things are better left in the past."

Sophie rose to go and thanked Mrs. Hunter for seeing her. She told no one in the family about her visit, but the one thing she had not expected happened a few days later.

One morning, a handwritten note addressed to Millie was brought to the door of the cottage. She took it into the parlour to read and then immediately came out with the letter in her hand, looking angry. In a raised voice she said, "Sophie, what is the meaning of this letter from Mrs. Hunter?"

Sophie looked alarmed. She hadn't expected news of her visit to be revealed in this way. She could see straight away that Millie wanted nothing to do with Mrs. Hunter.

"Did you go to see that woman?"

Sophie nodded silently.

"How dare you do such a thing without asking me first? You had no right!"

At that moment, Ben came in with an armful of logs and stood in the doorway. Fortunately, Billy was still playing outside.

"What's this about?" he asked. When he had been told, he turned to Sophie. "You shouldn't have gone there without Millie's permission."

Now Sophie was distraught. She could see that they were both against her, the two people she loved. She knew Ben had a vehement dislike of the rector and his wife. It was obvious he would side with his sister.

Ben took the letter from Millie and read it. "She says she wants to see her grandson," he informed Sophie, "and now you will have to tell her it is impossible."

Sophie turned to Millie. "I didn't ask you because I knew you would refuse and then I couldn't try to bring you together. Billy needs his grandmother even more now, and I hoped she would find comfort in her grief getting to know him."

Millie stormed out, and the door banged behind her.

"Sophie, how could you do this after what Millie has been through?" asked Ben, putting down his pile of logs and looking at her sternly.

Sophie began to silently cry. Her best intentions had gone wrong, and now she had to remedy the situation. Whatever was she going to say to Mrs. Hunter?

CHAPTER TWENTY

RECONCILIATION

SOPHIE KNEW THAT MILLIE HAD probably gone to see Harry's mother, Mildred. She had told Sophie that she had often gone there after her mother had died and her father's behaviour had got too violent. Mildred had helped Millie in the early stages of motherhood, giving her guidance and support. She had not been well for some time, and Millie had been going regularly to see her.

Sophie loved Millie, and she knew she had angered her. Now she had caused her more anguish after losing Frank. She had to ask her forgiveness as well as tell Mrs. Hunter she could not see her grandson.

When Millie returned, Sophie was working in the kitchen, as Billy's lessons were finished for the morning and he was helping Ben in the forge. Before she could speak, Sophie said, "Millie, I am so sorry I have upset you like this. You and Ben are right. I should have spoken to you first, and I offer you my sincere apologies. Please can we be as we were?"

"Yes, I forgive you, and you can take Billy to see his grandmother. I shall not be going, though."

Sophie wondered why Millie had suddenly agreed. "Have you been to see Mildred?"

"Yes. She said I should soften my heart and forgive Mrs. Hunter. I cannot do that yet, but I will try for Billy's sake."

"I understand," replied Sophie. *I know what it's like trying to forgive when you have been wronged.*

Millie gave her the letter to read. Mrs. Hunter had written that after Sophie's visit she had decided that she would like to see her grandson before she left the village and hoped that a meeting could be arranged soon.

Sophie wrote back asking if Billy could come one afternoon, as he had his lessons in the mornings. She then went round to the forge and told Ben that Millie had returned and had agreed to a visit. Ben read the letter and said he didn't really want Billy going there but that it wasn't his decision. *The Brownes are certainly slow to forgive,* thought Sophie as she walked to the rectory to deliver her letter.

A reply came suggesting a visit the following day at three o'clock. Millie took it on herself to talk to Billy about his grandmother. Sophie noticed that she spent some time getting him ready the next afternoon. Poor Billy had to submit to being bathed and smartly dressed, his hair wetted, parted, and smoothed down. He looked very grown up when it was time to go.

Sophie explained to him how he should behave. "Your grandmother is a refined lady, and you must be very polite," she said.

Millie watched as the two of them set off. Sophie had dressed smartly and put on her best hat. She enjoyed the feeling of going into society again. When they arrived, they were shown into Mrs. Hunter's drawing room, and she rose to greet them. Billy said "how do you do" as instructed, and Mrs. Hunter looked at him and gave a little gasp. "He is so like his father!" she exclaimed.

Sophie was relieved that Millie wasn't there to hear her remark. Mrs. Hunter couldn't take her eyes off her grandson. She bent down and said, "Hello, Billy. How very nice to meet with you at last."

At that moment, Sophie knew she had been right and began to relax.

Mrs. Hunter took Billy's hand and led him across the room. "I have put some playthings out for you. I hope you like them."

"Thank you, ma'am," replied Billy.

Sophie was pleased he was remembering what he had been told.

On the floor beside Mrs. Hunter's chair were several toys, puzzles and picture books. Some were too young for him, but even so, he enjoyed playing with them.

Mrs. Hunter watched him intently. She appeared to have forgotten about Sophie, but suddenly she remembered her manners and invited her to sit down.

"He is a fine young man Mrs. Browne, a fine young man!" Her eyes were shining, and Sophie could see how much pleasure Billy was giving her.

"I'm afraid his mother was unable to come, ma'am," said Sophie, hoping no other explanation was needed.

Mrs. Hunter nodded. "I do understand," she replied.

They sat and talked together. Sophie told her about Billy and how he was doing well at his lessons.

"He gets that from his father," observed Mrs. Hunter, and again Sophie was glad Millie wasn't there.

Mrs. Hunter raised the question about Billy's education. "Will he be going to school?" she asked.

Sophie knew that she meant a private school. It was something she and Millie had never discussed. "I don't know, ma'am. Nothing has been decided yet."

"His father went to Hillside School near Exeter, you know," Mrs. Hunter went on. "It would be good if he went there too. As his father was a pupil, they would give him priority."

Sophie felt ill at ease, as she knew that Billy did not officially have his father's name. "I'll mention it to his mother." she said.

Mrs. Hunter rang for tea, and the maid came in with a tray laden with good things. Billy was invited to sit down, and Mrs. Hunter poured him a cup of milk. Sophie had told Billy not to help himself, and she was relieved when Mrs. Hunter put a selection of sandwiches and cakes on a plate and gave it to him.

"I can remember little boys' appetites!" She laughed.

Sophie was surprised at seeing this less formal side of Mrs. Hunter and began to warm to her. Mrs. Hunter poured the tea elegantly and handed Sophie her cup. She was offered a sandwich and invited to help herself.

After tea, Mrs. Hunter spoke to Billy and told him he was a very well-behaved little boy. When it was time to leave, she addressed Sophie.

"I hope his mother will think about his schooling. I would like to help towards paying the fees."

Sophie expressed her appreciation, and Billy thanked Mrs. Hunter.

"I hope you will come and see your grandmama again," she replied and bent down to kiss his head.

As they walked home, Sophie asked Billy if he had enjoyed his visit.

"Yes!" he replied. "It was a scrumptious tea!"

Billy went to see his grandmama on two more occasions. Sophie had explained to Millie about Mrs. Hunter's offer to pay Billy's school fees, and Millie said she would think about it. Sophie always went with him, as Millie still refused to go, and she was surprised to find herself chatting away amicably with Mrs. Hunter. However, the visits ceased at Sophie's confinement, and by then Mrs. Hunter had left for her new home. She had given Sophie her new address and, as it was not far, said she hoped they would be able to come and see her again.

Sophie had her baby towards the end of August. It was a little girl, and they named her Florence, to be known as Florrie. Sophie had her hands full with a toddler and a new baby and was glad to have Millie there to help.

Ben had a few fares with his horse and trap over the summer months, mostly to Kingsbridge. The villagers were very appreciative of the opportunity to hire him for shopping trips or visits to the doctor.

Several weeks after the birth of his daughter, he had to take a fare to Newton Abbot, which meant an overnight stay. He told Sophie that it worried him to leave his family behind. She told him he was worrying unnecessarily, as she had Millie and there was always Harry to call on. Ben set off early in the morning to collect his passenger and said he would see them later the following day.

That morning Billy had his lessons as usual, and after lunch he went out to play. Millie went to see Mildred in the afternoon, and Sophie settled down to feed Florrie. Charles was amusing himself with some of Billy's old toys, and Sophie felt happy and contented.

Suddenly Billy appeared at the door, his face pale as if he was very frightened.

"Billy! Whatever is the matter?"

"Forge is on fire!" he shouted.

"Quickly!" she cried. "Run to the farm and get help. Tell them to bring poles!"

Billy sped off faster than he had ever run before.

Sophie put Florrie carefully into her cradle, shut Charles in the parlour away from the range and hurried round to the forge. She saw that the overhanging thatched roof was alight. The flames were crackling, and smoke was rising rapidly upwards, swirled by the wind. Sophie was thankful it was blowing away from the cottage. She suddenly remembered the horses and ran round to the back to the stables. She could hear them getting restless, having smelled the smoke. They were whinnying and stamping their feet.

She put a halter on Rascal and led him out, and the other horses followed. She put them into the orchard and ran back to see what she could do about the fire.

There was a trough with a bucket outside the forge, ready for any fire that might occur. She filled it and tried to throw the water over the roof, but she couldn't reach up high enough. The fire was now taking a hold and was halfway across the roof. She felt helpless, but then she heard the men from the farm shouting as they ran up the lane towards her.

"Stay back, miss! We'll deal with this now!"

They attacked the roof with their poles and began pulling the straw down, and it fell in burning clumps onto the ground. As Sophie walked back to the cottage in a daze, she saw Billy standing in the lane, watching the fire. She was about to call him when he saw her and ran off. Sophie began to wonder—had he been responsible for what happened, or was he just frightened? She went back inside and sat with Florrie and Charles and waited.

After some time, the men came round to the door. One of them looked in and said, "I'm sorry, miss. We've done our best, but the roof's gone, and some of the rafters. That thatch always goes up like tinder, and there's no stopping it. The fire's all out, but best go round and check it now and again to make sure."

Sophie thanked them gratefully and promised Ben would buy them a few ales next time he saw them. The men set off down the lane back to the farm with their poles over their shoulders, but there was no sign of Billy. Sophie sat down at the table to get over the shock. Whatever would Ben do now? The forge was ruined, which meant they had lost their main livelihood. Young Albert had left and moved away earlier in the summer, and Ben had been running it on his own for a few days a week now.

Just then, Millie burst through the door. "Oh my God! What has happened, Sophie? How on earth did the forge catch fire? Are you all right? Where's Billy?" Her voice rose in panic.

"We are all safe, thank goodness, Millie. The men from the farm put it out. Billy has run off."

"Is he responsible?" she asked, startled.

"Possibly. He came to tell me the forge was on fire. I don't really know what happened."

"What will Ben say, Sophie? Whatever will Ben say?"

She sat down, and Sophie could see that she was frightened. "Millie, I'm sure it was some sort of accident. Billy wouldn't do anything like that on purpose. He was probably just messing about."

Millie looked distraught. "But what will Ben do now?"

"We can repair the damage. We still have Frank's money."

Millie looked as if it was all too much. "I do miss my Frank," she said and began sobbing.

"Millie, Millie, I am so sorry. You poor thing," said Sophie and put her arms round her. Millie gradually calmed down, and Sophie said she would look for Billy. She went outside, and sure enough, he was standing in the lane.

"Billy," she called out, "come inside and comfort your mama!"

Billy ran straight past her into the cottage. When she went inside, he was hugging his mother tightly. Sophie began to prepare supper, but no one had much appetite, so there would be lots left for Ben the next day. They were all dreading his return. Neither of them felt like tackling Billy over what happened, and they decided to leave it to Ben. If the boy had been involved, he would have to account for his actions to his uncle the next day.

Nobody slept well, and they were all subdued in the morning. News had reached the village, and there were a few sightseers, mostly children, the next day. One or two villagers called to see if they could help, and Sophie thought how kind they were.

She was putting Florrie down for a sleep that afternoon when Billy raced in and fled upstairs, then Ben rushed in.

"Sophie! Thank God you're safe! Is everyone safe?"

"Yes, we are. There was no danger to any of us."

He hugged and kissed her and then his children. "Thank goodness you are all safe!"

After Sophie described to him what had happened, he looked round. "Where is Billy?" he asked.

"He's upstairs, hiding probably," she replied.

"Will you go and fetch him, please, Sophie?" asked Ben.

Sophie went slowly upstairs. She knew Billy would hear every creaking step. Sure enough, he was hiding under the bedcovers.

"Billy, come downstairs. Uncle Ben is home, and he wants to speak to you."

Billy reluctantly came out and followed Sophie downstairs, his head bowed. Ben was sitting in his chair, and Billy stood silently in front of him.

Ben put both hands on Billy's shoulders, looked straight at him and said quietly, "Now, young man, have you got something to say to me?"

Billy looked mesmerised. "I…I am sorry for burning down your forge, Uncle Ben."

The dreaded words had been spoken.

"And are you going to tell me what happened?"

Billy looked down at the floor, unable to look at Ben any longer. "Well, I went to play in the forge after you had gone, and I poked the fire with a stick, and some sparks came out, and I held my stick like that"—he put his arm out as if he was holding the stick in front of him—"and it burned! Then I came out of the forge, and I waved it about to see the sparks, and then"—his voice faltered—"the roof caught fire."

"You say the fire in the forge was still alight?" he asked.

Billy nodded.

Ben looked at Sophie. "I must have left in a hurry without making sure the fire was out," he said. He looked sternly at his nephew. "I think you now know, Billy, that fire must not be played with. It's a good servant but a terrible master, and you must never forget that. I will forgive you, Billy, as I see it was an accident. I am also to blame, because I should have made sure the fire was out before I left yesterday. At least it is only the roof. If the wind had been stronger, the cottage might have gone up too. Tomorrow we will set to and clear the mess, if Aunt Sophie will agree to let you off your lessons?"

He looked at Sophie, who nodded and smiled.

CHAPTER TWENTY-ONE

AFTERMATH

THE NEXT DAY, SOPHIE AND Ben went to inspect the fire damage properly. The farm hands had done their best, and they could see that, without their intervention, it would have been a lot worse. Billy followed them round and was on his best behaviour, apparently determined to do all that was asked of him. They cleared away all the burnt straw outside on the ground, and Ben examined the burnt rafters. He told Sophie that they would have to be replaced and this time he would have a tiled roof put on, which he said he had always wanted. He needed to find a builder and said he would ask round for one when he went to the Two Foxes.

The metal tools and contents of the forge were not damaged, just covered in ash. Everything needed removing and cleaning, so after Ben had checked there was no burning debris inside, he allowed Billy to gather up some of the smaller items with Sophie's help.

She had asked Millie to look after the children so she could give Ben a hand. The forge hadn't had a good clean in a long time, if ever.

Ben was at the back rummaging about when he saw something he recognised. It was Frank's leg iron, which he showed to Sophie.

Billy came running over. "Uncle Ben! That was Papa's!" he exclaimed.

"Yes, I know, Billy. What should we do with it?"

"He won't need it anymore, Uncle. You said he would get better in heaven."

"No, he won't ever need it again, so I will keep it in the forge so we can remember him."

Billy nodded enthusiastically.

They continued to clear up all morning, making piles of things to keep and throw away. When they came in for lunch, they were covered in dirt and ash.

"Baths later!" Sophie said.

Ben found a builder in Kingsbridge who came over to discuss what needed to be done. He suggested that they do away with the overhanging roof and put in a wide double doorway. He would replace the roof beams and tile the whole building. The walls, thankfully, were intact.

Harry came round and said he was glad the stables had escaped being damaged. He was impressed when Sophie told him about rescuing the horses and said her actions had probably saved them. He was making a habit of coming round, and he and Ben would often drink their ale in the parlour while Sophie worked at her sewing machine in the kitchen. Sophie could hear them talking quietly and often wondered what it was they were saying. There was little laughter, and it all sounded rather serious.

One evening before he left, Harry asked Sophie if he could "have a word." Ben had gone out to check the horses as he did every night.

"Miss," began Harry hesitantly, "do you think I have a chance with Millie?"

Sophie was surprised, as Millie had been widowed only recently. "Well, she certainly needs a good friend at this moment, Harry, as she is still grieving. Be a friend to her, and don't rush things. Give it time, lots of time."

Harry looked relieved, but he was also in a dilemma. "I know what you are saying, Sophie, but I have always wanted Millie as a sweetheart since way back when we walked to school together. I had waited to ask her because I thought she was too young, and then Jonathan got there first. I must admit I was shocked when I found out about her pregnancy, but like the rest of the village, I blamed Jonathan. When I was ready to ask her again, Frank had come along, so I lost out again."

Sophie had every sympathy for the worried young man before her. She remembered the time Ben had told her that Harry had developed an admiration for her. She realised that poor Harry had not had much luck in his love life.

"Don't give up, Harry," she said. "Just take it slowly."

One evening, Ben and Harry emerged from the parlour looking excited. Harry had some papers in his hand and had obviously been writing something down.

Sophie looked up from her sewing. "What are you two looking so pleased about?" she asked.

The two men looked at each other and grinned.

"We have been making plans," said Ben. "We are going into partnership."

"Well, yes, eventually," added Harry.

Millie stopped reading and looked up. Ben explained that, as blacksmithing had a limited future, he was thinking of getting involved in bicycles. He had seen them growing in popularity and was hoping to set up a workshop to repair them. Now that the forge was being rebuilt, it was the perfect time to make changes. Harry was to obtain materials and sell the bicycles, and Ben would do the practical side of things, such as designing, making and repairing. He would still do his farrier work and some blacksmithing jobs but hoped these would diminish in time. Harry would continue his work as a groom until the business grew and work with Ben in his spare time. Eventually Harry would look after the livery and hiring side of the business, which they hoped would continue to develop.

Sophie and Millie looked at each other. It all sounded exciting if it worked out. Both men waited for a response.

"I think that sounds a wonderful idea!" said Sophie.

"I agree—if you make me a bicycle first!" added Millie.

She told Sophie she had always fancied riding a bicycle, and she had seen several ladies riding them.

There was a bicycle shop in Kingsbridge, and Ben and Harry went to see it, wanting to speak with the owner, Mike Harding. When they returned, Ben explained that the meeting had been very useful. "Mike said that he could do with someone to help with the repair work. He gets several bicycles needing repairs every week. He does the simple jobs but sends the others down to Plymouth, and they apparently take ages to come back. He told us that there are new designs coming out and he has a pile of old bicycles that need updating. He will buy and then sell on any bicycles I can adapt or build."

"I think that all sounds very promising," Sophie said enthusiastically.

"One more thing," added Ben. "He suggested that we think about setting up one of these bicycle touring stops. There's an association now, and folks have formed clubs. They like exploring the villages round here at the weekends and are always on the lookout for a tearoom. This would involve you and Millie if you were interested."

Sophie thought about all the work she already had running their home and looking after two young children. "I'll have to think about that," she replied, "and what exactly it would entail."

From then on Ben, could talk of little else than bicycles. Sophie could see that this new venture would give him more challenging work.

That evening, Harry came over for supper and there was an animated discussion about what they could do and how to set it all up. Ben said he thought he knew how to adapt the forge and that he would train Harry so he could help with the repair work. Harry observed that working with bicycles would be a lot easier than temperamental horses. "And they don't kick either!" he added.

Ben said he would find a solicitor in Kingsbridge to sort out all the legal requirements for setting up his business. He suggested that they have a new name above the forge: Browne and Coates Bicycles and Repairs.

Ben worked hard on his new workshop, and Sophie often had to go and find him to remind him it was time for his lunch or supper. She would find him furiously sawing wood, and soon he had the old forge looking transformed, having set up a large workbench and a rack for the bicycles. She could see that things were moving ahead fast, and it made her think about how she could contribute to the new business.

She had two ideas to consider. One of these was to design clothes for cyclists. They had become popular, especially for women. She would try and obtain some paper patterns. Secondly, she decided that with Millie's help they could do teas at the weekends for the touring bicycle groups, as Ben had suggested. They could use the garden and orchard, or the kitchen if the weather was bad. It would mean a lot of baking, which she enjoyed. She asked Millie what she thought.

"Well, I don't really like baking, as you know, but I can serve the teas. I think I would enjoy that."

The work on the forge was finally completed, and it was decided to leave reroofing the cottage until the following summer, when the weather would be better. Ben got on with fitting up the workshop without delay. Harry came over when he could, but the evenings were drawing in now, and he usually only came at the weekends. After Ben had completed the workshop, Harry brought cartloads of materials and some old bicycles from Mike's shop. Sophie was pleased to see everything progressing so well.

One afternoon, Ben came round to the cottage and asked Sophie and Millie to come and see something. They stood at the gate and watched Harry wobbling hesitantly along the lane on one of their first bicycles with Billy chasing behind. He went to the top of the lane, turned and freewheeled back down with his long legs stretched out.

Millie ran forward to meet him. "Can I have a go now?" she asked excitedly.

Harry dismounted and held the machine for her to mount. She gathered up her skirts, and with Harry supporting her, she too wobbled along with them both laughing at her efforts. Sophie thought to herself, *Yes, they are getting closer, but is it just friendship on Millie's side?* It was good to see them together having fun.

Sophie finished making the first of her cycle outfits and decided to make Millie one for her Christmas present, given how keen she was to get on a bicycle. Sophie wondered if she would ever have the nerve to mount one herself.

Christmas was approaching, a time that Sophie loved, and it was going to be very different from the previous year at the Lodge. She was beginning to make a few presents, and they had to be started early. She decided that they would have a small, decorated tree in the parlour. She needed to make a few shopping trips to Kingsbridge and would ask Millie to drive her there, as the men were far too busy.

The following week, a note addressed to Sophie from Mrs. Hunter arrived saying she would be pleased to receive a visit from her and Billy in the new year. Sophie was relieved that her home was in a nearby village, as she had been enjoying her afternoon teas with Billy at the rectory. It had given her an opportunity to mix with a different class, and she realised that she missed the kind of conversation it offered.

The new rector was installed just before Christmas, and the church was full when Sophie and Ben attended the candlelit service.

On Christmas morning Ben took Billy round to the workshop. When he got there, he found a small-sized bicycle. He was thrilled.

"Is that mine? Can I ride it now, please, Uncle?" he asked.

"Of course it's yours, Billy. Happy Christmas!" replied Ben.

Sophie looked out and saw them going down the lane together, Ben running behind, hanging on to the saddle and Billy shouting "Faster! Faster!"

CHAPTER TWENTY-TWO

A NEW FRIEND

SOPHIE HAD BEEN GIVEN A small, carefully wrapped present from Ben in bed on Christmas morning. When she opened it, she found it was a gold chain.

"Ben! It's lovely, but so costly!"

"I married a lady, and she deserves to dress like one," he said.

He told her he had noticed that she had enjoyed getting dressed up for her visits to Billy's grandmother, and he wanted her to look stylish. Sophie took the chain out of the box and fastened it round her neck.

"You look beautiful," he said as he undid her plaited hair and let it tumble down over her bare shoulders. He leant forward to kiss her gently. "I'll always love you," he said tenderly.

Sophie closed her eyes for a moment, forgetting all the heartache and feeling really loved. It left her calm and happy for the rest of the day, and her pleasure was increased when Millie opened her present and found it was a bicycle outfit.

"Sophie! Did you really make this? You're so clever!" she exclaimed. "Now I just need a bicycle!" She looked expectantly at her brother. He held his hands up in the air.

"I know, I know! I'll have one ready for you soon. I am working on a design for a ladies' machine."

Billy spent the morning practising riding up and down the lane until their few guests arrived for Christmas dinner, and afterwards Ben took everyone on a tour of his new workshop. Millie said it didn't look like "a dark hole" anymore. When they were shown her new clothes, Mildred told Mrs. Chambers that she thought Millie was very daring for dressing up to ride a bicycle.

With Christmas over, life at the forge workshop continued at a lively pace, and Ben and Harry were kept busy. Sophie wanted to take Billy to his grandmother's new house, and as the weather was mild, she asked Millie to drive them. When they arrived, they found it to be one of several Georgian terraced houses near the top of the steep High Street in the village of Modbury. Sophie and Billy alighted from the trap, and Millie gathered the reins, ready to drive on.

"Mama!" exclaimed Billy. "Why aren't you coming in?"

Millie looked at Sophie.

"I think it's time he was told," said Sophie.

"Mama will tell you that when we get home," his mother said to him and drove away.

Sophie knew Billy was eager to go in, as he'd said how much he loved his visits. There were always toys and lovely things to eat at Grandmama's.

They were shown into what was a much smaller house than the rectory, but it was still elegantly furnished. As she looked round, Sophie thought she would love to live in a house like this. Her cottage seemed so small and simple in comparison. Although their visit had been prearranged, they found that Mrs. Hunter had another visitor, a young woman of about Sophie's age. Mrs. Hunter introduced Sophie to her guest, Caroline Bailey.

Sophie settled Billy down and then addressed her new acquaintance. "I do hope we are not interrupting your visit," she said politely.

Caroline laughed. "No, not at all! I am here because I wanted to meet you, Mrs. Browne. I understand that you are a very good needlewoman."

"I wouldn't say that," said Sophie modestly. "I make quite simple garments—nothing fancy, I'm afraid."

Caroline continued. "That is just what I require. I have recently married a widower, a doctor, and I now have two stepdaughters who need some new clothes."

She went on to explain that the two girls had been in the care of an old aunt who had dressed them in old-fashioned garments, and she wanted to update their wardrobes. "I am eager to be a good stepmother," she added.

Sophie liked her. She had a relaxed, friendly manner. Caroline asked Sophie if she would come to see her two girls, Harriette and Dorothy, so that she could measure them and see what might suit them. She said she lived nearby, and Sophie arranged to come the following week.

"Why don't you bring Billy and leave him with me?" suggested Mrs. Hunter. "I'm sure I could manage him."

Caroline rose to go and said her farewells, saying she was very pleased to have made Sophie's acquaintance. After she had gone, Sophie took the opportunity to ask Mrs. Hunter if Jonathan knew about Billy's visits.

Mrs. Hunter replied that she had written to tell him. She didn't see Jonathan very often, because he was kept busy with his parish duties. "I understand that he visited you and your husband and asked for news of his son," she said.

Sophie explained that Millie had agreed that she could write to Jonathan from time to time to inform him of his son's progress.

Mrs. Hunter nodded and sighed. "You know he is desperate to see him," she said.

"I'm sorry, Mrs. Hunter, but that cannot be arranged at present. Perhaps there might be a meeting when he starts school? I know Millie would like Billy to have a good education. I am unable to promise anything, however."

When they were preparing to leave, Billy suddenly asked, "Is Jonathan my real papa?"

Mrs. Hunter and Sophie both looked surprised. Billy must have been listening to their conversation.

"Yes, Billy, he is," said his grandmama, "and I hope one day you will meet him."

Billy seemed content with this, and they took their leave. Sophie was not looking forward to telling Millie, as she knew how volatile she could be. She told Billy not to ask any more questions until they got home.

When they arrived back, Billy was told to join Ben in the workshop. Sophie took the opportunity to tell her sister-in-law about the conversation Billy had overheard. "I am so sorry. It was thoughtless of me."

"He needs to know some time," replied Millie. "When he goes to school, he will want to know who his real father is. I will tell him as best I can. Ben says I must not prevent him from having a good education."

Sophie was surprised how conciliatory Millie was. When Ben brought Billy back, his mother explained in simple terms the circumstances of his birth.

He had a few questions, however. "Was it before Uncle Ben married Aunt Sophie?" he asked.

"Yes. You were only three then."

"Where is my new papa now? Can I see him?"

"He lives quite a long way away, Billy. You will be able to meet him when you go to see your school."

Millie thought that was enough questioning for now, so she asked Sophie about her visit.

"Mrs. Hunter introduced me to an acquaintance of hers, Caroline Bailey. Her husband is the village doctor, and she is his second wife. She asked me whether I could make some dresses for her two stepdaughters. I need to go back to measure them and find out exactly what they need." Sophie sounded excited. "I think I have made a new friend. She's about my age."

She was surprised when Ben didn't seem that pleased for her. "Hadn't she any friends in the village?" he asked.

Millie took Sophie to visit Caroline the following week, and after dropping off Billy at his grandmama's, they arrived at Caroline's house. Her home was tastefully furnished but not ostentatious. There was a grand piano in the room they entered and tables with books strewn about.

Sophie introduced her sister-in-law and then asked the two girls what kind of dresses they would like. The older girl, Harriette, had very set ideas, but the younger girl, Dorothy, wasn't sure. She had red hair, so Sophie suggested a green colour would suit her best, and she readily agreed. Sophie made a few notes and sketches in her pocketbook and said she would bring round some samples next time. She hoped she wasn't taking on too much. She had a feeling she would be making clothes for this little family for some time.

Caroline was very friendly and asked Sophie a bit about herself. Sophie told her about their plans to set up a bicycling business. Caroline was very interested and said that her brother had a bicycle and had joined a club. "He goes off every weekend," she said. "I think there are girls who have joined too."

When they left, Sophie went to collect Billy, leaving Millie in the trap outside.

Mrs. Hunter told her that she had been teaching her grandson to play chess. "He's very good," she said. "He nearly beat me!" Her face was animated, showing that she had enjoyed his company that afternoon.

Sophie thought the two of them seemed to be getting on well, and she was glad she had brought them together. Whatever Ben thought, she felt she had found a good friend in Caroline. She was full of her visit when she returned and told Ben all about her commissions for the two daughters. Sophie felt cheered by her visit, because she was at last meeting people from her own social class and enjoyed the experience.

CHAPTER TWENTY-THREE

THE NEW BUSINESS

BEN TOLD SOPHIE THAT HIS friend Mike, the owner of the bicycle shop in Kingsbridge, had invited him to attend a dinner at the local chamber of commerce. He said it was an organisation that looked after the interests of local businessmen, and he wondered if he should go. "I hope it won't mean meeting a lot of upper-class, well-off men. I don't think I would fit in."

"They will be men who have created their own businesses, entrepreneurs like yourself," replied Sophie.

Sophie could see Ben looking blank, and she quickly explained to him what an entrepreneur was. He decided to go, and this led to a discussion about what to wear. Sophie thought he should get some new clothes, as he had put on a little weight since they married. They drove to the tailors in Kingsbridge, and this prompted her to ask him something that had been on her mind.

"Ben, can you or Millie teach me how to drive? I cannot expect either of you to take me where I need to go. You are very busy, and we may not always have Millie here."

Ben suggested Millie might have more time and then asked her why she thought Millie might not be with them much longer.

"Surely you have seen her and Harry together?"

"Oh, Sophie! They have known each other a long time. They are just good friends."

"I think it is something more, or at least I hope it is."

They continued their journey, and at the tailor's Ben submitted to being measured for his new suit. They went back to collect it a week later, and he tried it on in the shop's changing room. When he emerged, the tailor fussed about checking that it fitted correctly. Sophie could see that it gave her husband confidence, and she felt proud of him.

"Will this do?" he asked her as he stood in front of the long mirror.

She agreed he looked very smart, and he would blend in well.

"I don't want to look like an upper-class gentleman," he said, his eyes twinkling.

"There won't be any there," replied Sophie. "They don't mix with tradespeople."

Ben told her afterwards he did find himself in the company of other men like himself running small manufacturing businesses, service industries, shops, trades and even a farmer. He said he was glad there was a mutual support network helping them all. Sophie was glad it had gone well and told him he had gone up in the world.

She had by now completed the dresses for Caroline's daughters, and so one afternoon she set off with Millie sitting beside her, letting her drive. The horse knew the way, and it was much easier managing the reins than Sophie had thought.

The girls were very excited when they saw their dresses, and orders were immediately made for two more. Caroline invited Sophie and Millie to stay for tea and spoke of her appreciation at making "two delightful new friends." Millie said afterwards that she liked Caroline, and this pleased Sophie.

Before Easter, a lone rider stopped outside Forge Cottage. After dismounting, he introduced himself to Sophie as Arnold, Caroline's brother. Sophie welcomed him and asked if he would like to see Ben's workshop.

Sophie left Millie minding the children and took Arnold down to the forge. Ben shook his hand and asked him into the workshop. Sophie knew he was getting used to welcoming gentlemen customers. She had taken Ben's working clothes in hand, and he looked a lot smarter than he had in his blacksmithing days. He even had a new apron instead of his father's old filthy one.

Ben introduced Arnold to Harry, who was working inside. He told Arnold about the fire that had made them restart as a bicycling business. Arnold looked fascinated by all the old bicycles piled up at the back of the workshop. He showed them his new machine outside. Ben said he hadn't seen that model before and examined it carefully.

Just then, Millie came to tell them it was lunchtime, and Sophie saw Arnold regarding her with apparent interest. They were introduced, and Millie's face brightened as she looked at him and he gave her a beaming smile. Sophie asked Arnold if he would like to stay for lunch, but he politely declined and jumped back onto his bicycle and sped off up the lane.

"He's a bit of a show-off," observed Harry when he had gone.

The following day, Easter Sunday, Harry came over to the cottage to ask Millie if she would like to go for a walk. He said he wanted to gather some primroses for his mother for the holiday. Sophie thought he looked surprised when Millie accepted, but he happily walked up the lane with her. Sophie did not know they had returned until she went outside later to empty some vegetable peelings in the garden.

When she came back, she was animated. "Ben!" she said excitedly. "You will never guess what I have just seen!"

Ben looked up from his bicycle catalogue.

"Millie and Harry are down in the orchard, and they're kissing!"

"That's where they should be if they want a bit of peace and quiet together," he said, looking back down.

"Oh, Ben, aren't you excited? It means they're in love!"

Ben said nothing and continued reading.

A short time later, Millie and Harry came in holding hands, and Millie was smiling broadly. "Harry has asked me to marry him, and I have accepted," she announced.

Sophie clasped her hands together and told them how pleased she was.

"I hope you know what you are taking on," said Ben to Harry, but then he immediately got up and gave Millie a hug and shook Harry's hand warmly.

Sophie felt excited. This meant they would be losing Millie, but she would not be far away, and she knew Mildred would be delighted.

When Millie and Harry left to go to tell his mother, Sophie said, "I didn't expect it to be so soon."

"I think I know why," said Ben. "It has something to do with that young man's visit yesterday. I think Harry thought he was getting a rival."

"Poor Harry. I don't think he could bear to lose her again."

Harry finally gave in his notice at Clayden House. He was to take charge of the small livery and hiring side of their business as well as helping with the bicycle work. He was often to be found in the workshop, and Millie would often wander down there to chat to him while he worked. After work, they would sometimes go for a short stroll into the village and back. Sophie was pleased to see them both so happy.

She continued giving Billy his lessons in the week, and Millie would serve the bicycle clubs their teas when they arrived at the weekends. She noticed Mille was going less to the workshop and preferred to stay in the cottage looking after the children while Sophie got on with her sewing. She had also become quieter.

One day, Harry returned from his day's work and asked Millie to go for a walk with him. She told him she had to stay to be with Charles, who was nearly two now. Sophie encouraged her to go.

"I can manage now," she said, snipping off the thread from the garment she was machining.

Millie got up and went to get her shawl. Harry took her hand, and they went out.

A short while later, Harry surprised Sophie by suddenly arriving at the kitchen door looking distraught. He slumped into a chair at the table and bent over, his head on his arm.

"Harry! Whatever is the matter?" She sat down next to him.

"It's Millie. She's broken off the engagement. She says she's not ready to get married again," he stammered.

Sophie was not entirely surprised. "Harry, as I've said before, she needs time. She's been through such a lot, and not surprisingly, she still thinks of Frank and misses him every day. I know she loves you, but she cannot make changes in her heart quickly. It's not quite a year since Frank died. I'm sorry, but you will have to be patient."

"I'm tired of being patient! I just want to settle down and marry the girl I have wanted for so long! What am I to do, Sophie? What am I to do?"

She could see he was desperate. "Leave it to me. I'll speak to her. I'm sure we can sort this out. Go home, and I'll see you in the morning. Where is Millie now, Harry?"

"I don't know. She went off."

Harry left, and Sophie sighed heavily. She wasn't at all sure she would be able to sort it out. She would have to hear what Millie had to say, and she might not want her to interfere.

At suppertime, Ben came in, and he had Millie and Billy with him. She had been in the workshop crying and now went straight up to her room.

"I know what's happened," Ben said quietly to Sophie as he came in. He put a restraining hand on her arm as she was about to follow Millie. "Leave her for a while," he said.

Sophie nodded and continued with the supper while Ben had his wash. She needed time to prepare what to say. Millie came downstairs when the meal was ready, and they all sat down. Sophie was busy trying to get Charles settled at the table.

"Mama's been crying," announced Billy.

Sophie shushed him and told him to eat his supper, then they would cheer Mama up.

Afterwards, Ben took Billy round to see the horses and Sophie got up and put her arms round Millie. "Do you want to talk about it?" she asked gently.

Millie nodded, and they both went into the parlour. Sophie settled her two children down and turned her attention to her sister-in-law.

"Did Harry come here?" asked Millie.

"Yes."

"What did he tell you?"

"He said you had broken off the engagement, that you felt it was too soon to get married again," replied Sophie.

Millie just held Sophie's hand tightly.

"Perhaps I'd better tell you something," said Sophie, hoping she was doing the right thing. "Some time ago, Harry came to me and asked what I thought his chances were with you. I told him it was far too early and that he should be patient and wait. I said what you needed was a friend, and I think that's what he's been to you these last months. The other day he saw that Arnold making eyes at you and he panicked, afraid he would lose you again. He has been in love with you since you were at school together, you know."

"I wish he'd told me that," replied Millie.

"Do you love him, Millie?"

"Yes, yes, I do. It's just that he started talking about his plans for changing the rooms in his cottage for us and his mother, and I felt I'm not ready for it all. I want to stay living here for now, at least until Billy goes to school. Oh, I shall miss him, Sophie, when he goes away!" She burst into tears.

Sophie realised at that moment what the trouble really was about. "Why don't you put off the wedding until next year? You will have had time to grieve, and you can concentrate on settling Billy into his new school in the meantime. You can let your love grow, and there is nothing to stop you staying over at Harry's occasionally," she said, giving Millie a knowing smile.

Millie wiped her eyes. "I'll go and see Harry," she said.

CHAPTER TWENTY-FOUR

BILLY'S NEW SCHOOL

One day when Sophie was in the village, she saw some bicycle riders, and it reminded her the touring club teas would soon be out and about. On good weather days, they would be served outside. The horses had been put out to eat the grass in the orchard, and Sophie had scattered some flower seed about in the hope of having some colour in the garden later. Ben pruned some of the trees and tidied up the yard. The tiling of the cottage roof was put off until the autumn, and if the teas were successful, they would consider building a small extension to the side of the workshop.

Ben had made some simple tables and benches, which could be stored away in the winter months, and these were placed round the garden under the trees. Sophie had worked hard baking cakes and scones, and she had plenty of preserves stored in the pantry. She had gone to Kingsbridge to purchase some inexpensive cups, saucers, plates and two large teapots at the market. Ben had put a few flyers round the village to direct any cyclists to the forge.

Before long, the riders began to arrive. Arnold had certainly put the word around. There were groups of both men and women, and the teas were much enjoyed. Sophie and Millie were kept busy every weekend, and a few riders even turned up on weekdays. Sometimes, if it was particularly wet or windy, they would serve teas in the kitchen and would enjoy chatting to a stranger or two for half an hour.

Young Charles got plenty of attention from the visitors as he toddled among them, and Sophie thought that it made him less nervous and shy. She was glad he was gaining some confidence. She would often put Florrie in her baby carriage out in the garden, where the visitors made a fuss of her. Billy obviously liked working with his Uncle Ben and Harry and scampered off to the workshop straight after his lessons. Sophie was kept busy baking and with her sewing commitments, so she had little free time.

Sophie carefully saved the money she made, as she knew that Frank's donation would be needed for the new roof and they would need extra to see them through the winter months. When she gave Millie her share, she asked her if it was to be put towards her wedding.

"Yes, it will help to pay for all the extras. Harry and I had a long talk, and we have decided the wedding should be next year. There is no need to rush things. I am relieved, as I need more time to get over my Frank. I still feel guilty at getting married again so soon."

Sophie took her hand in hers. "Millie, Frank would want you to be happy and not miserable for the rest of your life. I'm sure he would have approved of Harry and would be glad that someone as kind as he will be looking after you and Billy."

Millie bowed her head and nodded, and Sophie hoped she has reassured her.

Sophie continued Billy's visits to his grandmama throughout the summer. Mrs. Hunter told her that she had contacted the school. With Millie's permission, a visit would be arranged soon, and Jonathan would be there. She said that Billy's birth name would not matter, as many of the boys had different names from their fathers. Jonathan would just be required to sign a document acknowledging Billy as his son. Ben said he would take his sister and Billy on the visit, and Sophie said she would remain at home with her two young children, but she would want to know all about it when they returned.

Millie was able to tell her that Hillside School was a large mansion built of stone situated in its own beautiful grounds. It had a long sweeping drive that curved round, and the school buildings were surrounded by trees. She said they were thrilled when they saw it and couldn't believe Billy was going there, but when they went inside, Billy had told her he was feeling afraid.

"I think we were all a bit scared," admitted Millie. "Thankfully the school bursar arrived and welcomed us. She was very friendly. We followed her up a huge marble staircase to the headmaster's study. When we entered, we found Jonathan there."

Sophie asked Millie how she felt at seeing him again.

"I didn't know what to say or do," admitted her sister-in-law. "Thankfully, Ben came to my rescue and asked me to introduce Billy to his father."

"That must have been very difficult for you."

"Yes, I was so worried about it, and I felt very embarrassed. Before I could say anything, Jonathan got up and took my hand and said he was so very sorry about the way he'd treated me. Then he introduced himself to our son. Billy seemed to be overawed, but Jonathan was so good with him. He told him all about the school tuckshop, and I could see that went down very well with Billy, as you can imagine! He told him he'd felt very afraid himself when he started school, but he was sure Billy would like it and make lots of new friends."

"How did you feel about him?" Sophie sounded concerned. She could see that Millie was feeling emotional, as her eyes were full of tears.

"You know, Sophie, Jonathan wasn't what I expected at all. He has grown into a fine young man, and I found myself feeling proud that he was Billy's father. Can you understand that?"

Sophie agreed, saying she had thought the same when he came to visit them. "Do you have any regrets that you did not get married to him?"

"Oh, Sophie, even if he had asked me, I could not have passed myself off as a lady! I am a country girl, a blacksmith's daughter. Apart from that, his parents would never have accepted me into the family. I would have ruined his life."

"I think you underestimate yourself. Millie. I think you would have done very well. You would have been a good wife to him, as you were to Frank, and he was a gentleman."

Millie shook her head firmly. "I'm glad I met my Frank and regret it did not last. I think my marriage to him worked because he was related to you, Sophie, and he felt welcome in our family."

"I am so glad you and Jonathan are reconciled." Sophie put out a hand and touched her arm.

"Mr. Dawlish, the headmaster, put us at ease and asked us all about ourselves." Millie continued. "I told him about the circumstances of my relationship with Jonathan and that my brother and I had raised Billy. He asked who had prepared him for the entrance exam, and Ben looked very proud saying it was you, Sophie, as you had been a governess."

Sophie felt pleased at this. She had worked so hard to educate Billy, and she knew he had done well.

"Mr. Dawlish seemed very interested and told us they get boys with various backgrounds. He told us he realised Billy had had a few changes in his short life. After our interview, Billy was taken away for his exam, and I'm afraid I felt very worried."

Sophie said she wasn't surprised, as she had felt nervous about it too.

"We were then given a tour of the school. Oh, Sophie, it's wonderful! He is going to receive an excellent education there. When he came back, he told us he thought he had done well. He had ink all over his fingers, but he was smiling!"

Sophie smiled. She felt proud of Billy.

"We were given a lovely tea, and when it was time to go, Jonathan said he would let us know the result. He said he looked forward to seeing Billy again soon."

"How do you feel about that?"

"I don't think I mind anymore, Sophie. I'm sorry I was so angry with you for contacting his grandmother. I see now it was the right thing to do for Billy."

Sophie felt very gratified. Going to this school would give her nephew so many opportunities. She wondered what he would eventually do in his life.

CHAPTER TWENTY-FIVE

FRIENDSHIP

Sophie received a letter from Caroline asking if she could drop by and collect the girls' dresses the next time she came to Kingsbridge. Sophie immediately answered, inviting them all to tea. They were coming on a weekday, and Sophie hoped there would be no cyclists arriving that afternoon, as she was looking forward to seeing her friend again. Millie had to go into Kingsbridge with Harry, and Ben was visiting Mike, so Sophie would be entertaining alone. She had baked a cake and laid the table in the parlour with a new tea set she had bought, and she thought it all looked very elegant. Caroline and her two daughters arrived, and Sophie showed them round.

When they came to the stables, Harriette and Dorothy made a fuss of Rascal and began begging their mama for ponies of their own. Caroline told them that their father would have to be asked, but when she was out of earshot of the girls, she asked Sophie about the possibility of keeping a pony for them there.

"They'll have to share one," she explained. She then asked, "Would they be able to have riding lessons?"

Sophie thought it would be just the thing. She could ask Harry, and it would be lovely to see her new friend on a regular basis when she brought the girls for their lessons.

"Ben's partner happens to be a groom," she told Caroline. "I will see what I can do."

Caroline looked pleased and continued. "The girls do need occupying after their lessons. It would be such a treat to come here, if we don't make a nuisance of ourselves."

Sophie assured her that she would welcome their visits. They returned to the cottage, and the girls played with Charles and little Florrie, leaving Sophie and Caroline to talk together while the kettle boiled on the range.

"Your kitchen is so cosy!" enthused Caroline, looking round at everything. "I love the dresser with all your lovely china plates. It reminds me of my grandmother's cottage. I used to visit when I was a little girl. I loved my time in the countryside."

She watched Sophie make the tea and then asked, "What made you marry a blacksmith, Sophie? I am intrigued!"

Sophie smiled and put the kettle down. She described to Caroline how she and Ben had met on her walks and how unhappy she had been as a governess. "Of course, I had my doubts," she explained. "Apart from the difference in our backgrounds, I was not used to village life. I couldn't clean or cook. I had such a lot to learn."

"Your life seems very interesting, if hard work," Caroline replied. "I have servants and a cook, and I find it hard to find enough to do. Women are not allowed to use their minds and skills, and things need to change. We middle-class women are a wasted resource, and we should be allowed to be better educated and given the same opportunities as men."

Sophie agreed wholeheartedly, and they both looked at each other and laughed at how serious they were becoming.

"I think women riding bicycles and adapting their way of dressing may be one way," said Sophie. "We have been passive for too long."

The girls came in for their tea, and Sophie was glad to see Charles making friends. He was now two and a half. They tried on their new dresses, and their mother told Sophie she was very pleased with her handiwork.

Before they left, Caroline said, "I understand my brother paid you a visit. He mentioned he'd met a pretty girl. Was that Millie?"

"Yes. She's just got engaged to be married."

"I'm afraid Arnold is a bit of a flirt," said Caroline. "He has joined his bicycling club to meet girls. He imagines they're all in love with him!"

Sophie smiled to herself and wished she could see Arnold's face when his sister told him that Millie was to be married.

After their visit, Sophie spoke to Ben about the possibility of stabling a pony and giving the girls riding lessons. He agreed it was a good idea and said he would speak to Harry about it.

Sophie had enjoyed seeing her friend and her daughters again, but her pleasure was cut short by a letter arriving from Lucinda. Her brother was getting married, but she was to remain living at the rectory for the time being. She said that Lionel was thriving. He would be two at the end of the year. Lucinda's letters to Ben always made Sophie a bit tense, but Ben seemed to be quite relaxed when he read the news. He said he was glad that William was giving her a home.

Sophie was more concerned that Billy would be going away the following month in September and that this would upset his mother. She had received a letter from Jonathan informing her that Billy had been awarded a place. He enclosed a list of items from the school that Billy would need when he boarded, and this meant a trip to Kingsbridge to buy a trunk. Billy was measured for a suit at the tailor's, and Sophie was amused when Ben called him "a right little gentleman." She was soon busy at her machine, making the rest of Billy's school clothes and labelling them.

On the last day of August, Millie packed Billy's trunk and checked that all was ready for his journey to school the next day. After supper that evening, Ben stood a rather nervous Billy before him. "There's no need to be afraid, young man. All the other boys in your form will be feeling the same, and you will soon make some friends. Remember, always stand up for yourself. If anyone tries to bully you, give them a good whack and they won't bother you again."

"Oh, Ben! You're telling him how to fight!" exclaimed Sophie.

Millie laughed and said to her, "It's obvious you never grew up in a village!"

"And another thing," Ben continued, warming to his own advice. "Never snitch on anyone. That will make you very unpopular. The masters will have to find out what happened themselves. Only tell if something serious happens, because then you are just being a witness."

"Anyone would think you've been to public school, Ben. You seem to know all about it," said Millie.

Ben gave his sister a look. "These are life's lessons. They apply anywhere."

Sophie could see he was getting defensive. She sighed. It was all becoming too fraught. By this time Billy looked confused, but he nodded seriously, which seemed to reassure everyone.

The next morning, Sophie and Millie stood outside Forge Cottage trying to control their emotions. Ben loaded the trunk into the trap, and Billy climbed in. He suddenly turned to his uncle.

"Uncle Ben, haven't you forgotten something?"

Ben looked puzzled. He was sure he hadn't.

Sophie looked at Millie. *What could it be,* she wondered.

"Pennies for the tuck shop!" said Billy triumphantly.

"Oh, how could I have forgotten something so important?" exclaimed Ben, and he put his hand in his waistcoat pocket and gave Billy a handful of coins. "Here you are, young man, and don't forget to treat someone who has no money."

After Billy's departure, Millie fretted for a while, but Harry came round, and she began to relax. She now had him all to herself.

It wasn't long before Billy's first letter arrived in his wobbly handwriting, saying that he was having a good time, but the masters were a bit strict and he didn't like the mashed potato. Sophie comforted Millie when she read it, as it made her cry. Ben told her Billy wasn't a baby anymore and he would be perfectly all right.

They were all relieved when Billy did come home for half term. Sophie could see he had changed. He had grown up and was full of schoolboy expressions. When he went round to the stables to see Rascal, he wanted to know who the new pony belonged to. When Sophie explained about Harriette and Dorothy's visits, he said he didn't mind if one of the girls rode Rascal as they had to share one pony, and Millie said that was generous of him.

CHAPTER TWENTY-SIX

LIONEL

A LETTER ARRIVED FROM LUCINDA INVITING Ben to come and see Lionel to celebrate his second birthday. Ben purchased some toys and set off with Harry. Sophie had agreed he could go and put on a smile, hoping as she saw them off that all would be well. When Ben came back, he was full of news about his son. Lionel had his colour hair and eyes, and he was growing into a big strong boy. Sophie couldn't help but think that he was the exact opposite of their own son, with his dark hair and serious eyes. Ben said he couldn't wait for the two brothers to meet each other, but Sophie was doubtful. She resented this persistent intrusion into her family.

Another letter arrived after Ben's visit in which Lucinda announced her engagement to a lawyer by the name of Samuel Wells. Her divorce had come through a few weeks before. They were to marry in the new year and then travel to the continent for a while. When they returned, they would be living in London, where her husband had his chambers.

As he read the letter out, Sophie could see Ben's face change, and he frowned.

"What concerns you, Ben?" she asked, noticing his reaction to the news.

"My son is to have a new father, and he will be living further away," he answered.

Sophie thought it might be better if they did all live further away. Then Ben wouldn't be able to travel up to London often.

"I would like to go and meet this man."

Sophie was horrified. "I don't think you should go," she said.

He looked annoyed. "Why is that?"

"It wouldn't be appropriate and would embarrass Lucinda. Besides, you don't know how much she has told him about you."

"I really don't understand. Why shouldn't I go? This man she is marrying is to be a father to my son. I have every right to go!" Ben answered, raising his voice.

Sophie had not often seen this side of Ben. She thought he did not realise the implications, so she braced herself and went on.

"Ben, if you do go, you'll regret it. Believe me."

There was silence, and Sophie hoped her words had been heeded. She knew she had been outspoken.

"Can't you allow me to see my son?" Ben pleaded. "Can't you trust me to go there after all the promises I've made you?"

"It isn't that. I just know it isn't the right thing to do."

Ben got up and walked out. Sophie knew she was right, and she had had just about enough of Ben and this child. Perhaps it would be better if Lionel had a stepfather. She tried to carry on with her housework, but eventually she sat down at the table and burst into tears.

Presently, she felt a little hand reach up and looked down. She saw little Florrie pulling herself round the table leg and holding on to the chair until she had got to her mother. She was nearly walking now. Sophie picked her up and cuddled her. How comforting she was with her little pink arms and bright eyes. Florrie put her hand on Sophie's wet face and laughed. Sophie laughed too and wiped her eyes. She rocked Florrie and sang quietly to her, which always brought smiles.

Why, oh, why, can't Ben be content with just our little family? she thought to herself. *Why does he always want to go to see Lionel?* She realised they would be two families now, families that would always be connected, and she had to face the fact.

Charles was playing in the parlour, and when he heard the singing, he came to join them, carrying a toy he gave to his sister. He had always been kind to Florrie and protective of her. Sophie knew he was a gentle boy, having none of the toughness of his father. She wondered if that was why Ben had never fully bonded with him and was bound to compare him with Lionel. Sophie put her other arm round Charles and told him he was a good boy.

The door opened, and Ben walked in. He stopped and looked over at his wife and children, then came over and put his arm round Sophie and kissed her cheek. "I'm sorry, I know all this is hard on you. I've been thinking, and you are right. It's best not to go."

Sophie put Florrie down. "Listen, Ben," she said. "I've had an idea. Why don't you go on a visit before the wedding and take a gift? You could make something in the workshop. I am sure they would treasure a handcrafted object."

She could see that Ben was delighted at her suggestion. He decided to make a candelabra, an upright one that stood on the floor, with twists and scrolls in the metalwork. He used his skills as a blacksmith to bend and craft the metal.

Ben delivered his gift before Christmas, and when he returned, he told Sophie that he had not been able to meet Lucinda's fiancé. She was very relieved.

They were both surprised when a letter arrived shortly afterwards from Lucinda thanking him for his gift but informing him that Samuel had forbidden him ever to visit again and that he intended to adopt Lionel as his own son. Her fiancé was clearly not happy about Ben's visit to his intended.

Sophie could see that this news hit Ben hard, but there was nothing he could do. Sophie thought to herself that it was probably all for the best. At least they would be able to get on with their own lives now, and she felt a burden had been lifted from her. She could begin to enjoy her life with her two lovely children and not worry about letters from Lucinda anymore.

They were in the kitchen having supper one evening when Charles spilled his mug of milk over himself and the floor. He started to cry, and Sophie fussed over him, telling him everything was all right and that it didn't matter.

"You mollycoddle that child," said Ben.

Sophie looked up and replied, "It's better than ignoring him."

"What's that supposed to mean?"

"Perhaps he needs a little more attention from his father."

"Are you saying I don't love my son?" he demanded.

"I'm saying that you seem preoccupied with your *other* child," Sophie replied. "I know Charles isn't the son you expected. He's not going to grow up hammering metal and punching people who annoy him. He's not like that, Ben, and never will be."

Sophie felt bitter. She knew Ben was fretting that he could not see Lionel again. Why couldn't he be content with their son? She mopped up the milk silently and comforted Charles.

"Sorry, Mama," said Charles, looking upset.

"Bedtime now," said Sophie and took Charles and Florrie upstairs.

Sophie heard the kitchen door bang shut, and when she came downstairs, Ben had gone out. She guessed it was to the Two Foxes.

Sophie went to bed early, but she was still lying wide awake when he returned. She watched as Ben silently got ready for bed. She sat up and said, "Ben, we must talk."

Ben sat on the bed, looking doleful. "I don't seem to get anything right, do I?" he said.

Sophie held his hand. "Tell me what's the matter, Ben. I want us to understand each other."

Ben sat quietly in thought for a few moments. "You are a good mother, but I feel you are doting on the children all the time, and to be honest, I feel left out. I work hard for you all, you know I do, and it hasn't been easy setting up a new business and making sure we have enough income. You must understand I have to support three of us and three children. I am doing my best, and I think I am a good father."

"I do understand, Ben, but this has to do with Lionel as well," responded Sophie. "I feel you compare him unfavourably with Charles."

Ben was silent, then he said, "Yes, maybe I do."

"Please try and accept him for what he is. He deserves his father's love and attention."

Ben nodded and got into bed.

"I'm sorry you are feeling neglected," said Sophie, putting her arms round him and drawing him to her. "We both need to change."

The next morning when Sophie woke, Ben was already up, so she dressed quickly and carried Florrie downstairs, and little Charles followed. When they got to the kitchen, Ben was dressed and had laid the table for breakfast, and he was sitting down with a cup of tea. Sophie settled the children while Ben poured her a cup.

"Aren't you going to the workshop this morning?" she asked.

"No," he answered, "I'm going into Kingsbridge. I might take Charles with me."

He looked over at Charles. "Would you like to have a ride with Papa?"

Charles stopped eating his porridge and smiled at his father.

"And we may visit the sweetie shop," he added.

At this, Charles looked very happy. Sophie was so relieved when Ben said this. At last he was giving Charles some attention. "That's a wonderful idea," she said. "Thank you, Ben."

She enjoyed her day not having to watch Charles all the time, and she was able to get on with her work when Florrie was put upstairs for her rest. At the end of the afternoon, Ben came in carrying Charles. Sophie looked alarmed.

"It's all right," he said. "He's asleep."

"You tired him out, then."

"He tired me out, more like," replied Ben. "He must wear you out, too."

Sophie smiled to herself. After she had put a very sleepy Charles to bed, she came back downstairs.

"Ben," she said, "I don't think I want too many more."

Ben reached across and kissed her cheek. "Well, that might be difficult," he said, smiling.

"No, Ben, I'm serious. I cannot help with this business if I'm knee-deep in children. Besides, our cottage is very small."

Ben drew back. "I do understand. It means I'll have to exercise some self-restraint then."

Sophie was relieved he had agreed so readily. "Where did you and Millie sleep when you were young?" she asked.

"Millie was in the room she has now, and I slept in the parlour," he said. "I was always up first anyway, as I had to light the fire in the forge."

"How old were you?"

"Just a bit older than Billy."

Sophie realised what a difficult childhood Ben had had. He had been deprived of his schooling and made to work from a very young age.

"Why didn't your father light the fire?"

"Oh, he was sleeping off the excesses of the night before, probably."

Sophie felt sorry for Ben and what he had been through. "Ben, you have done well for yourself. I'm proud of you."

"I could never have done it without you, my lovely Sophie," he replied.

CHAPTER TWENTY-SEVEN

FOUR YEARS LATER

It was New Year's Day, 1900, and Sophie was helping Ben gather up the bunting that had been put up to celebrate the beginning of the new century. She was thinking about the previous night, when they had all been in the parlour welcoming in the new year. Sophie had primed the lamps for their small gathering. She liked the smell of the oil lamps and the way the room took on a warmth from their gentle glow.

Harry and Millie had joined them. They had left Billy, who was now twelve, with his little brother Tom, in the care of a kind neighbour. They had been living with Harry's mother in the village since their marriage three years before, and now the cottage was theirs, Mildred having passed away the previous summer. Ben had poured each of them a drink of homemade wine and asked what they hoped for in the new century.

Harry glanced at Millie. "We want to open a village shop," he began.

Ben and Sophie looked surprised and waited in anticipation to hear what was planned.

"Of course, the cottage is far too small," added Millie. "We shall build a wooden chalet on the ground at the side. It will be in a good position next to the road."

Sophie was delighted. "How exciting!" she exclaimed. "It will be so convenient for the villagers to get their provisions from you instead of going into Kingsbridge all the time. What a wonderful idea!" She looked at Ben, her eyes shining.

"I wish you both every success," he said, raising his glass. "When do you think you will be able to open?"

"Sometime in early summer, I hope," Harry replied.

Sophie and Ben had raised their glasses and wished the venture well. Sophie said she hoped that the new century would bring health and happiness to them all, especially her three children. Charles was now seven years old, and Sophie was continuing to educate him at home. Florrie was six and would soon be joining her brother in their makeshift schoolroom. Little Rosa was three and was a lively child. Millie and Harry's little boy, Tom, was slightly younger than Rosa. Sophie knew she would probably be called on to look after him, as his mother would be busy running the shop.

As she stuffed the flags into a sack the following day, she wondered when they would be put out again. Perhaps when the shop opened? That would be quite an occasion. She felt the coming year was full of promise.

Ben told her later that he was relieved that Harry had decided to set up his own business. "I have been worried for some time that he has not had enough work," he went on. "There just haven't been enough fares since that livery opened in Kingsbridge. Harry has been useful helping in the workshop, but I can easily manage on my own."

Bicycle riding was still gaining popularity, and Ben and Harry had built up a thriving business assembling bicycles and getting their colleague, Mike Harding, to sell them in his shop in Kingsbridge. It had all been going very well for the last four years since they began. Ben worked hard building the bikes in his workshop. He was able to obtain manufactured parts, which he would weld together to make a complete bicycle. Harry had had sole responsibility for the livery side of his and Ben's business, but they had not had any horses to look after for over a year, and fewer local people wanted to use the horse and trap.

Sophie knew they needed more room in Forge Cottage for their family. The children could not all sleep in the one bedroom for much longer. She and Ben had discussed plans to extend the cottage. They wanted an extra bedroom and an extension to make the parlour bigger. Sophie looked at the accounts and decided that they could not really afford it just yet.

She loved her little family. She had done her best to forget Ben's other child, Lionel. Nothing had been heard from Lucinda for over four years.

Life continued as normal. Sophie took the children round to the village green, and they had watched the May Day celebrations. The sun was shining as the laughing children danced around the maypole. Afterwards, they walked round to Millie and Harry's to see how the new shop was progressing. The chalet was now built and was ready to be stocked with goods.

Sophie had enjoyed her day, telling Ben all about it that evening, after his work. Her contentment soon turned to dismay, however, when next day she heard a voice calling outside the kitchen door.

"Hello, Papa!"

She stopped what she was doing, wondering if she had imagined it. She knew it wasn't Charles. He was upstairs playing with his sisters. Putting down her mending, she opened the door. Standing there was a young boy of about six or seven with light ginger hair. He was wearing a belted jacket with knickerbocker trousers and a cap and had a broad grin on his face.

"Hello!" he said brightly. "Is my papa there? It's Lionel!"

Sophie was shocked at seeing him. He resembled Ben so much in looks. The colour drained from her face, and she was speechless for a moment. "Is your mother with you?" she finally managed to ask.

"Yes," he replied. "She's waiting in the lane."

Sophie regarded the boy before her and knew she must try and welcome him. Inside, her resentment towards his mother and Ben was welling up.

"This is a surprise to see you, Lionel. I am Sophie, your papa's wife. I will take you to see him. Come with me."

She led him to the workshop and called out to Ben. There was no answer, and peering inside, she could see he wasn't there. She immediately guessed where he was and strode down the lane and round the corner, with Lionel trotting behind her. There she saw Ben standing beside a trap, talking to Lucinda. He must have just missed seeing Lionel dashing up the lane to the cottage.

"Ben!" she called.

He swung round, and Lionel rushed over to him. Sophie watched her husband bend down and embrace his son. "Hello, young fellow!" he exclaimed. "My, what a grown-up young man you are!"

Lionel beamed. He seemed quite at ease with the father who had not seen him since he was a toddler.

When Sophie saw Lucinda looking at her, she turned and quickly ran back to the cottage. Minutes later, Ben followed her in and found her in tears. She shook her head and buried it in his shoulder and began to sob. He put his arms round her and continued to hold her, saying nothing. After a little while, she moved away, and they looked at each other.

"Sophie, don't cry. It's all over with her. Please believe me. I had no idea they were coming."

Sophie wiped her eyes. "You'd better ask them in, Ben. I'll be all right in a minute. It was such a shock."

Ben kissed her, and without any more encouragement, he went out to see his visitors. He returned with Lionel. "Lucinda says she'll wait in the lane," he said.

Sophie nodded, feeling relieved. "Well, Lionel," she said, turning to him, "I expect you would like to meet your brother and sisters."

Lionel gave an excited nod, and Sophie called Charles and the girls to come downstairs. When they arrived, they stood in the doorway, staring at this strange boy.

"See who we have here," said Ben proudly. "This is Lionel, your half-brother."

Charles came forward. "Hello, Lionel," he said, smiling, but then he turned to his father, looking puzzled.

"Lionel is my son, but he has a different mama, Charles. He is only a little younger than you."

"Hello, Charles!" replied Lionel confidently. "Do you play football?"

Charles didn't, but he nodded, glancing at his father again.

The two girls were regarding Lionel, wide-eyed.

"And this is Florrie and Rosa," explained Ben.

Florrie greeted Lionel hesitantly, but Rosa hid behind her. Sophie could see she did not understand who this stranger was.

"Charles," said Sophie, "why don't you take Lionel outside and show him round."

The boys dashed out, followed by the girls.

Sophie turned to Ben. "What did Lucinda say?"

"She has been staying with her aunt, and they decided to call in here on their return home. Apparently, Lionel has been pestering her to see his half-brother."

"He knows all about Charles, then?"

"Yes, I suppose he must have been told."

Sophie had often wondered if her children should know about their half-brother. It was something she and Ben had not discussed, as there had been no contact with him. Now it would have to be explained to them.

She and Ben went outside. The children were in the orchard, running round excitedly. Ben and Sophie watched them for a while. Ben left her side and went down to speak with his son. Sophie could tell he was thrilled at seeing him again, but she could not feel the same. Suddenly her life had been turned upside down, and her memories came flooding back to her. Eventually Ben returned with his arm round Lionel's shoulder, saying that he shouldn't keep his mother waiting any longer. He called the children over to say their farewells.

Lionel looked at his brother and sisters and suddenly jumped up in the air, gave a whoop of delight and exclaimed, "I have such a big family!"

Before Ben took him back up the lane, he asked Sophie if Lionel could come again. His eyes pleaded with her.

"Yes, he can," she answered somewhat reluctantly.

CHAPTER TWENTY-EIGHT

THE TWO BROTHERS

A WEEK LATER, SOPHIE WAS IN the kitchen one afternoon when there was a sudden loud banging on the door. It startled her, as anyone who came to see them would usually knock and then enter straight away. She opened it tentatively and saw a well-dressed gentleman standing there, looking angry.

"I am looking for Lucinda Wells. Is she here?" he demanded.

Sophie was unsure what to say, but Ben, having heard the banging, appeared at that moment. "Can I help you, sir?" he asked.

The man swung round. "I've reason to suspect that my wife may be here."

"No, she is not," answered Ben. "Won't you come in for a moment?"

The man entered, and Sophie led him into the parlour and invited him to sit down.

Ben followed him in. "I am Ben Browne, and this is my wife, Sophie. Who do I have the honour of addressing, sir?"

The man jumped up, suddenly remembering his manners. "I do apologise. I am Samuel Wells, Lucinda's husband. How do you do."

Ben shook his hand, and Sophie nodded an acknowledgment. "How can we help?" asked Ben.

Lucinda's husband sat down again and sighed. By now the three children were standing in a row, staring at the visitor. Sophie ushered them into the kitchen, closed the door and came back into the parlour.

She was intrigued to find out why Lucinda's husband had come to see them and seemed so agitated.

He began to explain. "A few days ago, my wife and I had a slight disagreement, and yes, it was about Lionel. He has become difficult lately, and I found out that Lucinda had brought him here to see you."

"Yes, that is so," said Ben.

"When I returned home yesterday, I found that my wife had left with Lionel. I have no idea where they have gone. I have tried to be a good father to Lionel, but his mother does spoil him, and I have to introduce some discipline."

Sophie saw Ben's face tense.

"I have been to her brother's house, but he has not seen her, so I presumed she must have come here."

"She has an aunt," interrupted Sophie. "She may have gone there. Ben told me she was at Lucinda's confinement. We do not know where she lives, but her brother might have her address."

Sophie observed that both Lucinda's husband and Ben were looking bewildered. *These two men have a lot in common,* she thought to herself. *They have both been taken in by this beautiful, impulsive woman and now seem unable to know what to do.*

Ben got out the brandy and two glasses, then poured Samuel and himself a drink and sat down again. "If she does come here, I shall tell her she must return home to you. Have no doubt about that," said Ben.

Samuel nodded and swallowed his drink in one go.

"Mr. Wells, would you like some supper with us?" asked Sophie. "You have obviously had a long journey."

"That's very kind of you, but I will continue to Kingsbridge and stay at an inn," replied Samuel. "I apologise for my behaviour. I was convinced she was here." He regarded Ben with apparent interest, then left.

Afterwards Sophie said, "I hope she doesn't come here. I don't want us getting involved in her marriage problems."

Ben was silent, so Sophie left him to his thoughts. She went to see to the children, who were asking questions about who the man had been and what he wanted.

"That was Lionel's stepfather," she said. "He is looking for Lionel and his mama. We do not know where they have gone."

Sophie saw that Charles looked concerned. "Do you think they will be all right?" he asked.

Sophie reassured him. "His mama will take care of him," she said. "He will be safe."

The following day, Ben returned from the village with a letter from Lucinda. When he opened it, Sophie asked him who it was from. He handed it to her, and she read it out to him. Sophie had been right. Lucinda was at her aunt's house. She warned them to expect a visit from her husband. She said he was convinced she was in contact with Ben and had found out about her and Lionel's visit. She ended by saying that she was unsure what to do but wanted the brothers to meet again.

Sophie folded the letter and put it back into the envelope, saying nothing.

"Well, there's nothing we can do," said Ben. "I hope that's the end of the matter."

Sophie was left to her own thoughts.

Ever since Lucinda's marriage, life had been peaceful, as Ben had settled down to concentrate on his family. His relationship with Charles had improved, and he loved his little girls. Now their lives were up in the air again. Sophie knew that as the brothers grew, they would be curious about each other.

A week later, Ben had another letter from Lucinda, which he showed to Sophie. It informed them that things had settled down. It had been decided that she and Lionel were to move from London and live nearer to her brother. Samuel was to continue his work in London but would come home at weekends, and he had agreed that Lionel could see Charles from time to time. There was another surprising announcement in that Lionel was to go to Hillside School in Exeter.

Sophie was perplexed. This meant Lucinda would be living nearer to them. Ben did not want Lucinda bothering him, but he was glad that Lionel would be nearer. Sophie was wary of Lucinda. She had always felt that there was an ulterior motive behind her actions. Or was she misjudging her? Was she really wanting the brothers to know each other better, or was she wanting to be near Ben?

They decided to tell Charles that his half-brother was coming to live nearer and that they might be able to make contact again. Sophie knew it would give her son some much needed friendship.

The mention of the school opened a discussion between Ben and Sophie about Charles's education. Ben was keen for him to go to the Exeter school too, but the fees were beyond their means. Ben's business had grown steadily, but if the fad for bicycles was ever to come to an end, Sophie knew they would be in dire straits. Unless they could find a way of raising the money, they would have to consider other ways of educating Charles. Sophie said she was unsure that Hillside would suit Charles anyway. He had always been a quiet, thoughtful child, kind and caring, and he would probably get bullied.

"I think it's time he should learn to stand up for himself," stated Ben. "You protect him too much, Sophie. You always have done."

"I think that is unfair. I have tried to give him confidence. He is an intelligent boy, and because he notices things, it can make him fearful."

Ben shook his head to show he didn't agree.

"How about applying for a scholarship to Kingsbridge Grammar School?" she suggested "He can be a day student. I am sure he would get a place. Lionel can always stay here for the holidays, and they can see a lot of each other that way."

They let the matter rest for the time being, as there were a few years to wait until Charles was old enough to go there. Sophie enjoyed tutoring him and knew he would do well. She often wondered what he would be when he was older. She knew he was academic. She thought of Ben and how he had struggled to better himself. Charles would have every opportunity to be whatever he wanted.

Sophie had felt very unsettled after Lucinda's husband's surprise appearance. She realised that if Lucinda lived nearer, things would be difficult for her, and Lionel's visits would be an intrusion into their family life. She knew she had to accept that Lionel was part of their family, and she struggled to come to terms with this.

One night after supper, when they were sitting by the fire in the parlour, Ben took hold of her hand and said, "Sophie, I think we ought to talk about Lionel."

She removed her hand from his and remained silent.

"I shan't know what to do if you won't talk to me, Sophie."

She looked at the burning logs in the fireplace, wishing it would all go away. Finally, she said, "I won't find it easy when Lucinda moves nearer and Lionel comes to see us, but I can see Charles likes him, and he needs friends of his own age. I know he spends too much time with me. I do want him to do more things with you and his brother."

"I can fetch Lionel for his visits and return him to his school," Ben suggested. "If he must be collected from his home, I can always ask Harry, if that is worrying you. I am happy to have as little to do with Lucinda as possible. She is married now, and if there are any difficulties, I shall speak to her husband straight away."

Sophie felt better. She knew she couldn't go through any more heart-ache. She took hold of Ben's hand again, and he held hers tightly. "My family are everything to me," he said. "I shall never again do anything to hurt any of you."

CHAPTER TWENTY-NINE

AN INVENTION

HARRY AND MILLIE WERE READY to set up the village shop, which was to open at Whitsuntide at the end of May. Sophie and Ben helped to stock the shelves with tins and packets, the new "convenience foods" of the time. The wide wooden counter held a pair of large scales, a cheese wire cutter, a slab of marble for the butter and a large knife for cutting bacon. An upright till had been obtained by Harry from a shop that had closed in Kingsbridge.

Behind the counter was a row of large glass jars containing sweets that were to be weighed out and then wrapped in twists of paper, ready for the children to buy. Sacks containing potatoes, flour and other food staples were propped round the sides of the shop. Harry had put a variety of household items outside, such as brooms, mops, buckets and even a small tin bath. Finally, they were ready for the grand opening.

Sophie got out the sack of bunting again, and Harry festooned it round the veranda. The shop was well stocked with cakes and bread, made by Sophie, and some garden produce. Harry still cultivated the garden at Forge Cottage, supplying vegetables to Sophie and her family as well as the shop. The villagers arrived on opening day with their large wicker baskets over their arms, and the till rang all day as they made their purchases. Millie gave away complimentary sweets and pieces of cake, and the day was a huge success.

Millie and Harry were hoping that the cyclists would call into the shop when they came to teas at Forge Cottage. With the better weather, the cycling clubs were beginning to arrive.

At lunch one day, Ben asked Sophie to come round to the workshop, as he had something to show her. "Bicycles need to be more comfortable," he said. "Folk are riding longer distances, and I realised they need better saddles."

He showed her one he had made. "I have come up with this design. I contacted a saddler in Kingsbridge, and he made me a leather padded one, which I fitted up with a couple of springs underneath."

"It certainly looks a lot more comfortable than those hard ones," observed Sophie.

"I have been thinking of getting some made ready for the cycle clubs. I don't have to sell them a whole new bicycle—I can just fit one of these on."

They proved to be popular with his customers, and it provided Ben with a lucrative sideline. Sophie mentioned to Ben that she had seen a woman's bicycle at the shop one day and it had a basket tied onto the handlebars. This gave him another idea, and he fitted some of the bicycles with baskets, which he had specially made by a local basket-maker.

Lionel had almost been forgotten in all the excitement of the village store opening when a letter came suggesting a visit. Sophie had resigned herself to him coming and almost looked forward to his arrival.

When Charles was told, he said he couldn't wait to see him again and asked his papa to teach him to play football. Ben took him out to the lane one afternoon to practise, and Sophie watched over the gate. She could soon see that Charles would need a lot of coaching.

Harry went to collect Lionel, and when he brought him back to Forge Cottage, Sophie gave him a warm welcome. It was late, so it was supper, then bedtime. Sophie had moved the girls into her bedroom so the boys could have a room to themselves during Lionel's stay. It was a tight squeeze, and this led to a discussion with Ben about the pressing need for another bedroom. They still had some of Frank's money to put towards the building costs, and Sophie had savings from her teas and sewing, but it was still not enough.

Ben went out the following morning, not telling Sophie where he was going. Later he burst into the kitchen, red-faced.

"Whatever is the matter—what has happened?" asked Sophie, slightly alarmed. Her hands were covered in flour, as she was making bread. She brushed it off quickly and settled Ben down in his chair.

"That man!" exclaimed Ben. "I could have punched him in the face!"

Sophie knew by now that anger usually produced this reaction in her husband. "What man? What did he do?" she asked, mystified.

Ben began to calm down. "I have just been to the bank in Kingsbridge to try and get us a loan," he explained. "Who should I see but that awful man, Wilmott-Smith. He didn't recognise me at first, but when he did, he said he did not give loans for buildings and showed me the door."

Sophie put her hand to her mouth but was unable to stop herself laughing.

"It wasn't funny, Sophie!"

She knelt beside him and put her arm round him. "Sorry, Ben. I just saw the funny side when you two recognised each other."

Ben looked at her, then he too laughed.

"We'll manage without him, Ben. We have enough to get some of the work done, and then we can save up for the next bit."

Ben nodded in agreement. "I'm glad you can laugh about him, Sophie. He was so unkind to you. I still feel angry at the way he treated you."

He kissed her, and she got up and went back to the table to give her dough a good thumping.

Sophie told Millie all about the incident when she saw her the next day at the shop. Later, Harry came round and offered to provide the loan, and Ben gratefully accepted.

Forge Cottage came alive when Lionel was there. Sophie saw a different side to Charles when he was with his brother. Lionel asked if he could ride Rascal, so Sophie arranged for Harry to come round and give the boys riding lessons. Lionel mounted Rascal first and was soon able to ride him confidently.

"Your turn now," he said to Charles, who was looking very reluctant.

"No, you carry on for a while," said Charles.

Harry encouraged Charles to climb onto Rascal's back. He kept hold of the reins as he led him along, and Charles began to relax. The boys took turns riding up and down the lane. Sophie had come out to watch, and she could see that Lionel was being a good example to Charles, helping him do things he might never have done otherwise.

When he thought they were ready, Harry asked Sophie if the boys could go on a hack, taking it in turns to ride Rascal. Sophie was pleased with the change in her son, and she began to regard Lionel more sympathetically. Up until then she had seen him as a rival and had resented Ben's love for him. Now her feelings were changing, and she began to see the benefits of his visits.

Lionel was also responsible for fostering another friendship. Sophie and Caroline had continued to see each other from time to time. Caroline's daughters were now at their Quaker boarding school and only able to visit Sophie in the holidays. Their pony was still in livery at the forge stables. The older girl had lost interest, and only Dorothy wanted to ride. Sophie had written to Caroline asking her if the boys could ride their pony, Beauty. She invited them all to come over and meet Lionel.

Caroline arrived one afternoon with Dorothy, and they followed Sophie round to the stables. The boys were already there, and Billy had arrived earlier and was saddling up Rascal. The younger children looked up to Billy, who was eleven now. Sophie introduced Lionel and Billy to her friend and her daughter. Caroline had been told about Lionel's relationship with Ben's family. Sophie had told her in confidence, knowing her friend well enough to know she would understand.

Billy regarded Dorothy with some interest while she was petting Beauty. "Is that your pony?" he asked.

Dorothy answered that she shared the pony with her sister.

"Do you like riding?" he asked.

"Yes."

"Will you come riding with me one day?"

"Yes," she replied.

Sophie noticed Dorothy had avoided eye contact with the young man in front of her. She thought it was rather touching that Billy wanted to go riding with her. Lionel asked politely if he could ride Beauty, and

Dorothy agreed. Billy finished saddling up both ponies and then led them out to the lane.

Sophie and Caroline followed with the girls and watched as the boys had fun riding up and down. They went in for tea, and Billy took both ponies back to the stables. Sophie noticed that Dorothy followed him, with the excuse that she wanted to say goodbye to Beauty.

Sophie liked the cottage to be full of children. Their faces, arms and legs were tanned by the sun, and they all had healthy appetites when they came back from their play. The boys played together, and Florrie would join them. This left Rosa on her own, so she tended to stay with her mother in the kitchen. On the days when Sophie looked after Harry and Millie's son Tom, he and Rosa would play together.

When it was time for Lionel to return home, Harry's help was again enlisted. Ben said his friend liked getting out of the village and seeing something of the outside world.

When he returned, he had some news. "I think I should tell you that Lucinda looks as if she is expecting."

Sophie saw that Ben looked surprised. She was glad, as she saw it as an indication that Lucinda's marriage had settled down. "I expect Lionel will be pleased," she said.

Ben did not reply.

CHAPTER THIRTY

PATENTS

In September, a builder began work on the extension to Forge Cottage. Sophie was kept busy with her dressmaking and her visits to Caroline. She also continued taking Billy to see his grandmother in the holidays and would leave him there while she went to see her friend.

It was half term, and she was driving Billy on his visit when he suddenly asked, "Aunt Sophie, why does my mama not want to see Grandmama?"

Sophie had been expecting this question for some time. "When your mama had you, Billy, she hoped that your father's family would help her. They refused, and she has never forgiven them."

"But she spoke to my papa at my school," he observed.

Sophie agreed and asked Billy what had made him ask her about this.

He was silent for a while and then said, "When I last went to see Grandmama, my father was there." Then he added quickly, "My real father, that is."

Sophie was surprised he had not mentioned it before. "Do you think he may be there today?" she asked.

"I don't know," replied Billy. "I do have rather a lot of papas, don't I?" He turned to her and laughed.

They both continued their journey, enjoying this unusual fact together. When they arrived, Billy alighted, and just before he went into his grandmama's house, Sophie asked him if he would walk round to Mrs. Bailey's to meet her there afterwards. Billy usually stayed for just over an hour, as his grandmama had to have her afternoon rest. He had told Sophie that they would often play chess or cards and that he had taught her some of the card tricks Frank had shown him. He said this amused his grandmother a great deal, and she had called him "a little showman."

Caroline had invited Sophie to tea, as the girls were at home. Later, Billy arrived as arranged and found Harriette sitting in a large armchair, reading. Dorothy was at a table cutting out some paper shapes. Caroline suggested Billy help her, so he went and sat next to Dorothy.

"What are you making?" he asked enthusiastically.

"Paper garlands," she explained. "You fold a piece paper in half and in half again, draw on a figure and cut round it. Then you unfold it, and they all join up, like this." She proceeded to hold up her handiwork.

Sophie and Caroline were very amused when Billy held up his garland and it fell apart when he opened it out.

"You have cut through the fold, silly!" exclaimed Dorothy, laughing at him.

As they worked together, Sophie and Caroline heard him tell her about his school.

"Do you ever get homesick?" she asked.

"I did at first," he replied, "but when I got to know everybody, it wasn't so bad."

Dorothy nodded and told him she had just started school.

"Will you write to me?" Billy asked. "I like getting letters when I'm away."

Dorothy said she would, so he wrote the school's address on a piece of spare paper.

"I could write back if you want," he added.

Sophie smiled to herself as she watched them with their heads bent down, concentrating on their task. She wondered if a special friendship was growing between them. She realised Billy had coped with a lot in his life and had turned out well. She thought Dorothy was a sweet, gentle girl and they seemed well suited. She would have to tell Millie about Billy's new friend.

When she next visited Millie, she was busy serving in the shop. As there were no customers, she and Sophie chatted about her visit the previous day, and Sophie mentioned Billy's obvious attentions towards Dorothy.

"He's very young," replied Millie dismissively. "I'm sure he was just being friendly."

Sophie thought otherwise. She had seen there was an attraction by the way they kept to themselves all afternoon.

"I have some news for you," said Millie, looking please with herself. "I'm expecting again."

Sophie clasped her hands together. "Oh wonderful! Congratulations!" She ran forward to stop Rosa from taking an apple and trying to eat it.

"Yes. I have something to ask you. Could you take on doing our accounts? I won't have time when I have this baby. I know you have training. I've been doing them—Harry is a bit useless."

Sophie said she would like to help and could work on them in the evenings when the children were in bed. Her days were much too busy.

One morning, two visitors arrived at Forge Cottage asking to see Mr. Browne. The two men were smartly dressed, wearing bowler hats, and carrying briefcases. Sophie was in the middle of giving Charles his lessons. She asked them in and told Charles to fetch his papa. When Ben arrived, he looked puzzled.

"Mr. Browne?" enquired one of the men.

Ben acknowledged that he was, and they shook hands.

The men introduced themselves, and one of them said, "Mr. Browne, we are from the patent office. Is there somewhere we can talk?"

Ben showed them into the parlour and closed the door. Sophie felt uneasy. What did they want? She tried to continue with Charles's lesson but could not concentrate, so she ended it early and told him to play outside. His sisters were upstairs in their bedroom. She could hear the low mumbling of voices but was unable to hear what was being said.

Finally, the door opened, and the men emerged, followed by Ben. The two men bade Sophie good day as they passed and left.

Ben frowned. "Sit down, Sophie, and I'll tell you what this is all about."

Sophie did so, fixing her eyes on Ben.

"As you heard them say, they are from the patent office. Are you aware what a patent is?"

Sophie nodded. Her father had told her all about them.

"It appears that I was supposed to take out a patent for any design I make if I am to use it to sell my bicycles. They say that the design of my saddle is not mine and that this type was already being used elsewhere and was registered with the Patents Office some years ago. Someone has complained that I have stolen his design to make a profit."

"But you had no idea someone else had designed a padded saddle. Surely people often think of the same idea quite independently."

"My mistake is that I did not apply for a patent before I sold the bicycles."

"What else did they say?"

"They asked me how I came about the design. I told them the truth, that it just occurred to me, and I went ahead with it. I explained to them that I decided to design a more comfortable saddle and had refined the design by adding springs underneath. They then said I should stop using it immediately and that there is the possibility the owner of the patent might take me to court."

"Oh, surely not! You have done nothing wrong intentionally."

"That is no excuse, apparently."

Sophie was speechless. She knew only too well this might cost them dearly. Not only would they forfeit the proceeds from the sale of the bicycles, but they might have to pay compensation if it went to court.

Ben was silent too, and she could see he was perplexed.

"Oh, Ben, what are you going to do?"

"Nothing," he said resolutely and went back to his work.

Ben came in for his lunch early after washing his hands in the scullery. Sophie had just finished the lesson and was putting the books away. The girls were in their bedroom playing with their dolls. They were not allowed in the "school room."

"What have you been learning about this morning, Charles?" Ben asked.

Charles did not answer immediately, and Sophie quickly replied, "We have been doing history, the Trojan wars."

Ben looked slightly annoyed. "You shouldn't answer for the boy, Sophie. He won't always have you to answer for him."

Sophie knew Ben was right and she was overprotecting Charles again. "You should answer your papa when he asks you a question," she said.

Ben sat down and smiled at Charles. "Can you tell me about it, Charles? I would like to know."

Charles looked up. "The Greeks built this enormous wooden horse, and all the Greek soldiers hid inside and then they all jumped out and won the city of Troy."

Ben was impressed. "I didn't know history was so exciting," he said.

"Mama said I could draw a picture of it next time," Charles added.

"I'd love to see it," said Ben.

They continued to converse happily, and Sophie was glad that they were getting on well together.

"The Greeks invented the wooden horse to win the war," continued Charles. "I think it was jolly clever of them."

Ben agreed.

"Have you ever invented anything, Papa?"

"Well, yes, I have actually."

Charles looked impressed. "What was it?" he asked.

"It's funny you should ask me that this morning. I have invented a more comfortable saddle for people when they ride their bicycles. Unfortunately, another man invented one, too, and he wants me to stop making mine and maybe give him some money."

"Is that what those two men came about?" asked Charles.

Ben told him the purpose of the men's visit.

"You mustn't worry, Charles. Papa will sort it out," Sophie said quickly.

It was nearing the end of the summer, and Ben suggested they have a short holiday.

"Where were you thinking of going?" asked Sophie.

"Mike has a small cabin in a field near a farm. It's fairly near the estuary and not far from the coast. It's a bit basic, but I think the children would love it there, as long as it doesn't rain all the time."

Sophie hadn't been very far from the village for several years. The next few days were spent preparing everything for their departure. They asked Harry to take care of the ponies while they were away, and Ben put a sign up on his workshop to indicate when he would be closed.

Ben loaded up the cart, and Sophie drove the trap with the children in the back. They arrived in good time to settle in before dark. The cabin had two rooms, and the children slept in the smaller one in bunk beds. Later that evening, Sophie and Ben sat in the candlelight, talking quietly. Sophie was still concerned that Ben might be prosecuted.

"Let's forget about all that for now, Sophie," said Ben. "We need to enjoy this holiday together."

They spent most of the time on the beach and let the children swim in the sea and build sandcastles. Ben chased and teased them, and there was a lot of laughter and fun. Sophie allowed herself a paddle at the edge of the waves, and little Rosa came and held her hand.

After a week they returned home, pleased that the children had enjoyed their first holiday together. Back at the cottage, Sophie was glad to see that the builder had nearly finished and was clearing the site. When he had gone, she asked Ben to decorate the third bedroom so it would be ready for Lionel's next visit in the Christmas holidays. Charles was to share it with him. Downstairs, the parlour was now twice as big, and Sophie set about rearranging the furniture.

At the end of November, an official looking envelope in neat copperplate writing arrived. It was addressed to "Mr. Browne, esq.," and Sophie immediately knew what it was. A wave of fear spread through her as she stood waiting for Ben to open it. It was as they had feared, a summons for Ben to appear in court to answer a privately sponsored lawsuit. Ben was accused of imitating a patented bicycle saddle design for private gain.

Sophie and Ben looked at each other. Neither of them knew what to say.

CHAPTER THIRTY-ONE

LAWSUIT

SOPHIE WAS SICK WITH WORRY over the impending lawsuit. She could think of nothing else, and she could see Ben was very troubled.

"I think we may lose this case," she said. "What will happen if we do?"

"We will have to pay compensation and court costs. We shall then be in debt and may have to sell up."

Sophie fetched the letter to examine it again. "It says he is accusing you of using his patent and that he will want compensation for infringing the copyright and for the bicycles you have already sold using his design." She put the letter down. "Oh Ben! How many bicycles have you sold with these saddles?"

Ben sat at the table and put his head in his hands. "I don't know. Quite a few."

"What are we going to do if we lose? You will have lost your reputation as well as your business, and we don't have any money to pay huge costs."

"I know. It could mean bankruptcy." He bowed his head as if in shame.

The enormity of the situation became clearer to Sophie, and it made her feel ill. The forge, their cottage—all would go. How would they live? How would they feed their children?

"I am so sorry, Sophie. I was only trying to improve my business."

Sophie put her arms round him. "I realise that, and I am proud of what you have achieved. We'll get through this somehow."

He hugged her tightly. "I don't want to let you all down."

Sophie had no idea how they were going to get through the next few weeks. She realised she would have to be strong. Samuel was bringing Lionel over the following morning. She wished they were not coming, but perhaps the distraction would be welcome.

The following day, Samuel arrived with his son, and Sophie felt herself relax a little.

"Lionel has been looking forward to his visit," he said. "And I see there have been some changes here."

Sophie welcomed them, and Ben showed them the new extension. When they returned, he tentatively asked if congratulations were in order.

"Thank you, yes," replied Samuel. "We are both very pleased and expect our new arrival in early March. Lionel is very excited and is looking forward to his growing family."

Sophie provided refreshments. She called the boys in, and the girls came downstairs. She introduced their son and two daughters to Samuel, who expressed his admiration for Ben's little family.

Lionel was full of chatter after playing with Charles in the garden. "Charles says his papa is going to court, Father," he said, addressing Samuel.

Sophie looked startled. She hadn't realised that Charles knew. How had he found out? They hadn't wanted anyone to know about it yet.

"Charles, there was no need to tell Lionel that," Ben said sternly.

Charles reddened.

"No, I'm glad he has," said Samuel. "May I ask what it is about?"

Ben reluctantly described the visit from the two men from the Patents Office.

Samuel listened carefully. "From what you tell me, it may be hard to prove, but I think I can help you. I don't personally deal with such cases, but you will need a lawyer. You cannot defend yourself. They will eat you up."

"I can't afford a lawyer," said Ben simply.

"If you win, you will not be liable for costs, as this case has been brought privately. It is all about making money, I'm afraid. The inventor wants your money, and the lawyers want it too. I have a junior barrister in my practice who could do with this sort of case to deal with, and if you give me all the details, I will arrange for him to represent you. It is, I'm afraid, all you can do."

Ben looked at Sophie. "I think we must agree," she said. "This is very good of you, Samuel. Thank you."

Samuel went on to tell Ben he would write to tell him what documentation he would need. "Can you arrange for your saddle to be photographed? The pictures will be integral for your defence. You will need to come up to London to discuss the case with your barrister, and this will, of course, be an extra expense."

Ben agreed and again thanked him.

"You won't be thanking me if you lose!" replied Samuel. "But I think you have a very good chance of winning. I have a nose for these things and am rarely wrong."

Sophie was relieved they would have some counsel to fight the case. She knew all about bankruptcy and its possible consequences, remembering what it had meant for her father.

Sophie was puzzled as to how Charles had found out. She suddenly remembered that she had left the opened letter on the dresser. He must have read it.

She spent the next few evenings sorting out their finances. *If only we hadn't got the loan to repay on top of possible legal costs and reimbursement,* she thought. She realised their finances were stretched. She had no idea what a lawyer would cost, but she knew they were expensive. All they had worked for could disappear.

When the photographer came to take pictures of the saddle later that week, Sophie suggested that they have a family photograph taken. They all visited the photographer's studio in Kingsbridge, including Lionel, and posed for a family photograph. Sophie had it framed to put up on the wall.

Billy would always come over whenever Lionel visited. Caroline also came one day and brought Dorothy with her. Sophie confided in her friend about their troubles, and Caroline said how hard it was on them all and wished she could do something to help. She told Sophie that a good lawyer might be able to win the case, and Sophie reassured her that they were hiring one.

That afternoon, Billy and Dorothy went riding together. Lionel and Charles had gone fishing, and Florrie came into the kitchen and moped about with a disgruntled look on her face.

Sophie had been busy talking to Caroline when she heard Ben say, "What's wrong, Florrie-face?"

"Don't call her that, Ben!" said Sophie.

Florrie burst into tears.

"I was only teasing!" said Ben, holding out his hands in surprise.

Sophie found Ben tiresome sometimes, and she felt embarrassed in front of her friend. Why didn't he realise the children had feelings? She went to comfort Florrie and asked her what the matter was.

"Charles and Lionel went off without me," she complained.

"Never mind," said Sophie. "Come with me to the shop. I am sure Mrs. Bailey would like to see it. If we see Uncle Harry, I will ask him to start your riding lessons if it doesn't turn too cold, and I'll let you choose some sweets."

A few days after the end of Lionel's visit, a letter arrived stating the date of the court case and that it was to be heard at the local assizes in Exeter. Samuel had written to ask Ben to have the documents ready for his defence. Sophie helped him to collect them. Then all they could do was wait.

Samuel had arranged for Ben to meet up with his barrister, and he had to go to Samuel's office in London. When he returned, he told Sophie that he had been met by Samuel when he arrived and invited to stay in his rooms in the Inner Temple, where they had dinner together. The following day, he met with his counsel, and they went through the case together.

"He told me I was to just answer the questions simply and honestly when cross-examined. He will do all the arguing. Honestly, Sophie, I'm dreading it."

"You will be fine," replied Sophie. "I'm sure the magistrate will appreciate your honesty. It's all you can do."

Privately, she hoped Ben would be able to hold his nerve and not get flustered or angry.

On the day of the court case, Ben caught the train to Exeter. Sophie saw him off with a very heavy heart. She felt their whole life was on hold, and the day dragged on as she went about her chores. All she could think of was the case and how it was proceeding. She was sitting in the kitchen late that evening, watching the candles flicker as she thought through what it would mean if they lost. They would be destitute, although she knew Millie and Harry would do everything they could to help. Perhaps she could find work. Would Ben allow her? What would he do when all his stock and equipment had been sold?

It was late that night before Ben finally returned. She had sat up waiting for him, sick with fear. She started as Ben came through the door.

He looked shattered. Putting his bag on the table, he said quietly, "I have been acquitted."

"Oh, thank God!" exclaimed Sophie, jumping up and flinging her arms round him. "Well done, Ben! You did it! You won!"

They both sat down. "I am not required to pay any costs, thank goodness. It's over, Sophie. It's over."

Ben looked haggard and tired. He said he had had little sleep on the train. He reached out and clasped her hand, looking at her intently. "Thank you for your love and support, my Sophie, and for believing in me. I know I have failed you in the past, and I hope you have forgiven me."

"Yes, I have forgiven you," she replied.

Before she could say more, the door opened, and Charles had come downstairs. "Pa! You're home!" He ran to greet his father, and Ben put his arms round him.

"Is everything going to be all right now?" asked Charles anxiously.

"Yes, it is." He drew his son closer to him, reassuring him.

Sophie felt full of emotion. It was like a wave flowing over her. She could see how much Ben loved their son, and she was confident of his love and loyalty for her and their children. She realised that Ben's love child and his family were also becoming part of their lives now and wondered what the future would hold for them all.

TO BE CONTINUED...

DID YOU KNOW?

Many blacksmiths in Victorian times combined the skills of tool making and shoeing horses (farriers), but times were changing, and the blacksmiths had to change too. Although horses were still the main mode of transportation, automation was progressing rapidly. In the 1890s, there were great changes on the roads with the growing craze for cycling and the first early motor carriages. Cyclists often required help with puncture repairs and wheel straightening. Many blacksmiths became involved by offering services to do repairs and supply parts for cycles and early motor cars and some even added a garage business to their forges.

ABOUT THE AUTHOR

Penelope Abbott is a retired teacher who lives in the Chilterns with her husband. She has two grown up children, a son James, and a daughter Ros. Her hobbies are painting, gardening, and playing her violin. This is her first book.

Milton Keynes UK
Ingram Content Group UK Ltd.
UKHW012137131223
434291UK00001B/151